a novel by **Joanne Schwehm**

THE CRITIC

choose your words wisely.

Credits:
Cover Model: Erik Fellows, Actor
Cover Art: Sommer Stein, Perfect Pear Creative Covers
Cover Photographer: ©Otilia Villar Baker (About Time
Photography)
Editor: Cassie Cox
Proofreader: Devon Burke
Interior Designer: Integrity Formatting

DEDICATION

This book is dedicated to all the dreamers in the world.

TABLE OF CONTENTS

PROLOGUE

Bentley

Stunning. Absolutely drop dead gorgeous, make-me-hard-as-a-rock beautiful, and familiar as hell. When I saw Andrea Jordan's picture in the *Playbill*, I knew I'd seen her face before. When it hit me, my lips curled into a smile. Two days ago, I had been grabbing a paper at the corner store, and standing next to me was a beautiful woman buying a magazine.

As she exchanged pleasantries with the cashier, her melodious giggle made my breath falter. Her hair fell forward when she lowered her head to put her change away. Damn, she was beautiful. She must have sensed my stare because she glanced at me from the corner of her eye. I grinned, almost caught in the act of taking in her slight curves and her fine ass nestled in a pair of dark jeans. The woman was close to perfect.

A shiny penny slipped and fell at my feet. I couldn't help the smile that crept across my lips as I looked at Lincoln's head. I crouched down to get it and once I had it between my thumb and forefinger, I held it up and smirked. "Must be my lucky day." Not the most original line, but it fit the current scenario. I was hoping to hear her voice or a witty comment.

Instead, she just waved me off. "Then keep it. I wouldn't want to be the source of your bad luck."

She hardly looked at me when she spoke, but I noticed her flowing brown hair, beautiful eyes, and a smile that could stop traffic in a New York minute. But before I could get her name, she was gone.

Now, a mere forty-eight hours later, I was looking at a picture of the dark-haired beauty with a smile that could bring me to my knees. When I graduated top of my class with a journalism degree and entered the workforce, I'd expected to be reviewing prestigious performances. I'd been hired by a trade journal, *Spotlight,* which was a subsidiary of the *Edge.* Although the journal was based in New York City, I was sitting next to my new boss and mentor in the Garden State, about to critique my first off-Broadway play, *Love Entirely,* in a small theater. Even if it wasn't the Big Apple, everyone had to start somewhere, so I sucked it up. This was my job, regardless of location, and I planned on writing the best goddamn review I could. I hoped it would get me to where I wanted to be, leading the way in my field and making a name for myself. Word on the street was the lead actress, Andrea Jordan, would be the next big thing, so at least I'd found something encouraging about being there.

Scott, my boss, nudged me. "Remember, when the curtain goes up, you *must* focus. The dramatics the actors portray should transport you into the story, but keep the stage design, costumes, and lighting in your thoughts as well. Take good notes, and don't pay too much attention to any one actor; this isn't a one-woman or one-man show. It's a collection of artists coming together to bring life to characters." He sounded as if I were going to witness a life-changing event.

Nodding, I smiled while knowing my eyes would be trained on Andrea. However, I knew he was right. If I wanted to excel and leave my mark on the theater world, I'd be wise to listen to him.

A few minutes after the house lights dimmed, the curtain rose. Regardless of the instructions Scott had just given me, she became my sole focus. She was breathtaking. My internal temperature rose, and all I could focus on was her as my dick came to life. The pull I had toward this stranger was odd.

As her co-star and the secondary actors spoke, she began to fade away. Not physically but internally. Her voice grew softer, she appeared smaller, and the heat I felt when I first saw her slowly cooled off. It was as if I could see her mercury declining.

I jotted down scattered notes, trying not to lose focus on Ms. Jordan. I willed her to do better, to come out of the shell encompassing her. My elbows rested on my knees as I leaned forward, waiting for brilliance. I fixated on her lips as she spoke. I wondered what my name would sound like when she said it because if I had anything to say about it, she'd be mine someday. Not only would she say my name, she'd scream it in pure ecstasy. But I needed to get back to the task at hand. I continued scribbling words in my notebook.

During the intermission, Scott leaned in and said, "She's pretty, but I don't see her as the next big thing."

For some reason, his remark felt personal. His opinion of Ms. Jordan shouldn't have affected me, but my urge to tell him off was strong. I had to remind myself that he was my boss and I needed to reel it in or I'd never work with him at the *Edge*.

I wasn't sure what it was, but something about her called to me. My chest rose and fell with each word she spoke, and I found myself begging her to let go of whatever held her back. Her presence was bigger than the platform she stood on, but the stage engulfed her like a small fish in a giant wave. It curled around her and pulled her under until she was drowning. The more I watched, the more disappointed I became. I was borderline irritated that she wasn't capitalizing on this opportunity. Maybe she thought she was, but she wasn't.

At the end of the show, the house lights brightened, and people rose to their feet with thunderous applause. The cast came out in order of importance, and as Ms. Jordan received a boisterous show of appreciation, I looked around the theater. I found it comical to watch people who believed they were witnessing the "next big thing" jump on the bandwagon to be one of the first supporters. Oh, how I wished I was on that wagon, but I trailed far behind it.

Scott and I left the theater and grabbed a cab to the train station. While seeing a show was entertaining, my night was far from over. I needed to write a review that would most likely piss people off, especially a certain Ms. Andrea Jordan.

When my review was submitted, I wondered if the proofreader would question my abrasiveness. I knew Scott wouldn't. I figured he'd be happy I hadn't titled my review, "Andrea Jordan Looked Totally Fuckable." Scott had told me to write with my brain and not my dick, so I did. All I could do was write the truth.

"*Love Entirely* Wasn't Entirely Loved" ended up being

my title, and what sucked was that I knew once Andrea Jordan had read the review, she'd hate me. That wasn't exactly the way I'd wanted to start my career or make my first impression on her, but being an honest critic was important.

Over time, that review, and several others that were referred to as "spot-on," won me critical acclaim, and thus the critic was born. I was no longer just Bentley Chambers, theater critic for the *Edge*. I was *the one* producers, actors, and theater patrons looked to. To me, my words were just an opinion, but to them, my opinion was so much more. Some hated me, while others praised me, but through it all, I wanted to see one person flourish and succeed: the woman who often starred in my dreams, both awake and asleep—Andrea Jordan. All I could do was hope that I'd witness it and be able to write about it.

CHAPTER 1

Five Years Later

Andi

I stood center stage and stared at the empty theater. The burgundy seats, which would soon be filled with theater-goers, made my heart race. The Xs and lines for blocking and positioning were laid down on the shiny wood floor, and everything was ready for tonight's preview show. But was I? Being front and center as a lead was all I'd dreamt of, and the time had come for that dream to become reality. My nerves spiked, and my palms grew sweaty as I walked from spot to spot, practicing my lines in my head.

If my prayers were answered, this small production would turn into the biggest chance of my life. I hadn't had an opportunity this big in half a decade thanks to the scathing reviews I'd received. Thankfully, not all my reviews had been horrible, but I had the lead now, and I wouldn't fuck it up. Nope, no way would I blow it. When I'd auditioned, our director, Mack, told me I'd only edged out my understudy by a few lines. I needed to be as good as I could be. No, I needed to be spectacular, or funding would be pulled.

As my lines swirled through my brain and my feet traveled from mark to mark, I swung my right hand and hit a muscular chest. I looked up to see Seth, one of my closest friends and our set designer.

"Sorry, Andi. I didn't know you were rehearsing. I hope I didn't interrupt. Mack wanted me to check the sets." Seth's calm voice soothed me.

"I'm just taking it all in. You guys did an amazing job. If I didn't know we were in Jersey, I'd believe we were on North Michigan Avenue in Chicago." I nudged Seth with my shoulder.

"Thanks, that means a lot to me. I'll say this crew is top notch. They really outdid themselves." A prideful smile grew across his handsome face.

"Yes, they did, but they had you to lead them. That says a lot too."

He blushed, which made me laugh. Seth was about my age and very easy on the eyes. His deep brown eyes lit up at my compliment even though he should have been used to them by now. I was his biggest fan.

"You look nervous. Are you okay?" His voice was laden with concern.

I stopped fidgeting with the hem of my shirt and half-smiled. "Yeah, I'm fine."

His brows rose forming frown lines on his forehead.

"Really, I am," I said.

Seth put his hands on my shoulders. "You're a wonderful actress. I don't know what it's like being in the spotlight, but I've watched you there before, and you make it look effortless and believable. Don't doubt your talent. I love you, and you got this." He placed a chaste kiss on my cheek.

I was comforted knowing that he'd be in the wings as I was center stage. "Thank you. That means the world to me. It's just this show depends on us being spot-on. If the reviews aren't good, we won't get the backing to leave Jersey. I need this . . . we all do." My heart constricted with the pressure riding on me. The thought of a show progressing to Broadway or not solely because of my work weighed on me, but I knew I could do it. I was a good actress, and I needed to remember that. If my confidence wavered, it would show.

"I have faith in you, and remember, you aren't the only one on the stage. Don't put all the stress on your shoulders," he said. "But if I don't check all these props, the Sears Tower may fall, and that wouldn't be good for the show, now would it?" He winked and walked off the stage.

I took one last look around at the empty seats, wondering where the critics would be. In a way, it was good I didn't know, because I didn't want to direct anything toward them. Once I was comfortable, I went to my dressing room to get ready for one of the biggest nights of my life.

⬥⬥⬥

Applause continued as we took our final bow, and the curtain lowered. I let out a deep breath that I was unaware I'd been holding. My fellow cast members hugged each other, and the cheers seeping through the thick blue velvet curtain were palpable. I stood stock-still, staring at the stage floor, wondering if I'd finally have my break. Could I make it to Broadway? Was I closer to having my dream come true? I saw Seth high-fiving his team, and he gave me a thumbs-up. I nodded and closed my eyes. I thought of bright lights and my name in theater programs, and a sense of joy enveloped me.

My best friend's shriek brought me out of my fantasy. "Andi, you were fantastic."

I smiled wide. The adrenaline of being on the big stage still coursed through my veins

"Do you really think so?"

She swatted my arm. "The audience loved you! Couldn't you hear them? That standing ovation should be a clue that you nailed it. You need to enjoy this. I'll meet you outside. I'm so excited for you!"

Gina's enthusiasm was contagious, and I loved her for it. She wasn't a stranger to the business. Although she was a makeup artist, she got critiqued in reviews as well.

"I'll be just a few minutes. I need to scrape off this pancake batter you artists paint our faces with."

"Can't blame me for this one." Gina rolled her eyes and smiled.

I returned her smile, but I was still uneasy about the show. Deep down, I knew I'd performed well, but art, no matter what form, was always subjective. There was one critic who needed to love it. He had made and ruined careers with his printed words, and that was Bentley Chambers. He wrote critiques for the *Edge*, a critically acclaimed newspaper that was like the Bible to the theater world.

Mr. Chambers had critiqued a couple shows I'd performed in, and his reviews weren't glowing. He'd once written that he "didn't connect with Andrea Jordan's performance." He wrote as if I'd done something personal to him. You need thick skin to be an actress, and although I felt as if mine should have the density of rawhide after all the shit reviews I'd received, it still bruised easily.

Thankfully, with this performance just being a preview, the only critics in attendance had been drama students from the local university, a few critics from local papers, and patrons with deep pockets. Our true opening night was over a week away. That was when I'd really worry about what Mr. Chambers would write—if he showed.

Mack waited for us offstage. He pulled my co-star, Justin, and me aside. His voice was as deep as the wrinkles on his forehead. "Great performance, you two. Let's hope it was enough."

He seemed to direct the last part of that comment toward me. I was probably just being paranoid, but it didn't resonate well.

"I'm sure they loved it." Justin rubbed my back.

"What's wrong, Mack? Don't you think they liked it?" I asked when I saw the worried look on my director's face. I could practically hear the gears turning in his skull. My heart raced, and I suddenly felt ill.

Mack swallowed hard and ran his hand back and forth over his shaved head as if a genie would emerge from his ears. "There was a critic from the city in the audience. I didn't see him, but one of the stagehands heard he was in attendance."

My eyes closed, and I wrapped my arms around my stomach. "Who?" My voice trembled.

"The one who matters: Bentley Chambers." Mack's voice was laced with uneasiness, which didn't help my current state.

"Oh my God, you have got to be kidding me." I'd have sworn that man was following me around just to destroy me. My voice became louder as I grew more irritated. "He hardly ever attends shows in Jersey!" If I didn't know better, I'd have thought that asshole had it in for me. I stared at Mack, trying to get some sense of reassurance that the show was good enough, but his tense smile spoke volumes.

"Like I said, I thought you both did fine, so let's assume he did as well," Mack said before he walked away.

Fine? We did fine? That word made my nausea worse. I needed to get out of there. Justin was new to the scene and four years my junior. Age in our industry was different for women. I knew that if something didn't happen for me soon, my time would dissipate. I looked as though I was in my early twenties, but I wasn't, and my resume said so. Why the hell would Mr. Chambers review our show? It was nothing in comparison to the ones in the city.

My heart thundered as I wondered what he'd thought about it. Could he finally like a show I was in? I needed to calm down and hope for the best.

Justin and I walked toward our dressing rooms. Gina was waiting for me out front, so I wanted to hurry and get cleaned up. The costumes were heavy, and my body was craving my jeans and T-shirt.

"So this Bentley guy sounds like a douche." Justin had an easy way about him, but he didn't seem very pleased by the news either.

"I think douche is too much of a compliment. He's horrid, wretched, and I hope that whoever saw him was wrong and he wasn't here." I pushed open my dressing room door as I turned to Justin. "I'm sure he loved your performance, so don't worry." As the door clicked shut behind me, I was greeted by my mirror. My reflection stated, "You're fucked. Pack your shit up now because you're done."

I wanted to find Seth to see who on his crew knew who the asshole was, but they were in a post-production meeting. I wanted to stick around to talk to him, but Gina was waiting for me. Due to the fact that Bentley Chambers spent a large amount of time ruining careers and trashing lives, his picture had never been attached to his reviews. I'd never seen the image of the man who seemed to have it in for me.

I made my way outside, into the crisp air, and saw Gina on the sidewalk with a bouquet of daisies, my favorite. My lips curled into a smile that I knew didn't touch my eyes. "Thank you for the flowers." I hugged her for longer than I should have, but she was more like a sister than a friend. At times, she seemed like the only family I had.

She pulled back and looked at me with worry in her eyes. "Okay, what's wrong? You were so happy a few minutes ago."

We walked toward her car to go to a small diner we hung out at after shows. I preferred to skip hanging out with the cast. I'd had enough of watching castmates drink themselves under a table while they chose their bedmates for the night. I understood actors needed to unwind and come off of their "stage high," but that wasn't for me.

Once inside her cute Jetta, she asked again, "What gives? Why are you acting so depressed?"

I fiddled with the petals on the daisies. "He was here. Why? What the hell is with that man? Can't he find someone else to ruin? I don't understand why he hates me so much." My voice cracked. I hated that a man I didn't even know despised me.

"You totally lost me. Who are you talking about?" Gina's tone was soft as she placed her hand on mine and glanced between me and the flowers.

I hadn't realized I was actually picking off the petals. I laid them on the backseat before they were just yellow nubs. "Bentley 'The Asshole' Chambers, that's who."

"He was here? Dammit, I wish I knew what he looked like. I would've spied for you." Gina knew about him from the reviews he'd written about me.

"Yeah, well, he's probably about seventy years old with nose hair that touches his top lip." My eyes caught hers, and we burst out laughing.

"Don't forget his white hair, which I'm sure is combed over to cover his bald spot." Gina started the car.

I giggled. "Yeah, or his pot belly hanging over his polyester pants."

"And a small dick." Gina winked.

My stomach rolled. "I don't want to think about his dick, but thanks for that image. I need to scrub my eyes now."

Our laughter continued as we headed down the road. We continued to bash Mr. Chambers's appearance until we walked into the diner.

The hostess greeted us and walked us to our table. "I heard your show was wonderful, dear."

"You did? Thank you, Sally. I hope so." The smell of

comfort food wafted through the small restaurant, making me feel at home and a bit more relaxed. Just knowing Sally had heard the play was good made me feel better too.

"Yes, I did, sugar. Some couples in here earlier said the show was hot. They were getting cozy in the booth over there." She tilted her head to the left. "So was this a sexy show?" She touched the tip of her pencil to her tongue as she grabbed her pad out of her apron pocket.

"Well, it was written to be sexy. It's about a couple who decides they are better off apart, but after being separated, they realize they still love each other. When they get back together . . . let's just say they're very happy about it." I winked and gave her a shy smile.

"Hmm, well, sounds sexy to me. At my age, a kiss is as good as it gets without the assistance of a little blue pill." She laughed. "Okay, what'll it be, girls?" She tapped her pencil on her pad.

"I'll have the apple pie and a coffee, please." I handed her my menu.

"Make that two, and the show was very steamy." Gina winked at Sally before she walked away. "So this Bentley guy. Do you really think he's going to review the show?"

"Who the hell knows? He's such a prick." I let out a huff as my eyes landed on a stranger at the door. He was gorgeous, and I swore my panties dampened at the sight of him. I shifted in my seat, trying to relieve the pressure growing between my legs.

Mr. Hot as Sin and Sexy as Hell walked across the checkerboard floor to a burgundy vinyl booth. He slid his fine ass in, and Sally blushed as she handed him a menu. Sally could've been his grandmother, but I figured she'd favor the title "cougar" when it came to that fine specimen of a man. His worn leather jacket was open, revealing a navy shirt that was snug enough to outline each muscle in his torso. Shit, he was sexy as fuck and vaguely familiar. Maybe he was a model from the city or an actor I'd seen in a show?

He peered over his menu, and our eyes locked. I watched his deep blues widen. He appeared rattled.

"Andi? Did you hear me?"

I looked back at Gina's. "I'm sorry, what?" I noticed my coffee in front of me and took a quick sip. I made a face at the bitterness before doctoring it with sweetener and cream.

Gina started laughing. "Who were you looking at?" She glanced over her shoulder. "Holy shit! Who is that, and can I order one to go? He's an orgasm walking!" She turned back to me. "My God, he's beautiful." She let out a sigh. "Is it wrong that I want to run my fingers through his hair? I bet it's soft." She giggled.

I glared at her. "Shhh, he'll hear you!" My eyes had a mind of their own. They seemed to just stare at him. "Man, he is just . . . wow."

We both snickered when Sally appeared at our table with our food. "He's not on the menu tonight, girls." She grabbed the pencil from behind her ear and straightened her pink uniform. "I need to go get his order. Enjoy your dessert." She walked away with a tad more sway to her hips than normal.

"Okay, so new topic. Your co-star is a major hottie. How're his lips?" Gina took a forkful of her pie and waggled her brows at me.

"His lips are nice. I don't know. I've kissed him so

many times that it just seems friendly." I shrugged. "It's like kissing a really close buddy."

Gina shook her head and sipped her coffee. "No, I don't know. Let's remember you're talking to me. I haven't kissed anyone since Derek left for California."

"You haven't kissed anyone in eight months? Oh my God!" I sucked my lips in between my teeth, realizing I'd said that louder than I should have. "Sorry."

"Yeah, thanks." Gina shook her head. "Announce it to everyone here. Maybe that hot guy will take pity on me and do me on the table."

As her hands rubbed the top of the table, an odd sense of ownership consumed me. All I could think of was, *I saw him first, so I have dibs.*

"Andi? Did you hear what I said?"

I looked up, and he was gone. My gaze darted around the diner, but he wasn't anywhere. For some reason, I felt disappointed. "You don't have to worry about that, because he left."

"Are you okay? I know you're worried about how the show went, but trust me, it was awesome. Truly." Gina beamed.

I tried to suppress a yawn, but it didn't work very well. The adrenaline coursing through my veins was gone, leaving me drained. "Let's get going. I can't wait to wake up and see what the asshole wrote about me." My words were sarcastic, but in some masochistic way, I meant them.

"Maybe he wasn't there, or he could've liked it. It was hot, and I still want to meet Justin. He does play for our team, right?" She snickered, and I shook my head.

I tossed a twenty-dollar bill on the table. "Yes, he

does. He has a girlfriend, and no offense, he's rather young."

"Hmm . . . well, Seth isn't too bad either." She wiped her hands on her napkin and placed it on the table.

Seth was quite a catch in my opinion. Gina had always liked him, but he and I were such close friends that she'd never wanted to pursue him.

After waving to Sally, we slid out of our booth. The ride home was quiet. I couldn't wait to get in bed and say a prayer that Mr. Chambers hadn't been at tonight's performance.

Bentley

Knowing my words would destroy her gutted me. Seeing her in that diner was the last thing I'd expected. When her eyes met mine, I knew I couldn't stay. How would she react to my review? I was just doing my job, but that meant putting in writing that she wasn't good at hers. It wasn't even that she hadn't been good—she had been—just not as good as she could've been. Hopefully, she'd take it as constructive criticism and strive to do better. It had just been a preview performance, so in essence, my review could help her. *Yeah, I'll go with that.*

When the waitress came to take my order, I made a lame excuse about why I had to leave. I hurried outside, fighting the urge to go meet the woman who had haunted my dreams for years. Instead, I hailed a cab, grabbed my cell phone from my backpack, and called my brother.

He answered after just one ring. "Hey, bro, what's up? Everything okay?" Brett's voice was muffled by the sound of people in the background.

"Hey, man, are you still at work?"

"Yeah, I need to get out of here though. It's not my night to close, but the ladies are in rare form." He let out a chuckle, making me smile.

Brett was a ladies' man, and he co-owned the hottest club in the city. He still worked as a bartender, so he never had a lack of pretty women tossing themselves at him. He had enough issues with women though, and I prayed he didn't add more to his plate—or bed. His last conquest was claiming to be pregnant with his child, so to say Brett's been on edge would be an understatement. I should be the one making him feel better, but right now, I didn't know how.

"You're still coming here this week, right?" I knew my voice wouldn't reassure him that everything was okay, but I didn't want him to worry either.

"I can get there early in the day, so we can go to lunch. Unless you need me sooner? I can talk to Alex and take time off." He sounded concerned.

The thought of him hopping on a train ran through my mind. But it was late. He should sleep for a change. We both kept shitty hours, and getting together at night never worked out.

"No, I don't want you to do that. It can wait." I was the big brother, and I needed to handle this on my own.

"Hold on." I heard movement and Brett greeting people, then it went quiet. "Okay, what's the deal? I'm in the office now, so talk."

I knew he wouldn't let it lie. I took a deep breath.

"Remember a few years ago, I told you about an actress that I couldn't get out of my head?" My chest constricted just thinking about her and the day I told Brett I'd fallen for a stranger.

"The one you had awesome sex with?" Brett let out a boisterous laugh.

"No, I've never had sex with Andrea." Just the thought of that made my heart palpitate.

"Andrea?"

From the confusion in his voice, I knew he didn't have a clue whom I was referring to. "Yeah, my first review I ever did. Andrea Jordan was the actress—"

"Oh, yeah! I remember that. You told me you had to take a cold shower after just looking at her picture."

Brett's deep chuckle made me want to hang up, but I had said that. I'd wanted to jerk off to her picture many times, but I kept that to myself. "Well, I went to another one of her shows tonight."

The cab pulled up to my hotel. I swiped my card to pay the fare and left without a word to the driver.

"Really? Did you finally meet her?" Brett asked. "Wait, isn't this, like, the third or fourth show of hers you've reviewed?"

"Fourth."

"And . . . did you give her a glowing critique? One that would make her want to jump all over you with gratification?" The humor in Brett's voice wasn't helping my situation.

I walked into my hotel room and tossed the key on the side table. "No, I couldn't do it."

"You couldn't review it, or you couldn't write a positive review?"

"She just wasn't good enough." I let out a frustrated sigh as I grabbed a beer from the mini-fridge. "I mean, she's a good actress, but I know she can do better."

"So the review you wrote, was it harsh?" He exhaled. "Maybe that was her best. How do you know she can do better?"

"I just know she can. Don't ask me how. I just do." I took a swig of my brew. "She won't like what I have to say, but it will be honest."

"Oh, bro, you need to add some positivity to your criticisms, or this chick is going to come at you with a knife someday." The humor in his voice turned to concern.

I slumped down on the recliner. "I won't lie, Brett. I write it as I see it, and from what I saw tonight . . . well, let's just say I hope her knife has a dull edge."

Brett laughed, and I could picture him shaking his head. "Look, I gotta go, but if you need me, I'll come there tonight."

"Nah, it's okay. I'll just see you later. Thanks for the talk."

"No problem."

Our call ended, and I felt worse than I had. I closed my eyes and remembered her kissing her co-star. I should've been consumed with jealousy, but instead I felt sorry for the boy. Maybe he didn't do it for her, but an audience member shouldn't be able to see that or feel it. If I had been kissing her, I wouldn't have stopped until she moaned in delight. Yeah . . . Andrea Jordan would be putty in my hands.

CHAPTER 2

Andi

All I heard was ringing. I realized it was the alarm on my phone that I had neglected to turn off, and I was so annoyed, since it was Sunday and I could sleep in before our afternoon rehearsal. But since I was up, I might as well get my day started.

After I put on my running gear and pulled my hair into a ponytail, I tucked my key and some money in the pocket on my shoe. With my headphones playing music, my joggers hit the pavement. The air was a bit warmer, and humidity had begun to blanket the day. I took a minute to look at the trees, and I couldn't help but smile at the budding leaves—summer wasn't far away. Once I'd rounded the block for the third time, I decided to head into the Brew Spot for a cup of coffee. Most runners drank sports drinks, but I needed caffeine.

The barista smiled as I walked in. After I'd ordered and paid for my coffee, she said, "Hey, aren't you that actress in *Together Again?*"

I felt my smile grow. I couldn't believe she

recognized me. "Yes, that's me. Did you see it?" My pulse quickened as I prayed that she'd enjoyed the show. I was borderline giddy and wondered if she wanted an autograph. My inner thespian curtsied in appreciation.

Her face fell. "No, but I saw your picture in the paper."

My heartbeat picked up more speed, making my nerves spike. "What picture? Wait, which paper?" *Please don't say it . . . please don't say it . . . it can't be.*

She handed me my coffee. "The *Edge.*"

Fuck. She said it.

"It's over there on the table if you want to see it." She gestured toward the table nestled in the corner surrounded by plush chairs. Her smile faded.

I knew I didn't want to read it, but I needed to nonetheless. "Thank you."

I walked over, grateful no other customers were there. I gingerly sat down, looked at the paper, and read the headline, "Vying for Broadway: Will *Together Again* Make It? Story on page 6."

A chill crept up my spine as I set down my cup and flipped to the page which held my future. My eyes nearly fell out of my head when I saw my picture next to the caption, "Bored Again." Pressure built behind my eyes, so I grabbed a napkin from the holder and reclined in the chair.

Joanne Schwehm

OFF-BROADWAY THEATER REVEW:
"Together Again" Hits the Stage with a Resounding Thud.
By: Bentley Chambers

The highly anticipated production, "Together Again," starring newcomer Justin Monroe as Jake Landon and a veteran of off-Broadway productions, Andrea Jordan as Katie Jackson, flopped. Writer and director, Mack McKenzie, had to be flailing offstage as he watched his preview of this production. The story was beautifully written and well directed, but the scenes that should have been full of passion were full of lethargy.

Jake and Katie are former lovers who always wanted someone to love and to be loved. They met when they were younger and shared many firsts. They were hopelessly in love. Then college happened, and they were separated by geography. But they never forgot what they once were, and no one who came after was enough. Jake and Katie reconnect online, and through various e-mails and instant messages, they decide to see each other again. Jake, who was in London, comes back to claim Katie and make her his own, and she's in desperate need of what he has to offer—well, that's what the writer intended.

Their reconciliation was so anticipated that sparks should have been radiating off them once their bodies and souls collided. I expected that. I predicted lust, heat, and the need to love resonating from the stage, but instead, the audience was presented with disenchantment and coolness. If I had been apart from my former lover for numerous years, the audience would have been able to feel it in their souls and other parts of their bodies. Sadly, I have more passion in my fountain pen than these two had on stage.

Despite their efforts, the actors just lacked chemistry. Ms. Jordan seemed stiff and robotic. I'm sure Mr. Monroe felt it every time their lips met. They should have produced enough sparks to illuminate the dimly lit theater. However, we remained in the dark.

The supporting cast, sound, and set were spot-on. Karen Garner as Constance Malloy and Matthew Little as Bill Hastings portrayed Katie and Jake's best friends, and although they weren't romantically involved, their chemistry surpassed that of the main characters.' Watching their performance was pleasurable, so kudos to them and the sound and stage crews.

Hopefully Director Mack McKenzie will see the gaps in performances and be able to bridge them so "Together Again" can head to Broadway.

THE CRITIC

I set the paper down and stared into space. Insurmountable embarrassment washed over me. The delicious aroma of coffee and baked goods was replaced with repulsion and my fear that everyone there had read the horrible review. Why was he doing this to me? My phone buzzed, and Gina's picture appeared on the caller ID.

I attempted to collect myself. "Hello." My voice was barely a whisper.

"Andi, where are you?" Her voice was full of concern. Great, she must have seen the review.

"I'm at Brew Spot, but I'm getting ready to leave." The feeling that everyone was staring at me was unnerving. I was sure they weren't, but I felt mortified and beyond upset. "Why?"

"Well, I was hoping to come over." She sounded sympathetic, and another piece of my heart splintered off.

"You saw it, didn't you?" Tears streamed down my face. I quickly wiped them away as my gaze darted around the small cafe.

After a long pause, she said, "Yes, but please don't believe a word of it. You said yourself that he's a douchebag. Mack knows you did an awesome job, so don't worry."

"I'm headed home if you want to meet me there."

"Okay, meet you there in an hour. I love you."

"Love you too."

I tossed my cup and left Brew Spot, but not before I'd snagged that wretched paper. My feet hit the pavement with force. If I hadn't had on my running shoes, I would've cracked a bone and most likely the concrete.

My neighbor, Mrs. Booker, came out of her apartment and shyly smiled at me. The old woman couldn't have read the *Edge* or seen my performance, could she? I'd become paranoid. My body felt clammy, and I needed to get inside.

I opened my door and hurried to the bathroom, where I stripped out of my clothes and jumped in the shower. The warm water didn't have its usual effect on me, so I bathed quickly. I wrapped myself in a plush towel and stepped onto the cool tile floor. I ran a brush through my hair, towel-dried it, and twisted it into a braid. My reflection was so different from just a few hours earlier, when I'd had a sense of pride and accomplishment in my features. After I dressed, I sat on the couch and stared at the paper now lying on my coffee table. The buzzer on my door sounded, and I got up to let Gina in.

She ran to me, practically knocking me over with a hug. "I'm so sorry." She rubbed my back in an attempt to offer me solace.

"Thank you. Can you even believe it?" I shut my door before Mrs. Booker could hear us. "I'm so pissed off. Seriously, did I suck? Do I really lack passion?" I flopped onto the couch and rested my head against the striped square cushions. She sat next to me, and I rolled my head toward her. "G, please tell me."

"No, you don't lack passion. You and Justin were hot. I wished I were you." Gina blushed and smiled.

"But would you wish you were Justin if you were a guy? Is that what Bentley Chambers meant? He said that Justin was good and the issue was me."

When was the last time I'd felt passion? I'd been with

my ex-boyfriend Marcus, and that was months ago. Justin was the most action I'd gotten since, and that wasn't really action. It was a job. Was that my problem? My mind was all over the place, and I couldn't stop the visuals that popped in and out of each thought.

"Mack would tell you if you didn't perform well, and Justin isn't that good of an actor," Gina said. "You radiate desire. Don't let this piece-of-shit critic bring you down."

I stood and tossed up my hands. "But he's *the* critic! Do you understand that? He's not just some nobody. Everyone listens to him, and he's well respected." My voice was sterner than I wanted it to be when I was speaking to my best friend. "I'm sorry for yelling, but I'm so annoyed."

Gina quirked her lips to the side. "So now what?"

"Well, I've been thinking about that, and I think I should confront this dickhead. You know, come face to face with the asshole who's set on ruining my career." I bounced around the room as if I were in a boxing ring and getting ready for the bell to sound. If I could just get inside his head and figure out what the fuck he wanted from me, then maybe, just maybe, he'd think I was worth the price of a Broadway ticket. "Yeah, I need to talk to this douchebag."

"How are you going to do that, and what are you going to say?" Gina went into the kitchen and grabbed us each a bottle of water.

I gripped the bottle and envisioned wrapping my hand around Chambers's neck. I spun off the top and took a long swig, making the plastic crinkle. "Well, I'm going to call his office tomorrow and ask to speak to the jackass."

"That could work." Gina rolled her eyes. "Then what are you going to do? Say, 'Hi, this is Andrea Jordan, and you're an asshole?'"

I sat on the couch and set my water next to the paper that was motivating me at the moment. Scenarios ran through my mind. I needed to decide which would be best. I was an actress for God's sake—I could totally do this. I just needed to select the words that would make me look as though I had conviction and not as if I were a whiney toddler. I wrung my hands, plotting my move.

"Andi?"

"Yeah, sorry." I came out of my reverie. "I'll figure it out. I just need to get him on the phone and schedule a meeting."

Gina nodded, but her face was full of worry. "I assume you have a plan?"

"Yeah, maybe. I'll have to wait until tomorrow to see if it will work." I let out a breath.

"Well, I hope your plan works, whatever it is. Andi, please remember that Mack is in charge, not Mr. Chambers."

"I know, it's so unnerving. Anyway, I have rehearsal soon, so if Mack saw the paper, which I'm sure he did, I'll know sooner than later what my fate is."

"Then I'm going to hit the road and let you get to it. Please try not to worry, and remember—you're an awesome actress." Gina hugged me. "Call me and let me know how it goes."

⇒◈◈◈⇐

Rehearsal went as well as it could have. My mind kept thinking of the review that had been given. I did my best not to have it affect my performance, but it wasn't very easy. I amped up the passion with Justin in hopes that if Mack had read the review, it would squash any reservations he may have had.

Mack gave no indication that there was a problem. So, I was able to breathe easier, until he approached me and Justin afterwards while we were chatting with fellow cast members.

"I'd like to see you two in my office please." His finger waved between Justin and me. "Now."

I looked at Justin, who just shrugged. This couldn't be a good sign. Mack's lips were in a fine line. If this wasn't bad news, he should be an actor.

Bentley

I held the paper and read the words I'd written. I couldn't help but wonder if she'd seen it yet. All I could imagine was a dart board with my article as the bull's-eye, Ms. Jordan hurling small spikes at it. When I write a review, I never intend to hurt anyone or be rude. I'm a professional.

My phone rang, interrupting the thoughts of sharp spikes being driven into my words. I'd expected it to be my editor telling me which show I needed to attend when I got back to the city, but it was my mother.

"Hi, Mom."

"Sweetheart, it's so good to hear your voice. Your brother told me you're still in Jersey?"

The surprise in her voice made me second-guess my decision to stay there. "Yeah."

"Bentley, sweetheart, I read your latest review. That poor girl." Her voice dripped with sympathy for Ms. Jordan. My mother didn't exactly appreciate my blunt reviews.

"Mom, it's my job. Should I have said she was superb and then looked like a fool when people spent their money on my recommendation? You're the one who taught me to respect the art of acting."

"Honey, respecting art is one thing, but I also taught you to respect people. How do you think that young lady feels now?"

I felt my mother's words in my chest. "That review was based on my opinion, which I am paid and respected for. Would you have preferred me to lie and say she was the best thing to grace a stage since Liza Minnelli?" I was getting defensive with my mother, which wasn't something I normally did, but I felt bad enough. Having the only woman I loved coming down on me wasn't helpful.

"No. All I'm saying is your opinion could be kinder," she said.

"Maybe we can agree to disagree because I can't change who I am. If I'd said that she was wonderful, that wouldn't help her or the show. When I wanted to play in the father-son golf tournament with Dad, do you remember who played with him?"

"Yes, dear, your brother did." Her voice relaxed as she sighed.

"And do you remember why?"

"Yes, because your father thought he was better."

"Right, and did I whine and cry about it?" I asked. "No. I took lessons and became better so the next time, he would pick me—which, if you can remember, he did." I ran my hand through my hair.

"But—"

"No buts, Mother. This is how you both raised me. I'm trying to help this woman. Honestly, what gives today? I gave my opinion, which you should respect like others do." I cringed as soon as the words left my lips.

"Bentley David, I am still your mother, and you will not speak to me that way. Now when you get home, please call me so you can voice your very important opinion at our monthly meeting. This quarter's funding is approaching, and we need to make some decisions. We're counting on you. Can you be there?"

"Yes, I'll be there," I said.

She was the president of the Shooting Stars Theater Guild, a group that prided themselves on funding shows that normally wouldn't make it to Broadway without their help. The last thing I wanted to do was sit through afternoon tea with the guild, but I knew they'd want me to select the show they helped. Apparently my opinion was needed even though, at that moment, she didn't appreciate it.

"Thank you," she said.

"You're welcome. I'll see you later. I love you."

"Love you too, dear."

I hung up and thought about which show I should select for them. If I had it figured out in advance, I wouldn't have to stay too long. I picked up a stack of theater programs from recent off-Broadway shows and tried to decide which were best for the guild.

CHAPTER 3

Andi

My shaking legs carried me across the room to Mack's office. I couldn't tell if I was actually breathing.

Mack's door swung open. "Come in, you two." Mack's words were curt.

Justin stood and motioned for me to go ahead of him. I swallowed hard and felt as if I were entering the principal's office to get expelled. I looked at Mack's desk and saw the *Edge*. The back of my neck grew warm, and I was sure I was going to faint. *Great.* We sat in front of his desk, and I couldn't pull my eyes away from the paper.

Mack must have noticed where I was staring. "I take it you've seen this?"

My head snapped up. "Yes, I saw it."

Justin's eyes darted between me and Mack. "I don't know what you're talking about. Seen what?"

Mack picked up the black-and-white paper and handed it to Justin. "This."

Justin read the review then stared at me, confused.

I decided I needed to know exactly what was going on. "Mack—"

"Andi, I don't know why Bentley Chambers was here, but I believe it was because of you," Mack said. "I know that he has critiqued your work before, and I didn't agree with him then. I don't completely agree with him now."

Wait . . . completely?

"When the stagehand told me he saw Chambers, I didn't really believe him. But he was here." Mack shrugged. "Now, you're probably wondering why I wanted to meet with both of you."

"Excuse me, Mack." My voice was unsteady at best. "Did you say completely? You don't *completely* agree with him?"

"Andi, you know I adore you and think you're very talented."

He hadn't answered my question, but I didn't dare ask again. I glanced at Justin.

His brows were lowered, and he rubbed the back of his neck. "Reviews are reviews, right? I know I'm green in this business, but I can assure you there was passion." Justin winked, making me smile.

"Well, kids, this is what we're going to do. Justin, you're definitely keeping the role of Jake." Mack turned his attention to me.

His sympathetic brown eyes bore into mine, and my chest heaved at what was coming next.

"Andi, as I said, I adore you, but I have an entire cast and crew depending on this show making it. If we don't receive the necessary funds, we'll be done before we start. That's why you and Lucy will be re-auditioning for the role this week." His face fell a little at his words, but not enough to mirror mine. I was sure mine was on the floor.

"Mack, I can do this." My spine stiffened, and my voice somehow was steady.

"If you do retain the role of Katie, make Bentley Chambers physically hard the next time he comes to see the show. According to his editor, he'll be at our next preview performance."

My mouth dropped open. I closed it, and my eyes widened. "Pardon me?"

"Sorry for my crassness, but you two need to work together and get this right. This man wants passion, so give it to him. Make him want you."

His nonchalant tone threw me. All I could do was stare at him. So much for my stiff spine, it was now a wet noodle. Make him hard? It wasn't a burlesque show. It was a romantic play, for Christ's sake.

"Mack, I know I can do this. I'll be better by the end of the week." I gave the best smile I could muster.

He stood and tossed the *Edge* in the aluminum trash bin. "I know you can, or we wouldn't have cast you. Do what you need to do, and let's get together next week. Come prepared. I want you in this role, but I can't make any promises right now."

Justin and I stood. Trying to sound confident, I reached for Mack's hand. "I promise I won't let you down." I scurried out of the small office, trying to rein in my nerves and squash my self-doubt. I leaned against the cool cement wall near the exit of the theater and took in a deep breath. I couldn't believe this was happening. All because of Bentley Chambers. *Who was this guy?* My breathing became shallow, and if I didn't calm down, I was sure to pass out. Beads of sweat formed on the back of my neck.

Justin stood across from me with one foot propped on the wall. "Andi, are you okay? Why don't we get together and rehearse." He hugged me tight. "You're the best actress I've worked with, and you deserve this part."

Justin had to be just over six feet tall, and in comparison to my five foot four, he towered over me. My cheek rested just under his shoulder, and his soft cotton shirt soothed me. I didn't want to leave mascara stains on it, so I steadied my resolve.

"Thank you. Let's get out of here." I told Justin I'd call him for extra rehearsal time. I didn't think I could have too much at that point.

I went home and called Gina to tell her the latest and not so greatest news.

"Hey, Andi."

Just hearing her voice calmed my nerves. Thank God I had her. "Hey, G. Well, Mack met with me and Justin after rehearsal." I let out a sigh.

"What happened? You don't sound very good. Do you want me to come over?"

My teeth grabbed my bottom lip. I tried not to burst into tears. "No, it's getting late, but thank you. So, he wants me to audition again."

"No way!" Gina's voice bellowed through the receiver.

"What am I going to do? Maybe this Bentley guy is right and I really can't act."

My stomach turned at that thought though. It was bullshit—I could act, and I did my job well. But I hadn't yet made it to Broadway . . . maybe the dickhead had some clue what he was talking about. That thought hurt just a little bit more. For some reason, he had a different idea of what acting was.

"You know that isn't true," Gina said. "You're awesome. Please try not to worry."

"I suppose I could teach." My head dropped in my hands. "It's over. I know it is." An instant headache overwhelmed me. I rubbed my temples to try to relieve the pressure, but I knew that wouldn't work. I wanted to curl up in bed and pray this was all a bad dream, that Bentley Chambers hadn't come to the show. "I'm so tired. The hours I put into perfecting this role were a waste because it wasn't perfect."

"Nothing is perfect, no matter how hard you try or how good you are. You don't know what Mack is going to do. Please try to relax and think positive thoughts. You got this."

I exhaled. I felt lost and overwhelmed. Sadness and self-doubt had settled in. "Thanks, G."

"I think you should rest. Being overtired isn't helping. Call me tomorrow, okay?"

"I will. Love you."

"Love you too," I said. Gina was my biggest cheerleader and someone else I didn't want to let down.

I rested my head on the pillow and mentally prepared myself for tomorrow, thinking of everything I wanted to say to this man. As defeated as I felt, I knew I had to take action.

The sun beamed through my blinds when I sat up in bed. *Today's the day.* The theater was closed on Mondays, so the day was mine. I knew exactly how I was going to spend it. It was time to figure out exactly what Mr. Chambers's problem was with me, and I could only think of one way to find out—ask.

I searched the web and found the number for the *Edge* and dialed. Once I got connected to his assistant, my heart began to race.

"Mr. Chambers's office, Vanessa speaking."

Her professional tone told me this wouldn't be an easy task.

"Hello, Vanessa, this is Helen from Mr. Chambers's doctor's office. I was hoping to speak to him." That was my brilliant plan—pretend to be someone else.

"Hello, Helen. I'm sorry, but he's out of the office. I can take a message if you'd like."

I could imagine her reaching for a pen and pad as she spoke. Fan-fucking-tastic. *Think, Andi . . .*

"Here's the thing." I lowered my voice to a step above a whisper. "Assistant to assistant, I was supposed to call him last week, and I didn't. It's imperative that I speak to him sooner rather than later. May I please have his cell phone number?"

"I'm not at liberty to give out that information. Don't you have his contact information on file?" Her voice became snippy and a bit skeptical.

Shit. "Yes, I'm sure we do, but our computer system is down. Thankfully this number was in his paper file."

"How about I give him your message? He should be calling in when he's done with lunch at the Brookstone."

She didn't realize she'd just given me the information I needed. My smile was so wide I thought it might reach around to the back of my head and tie into a perfect bow. "How about I try him at another time? Thank you." I hung up, got in my car, and drove to the posh Brookstone restaurant.

The streets were crowded and lined with cars on either side. A thousand different scenarios ran around my brain as I tried to think of what to say to this arrogant man. The curbside parking was full, but thankfully the restaurant had valet parking. I pulled my Accord over and hopped out. The valet, in his black-and-white uniform, looked at me from head to toe. My clothes weren't the norm for someone dining at this establishment, but I didn't care.

I tossed him the keys in exchange for a ticket. "I won't be long."

I took the carpeted stairs two at a time to the hostess station. The sound of flatware on china mixed with the delicious aroma of the diners' lunches.

The hostess was stunning. She had auburn hair and deep brown eyes that perused me as the valet's had. "May I help you?"

With a straight spine and my head held high, I said, "Yes, please. I'm here to meet Mr. Chambers."

She pursed her plump, and no doubt silicone-injected, lips as she looked at the reservation book on the wood-and-brass podium. "It doesn't say Bent—I mean, Mr. Chambers—is expecting anyone."

"Really? Well, I wouldn't want to be the one who made that mistake." I looked around as if I had a deep, dark secret to tell her. "You know how he gets when he doesn't get his way."

This woman obviously knew him. Her pouty, full lips turned into a snarl, and I realized she was probably a gold digger who had carnal knowledge of him. Just the thought of that made me queasy. He was probably old enough to be her grandfather.

"Yes, well, we don't make mistakes here, but I will take you to him." Her voice was a tad shakier now.

I felt a hint of guilt but not enough to tell her it wasn't an error. "Thank you."

I followed her through the crowded restaurant. I peered around her right shoulder and saw a stodgy-looking older man dining alone. He had to be about eighty. No wonder he didn't know what passion was. Did his dick even work anymore? Mack wanted our kiss to make him hard, but clearly the man needed a little pill for that. I stifled a laugh.

Just when I thought the hostess would stop at his table, she shifted to her left, exposing the most beautiful man I'd ever laid eyes on. Scratch that—I had seen him at the diner! My heart hammered as I tried to quash my nerves.

"Mr. Chambers, your guest is here."

Well, fuck me! My stomach was in knots as my breathing increased.

He gave her a confused look. Then he saw me, and his lips curled into a shit-eating grin. "Thank you, Melissa."

He winked, and her face reddened. She looked at me and grimaced before she left us. Yup, they definitely had carnal knowledge of each other. I rolled my eyes before his deep blue eyes locked on mine.

He wiped the corners of his mouth with the black linen napkin. "Ms. Jordan, what a wonderful surprise."

Sex oozed from him. He placed the napkin back on his lap and picked up what I assumed was a scotch neat and sipped it. I couldn't stop staring at his perfect lips as he licked the amber liquor off them. His crisp, perfectly pressed white shirt definitely contrasted with my Levi's and "I'm With The Band Raging Urge" T-shirt. I glanced down at my attire.

Shit. I needed to focus. I sat in the cushioned chair across from him and prayed my shaking legs didn't touch the table. He was more mouthwatering than the meals being served. Never in my wildest imagination had I pictured Bentley Chambers being the sexy man from the diner.

"I won't be here long." I peered back at Melissa's retreating back before returning my attention to him. "I wouldn't want to keep you from your dessert."

He chuckled as a waiter came up and offered me a menu, which I declined. He filled my water glass and left a small plate of lemon and lime wedges. I didn't bother with adding citrus to my water. My mood was sour enough.

"So what is it that I can I do for you, Ms. Jordan?" His voice was deep and made the fine hairs on my arms stand at attention.

Why couldn't he be the ugly old ogre I had envisioned? I mustered up all the courage I could and prayed my voice didn't tremble. I realized I was fidgeting with the edge of the white linen tablecloth, so I brought my hands to my lap. "You can tell me why you take pleasure in decimating my career."

He slid aside what was left of his lunch and leaned his elbows on the table. "Decimate? I don't find pleasure in decimating your career, nor do I feel that I have. I think you've done a fine job of that on your own." His features remained perfectly chiseled and impassive.

THE CRITIC

Stoic. Remain stoic. What a rude son of a bitch. I'd have been in tears if I wasn't so pissed. "Excuse me?"

"Look, Ms. Jordan, I don't know what you're doing here, but if you think I've ruined your career, then you need to take a look in the mirror." His tone didn't fluctuate as he reprimanded me.

I tried to swallow my heart, which was in my throat. "You're a theater critic, correct?"

"Yes. I thought that had been established." He sat back in his chair and crossed his arms, making his biceps flex.

"Have you ever taken an acting class, Mr. Chambers?" I'd become more irritated since I sat down. My elbows were firmly planted on the table.

"No, I'm a writer. I haven't been on stage since high school. That doesn't mean I can't see the difference between a good performance and poor one. Is this why you came here, to review my resume? How did you find me anyway?" He lifted his glass to his lips without wavering at all.

"Don't change the subject. So you're not an actor, yet you critique my work and say that I lack passion and talent? Who gave you the right to determine who's good and who's not?" I felt my shoulders roll forward in defeat, so I straightened my spine.

"Well, quite frankly, my employer does. Andrea—can I call you Andrea, or do you prefer Andi?"

"It's Ms. Jordan to you. My friends call me Andi." *How does he know my nickname?*

Before I could ask, he smirked, which made me want to reach across the table and slap his smug face. "Fine, Ms. Jordan. I didn't say you couldn't act. Well, not entirely. Deep down, you may have the passionate woman needed to play the role, but you aren't there yet. That doesn't mean I don't think you can't get there. I think you have it in you. Your coming here shows me that you want it. So tell me, when was the last time you were in the throes of passion?"

Was this guy for real? My eyes caught his, and I felt something different, unexplainable. I felt as though he looked through me rather than at me. My insides were in a knot a sailor would have been proud of. "I don't see how that is any of your business." I prayed my face wasn't beet red.

"Ahhh, I think I have my answer. You may have the passion for acting, but can you feel real passion—that's the question." He picked up his drink and took a taste. As he set the glass down, he grinned. "I could help you with that." He winked at me.

I abruptly stood, hitting my thigh on the underside of the square table and making it wobble. The audacity of this man! "You have some nerve! Who the hell do you think you are?" I spun around and noticed the other diners looking my way. I sarcastically smiled and felt like flipping them off. *Fuck this and all the pretentious assholes in here.*

As I speed-walked across the restaurant, dodging the wait staff and ignoring the stares, I prayed he wasn't following me. Melissa shook her head in disgust as I breezed by. I glared back at her and pushed through the revolving door. On the sidewalk, the valet walked up to me. With a shaky hand, I gave him the ticket for my car.

Standing on the corner with my arms crossed, I felt his presence behind me. My brain whirled with how arrogant he was, not to mention his stunning looks. Why did he have to be one of the most striking men I'd ever seen? When he'd asked me about passion, my body tingled with anticipation. I internally chastised myself for that betrayal.

"Ms. Jordan." His deep voice cut through my thoughts and not in a good way.

My focus remained on the passing cars while I waited for the valet.

"Ms. Jordan!" His voice was sterner, and that irritated me.

Not only was my mind abandoning my reason for being there, but hearing his voice call my name made my skin tingle. I'd said my piece, and now I needed to get the hell away from him.

I twisted to look at him. My head craned back to meet his eyes. "What? What do you want? Am I standing in the wrong spot? Do I have a hair out of place?" I ran my hand over my head in an exaggerated manner. "Didn't I look convincing when I gave the guy the ticket to retrieve my car?" People leaving the restaurant were looking at me as if I were crazy, so I tried to calm my nerves and took a deep breath. "So are you going to speak or just stand there looking pretty?"

He moved toward me swiftly and brought his hands to each side of my face. He pulled me to him which made me roll up on my toes and crashed his mouth onto mine. His grip became firmer as he tilted his head, making my lips part. His tongue slipped in, and I allowed it. I was totally and utterly gone. Our tongues tangled as his hands slid through my hair, and my hands went under his leather jacket to his strong back. He groaned and pressed his hips against mine. As soon as I felt what the kiss was doing to him, I backed off, looked into his deep blue eyes, and swung my hand at his face.

He grabbed my wrist, stopping the blow, and stared at me. "That is passion, Ms. Jordan." He trailed his thumb over the corner of his lips, wiping away the moisture that had gathered from our kiss.

I pulled my wrist out of his grasp. "No, Mr. Chambers, that's acting."

"Bring that to the stage, and you might keep your job," he growled without taking his eyes off me. His brows drew together, creating a small crease above his nose.

I squinted in the sunlight as he slid on a pair of aviators that made him look more like a biker than a critic. That, mixed with his perfect hair and overconfident charm, made me weak. All I could do was pray my expression didn't scream, "I want you." The valet pulled up with my car, and I was thankful I was wearing Converse sneaks instead of stilettos because I felt as if I could fall over. I sensed that passion in every cell of my body. Damn it, and damn him!

"Good-bye, Mr. Chambers." I walked behind the car and greeted the valet, who was holding my door open. My body trembled as I slid in.

He shut my door, and the passenger door opened. Mr. Arrogant slid in, shut the door, and buckled up.

"What the hell do you think you're doing?" My voice was so loud that the valet looked at me.

Bentley's eyes narrowed. "We're not done, and I think you know that as well as I do. Drive."

"Get out!" Was this guy kidding, just hopping in my car like that? His cologne had begun to permeate the air in my car, and I hurried to open a window so his scent wouldn't linger.

"Let me help you." He reached for my hand, which I quickly moved.

"What? With what?" It didn't matter—he irritated me more than a cold winter's day. "No! Get out!"

He didn't move. Instead he faced forward, grabbed his phone, and made a call. "Vanessa, it's me. Can you please clear my appointments for the rest of the week and send Michael to the shows I was going to review?" He paused, obviously listening to her response. "My doctor's office?" He glanced at me.

I tried to hide my smile and bit down on my lip.

"Hmm . . . I see. Well, if Helen should call again, tell her that I'll contact the office when I return to the city, but that won't be until next week. I'm staying in Jersey through Friday."

My mouth gaped as I looked at him. "No, you're not!" My knuckles whitened as I gripped the steering wheel.

He chuckled and focused on his call. "What? No, that was the maid. Yes, it's fine. Thank you. Have a good week."

"Get out of my damn car!"

As soon as the words left my mouth, a police officer pulled up alongside me and told me to move. *Damn it! What next?*

"I guess you'd better drive unless you want a ticket." That snarky smirk appeared again, making my blood boil.

The audacity of this man! I looked at the black-and-white car and waved to the officer before I pulled away. "Where are you staying? It better be close, or I'm dropping you at the corner." I should have dropped him there anyway.

"The Ritz on Belmont. You won't have to drive far."

A rush of relief, laced with a twinge of disappointment, passed over me. *What was wrong with me?* "Fine. I'll drive you there, and then I don't want to see you again—ever."

"Oh, you'll see me again. I'm going to stay here and help you, and you're going to let me."

"The hell I am!" I tried to keep my cool as I drove through the city streets. A few stoplights later, I was at the Ritz. I pulled into the semi-circle in front of the entrance and tossed my car in park, unlocking the doors. "Good-bye, Mr. Chambers."

He opened the door and got out. Before he closed it, he leaned into my car and handed me his business card. His fingers brushed mine. I didn't know what was happening to me, because my heart rate picked up and not because I was angry—he was turning me on.

"I know you don't like me and think I'm a horrible person, but deep down, I think you know I'm right. Don't lie to yourself and tell me you didn't feel the heat between us on the sidewalk. Think about it," he said, his confidence never wavering. "My cell phone number is on the other side. Ms. Jordan, my goal is not to ruin your career. In fact, I would love for the opposite to happen. If you need to go through your script, you have my number. I know you have Justin, but I don't think he evokes fire in your soul."

"Pfft! And you think you do?"

"Think about that. My reach in this industry is deep, Ms. Jordan. I'll expect your call." He was about to close the door when he leaned in. "By the way, this is for you." He handed me a penny. "I wouldn't want to be the source of your bad luck." He winked and shut the door.

My brows lowered as I watched him walk through the revolving door. I looked at the copper coin. *Bad luck?* As if a lightbulb had turned on, my mouth dropped open. I flashed back five years to a small store. That was him? No wonder he looked familiar! He remembered that? Holy shit, what had I gotten myself into?

I tossed the card into the cup holder in my center console and pulled away. My thumb pushed the phone button on my steering wheel. Wait until I told Gina about his nerve, not to mention the sureness and sexiness that he radiated. But my call went to voicemail. *Figures.*

"Gina, call me when you get this. The ogre was rather orgasmic." I clicked the off button and laughed. If that message didn't get her to call me, nothing would.

Bentley

She'd tasted sweeter than icing, better than I could've ever imagined. The fire that raged through her as she laid into me had made me hard as stone. Going after her and getting into her car while trying to hide my erection had taken effort.

The sight of her behind Melissa, a one-time conquest I wasn't proud of, had thrilled and scared me all at the same time. I thought of Brett's words and was happy the Brookstone didn't keep steak knives on the table. How that woman could get so passionate about my words and not about the words in her script was beyond me.

I sat at my desk and opened my laptop. I reread my review. I supposed it was harsh, but it was still honest. I couldn't change my opinion just because I wanted to make her mine. I'd rather her trust me and allow me to help her. *I'll prove to her we could be good together.*

Just thinking about her glaring at me and her tits in that worn T-shirt stirred me in a way no woman had before. I needed her like I needed my pen to write. We would be together someday, and she didn't even know it. I just needed to make it happen.

My phone chimed with a text from Brett.

Brett: Still on for tomorrow?

Bentley: Yeah at your favorite place?

Brett: Of course. Are you feeling better?

I laughed.

Bentley: Well, there weren't any knives in sight.

Brett: Oh shit. You saw her?

Bentley: She confronted me.

My phone rang, and I grinned. I'd known texting wouldn't suffice. "Hey."

"Don't 'hey' me, big brother. What's the deal with this chick?" Brett sounded annoyed and perhaps a bit scared for me.

I laughed. "Her deal is she hates me."

"And you find that funny?"

Yup. He's annoyed. "No, you calling her 'chick' is funny. I had an immediate vision of Andrea kicking your ass."

"Yeah, like she could do that." Brett chuckled, but he hadn't met her yet.

"Call her that to her face someday and find out." I cleared my throat. "Anyway, she confronted me and then drove me to my hotel."

"Ahhh . . . there's my brother. How was she between the sheets?"

I could picture him waggling his brows. "I didn't fuck her. She gave me a ride. I did, however, offer her my services."

"Is that what they're calling it now?" Brett was finding too much pleasure in my discomfort.

"I'm glad you're finding this funny. All I did was offer to help her. You know my rule—I don't sleep with actresses." But I'd wanted her since I saw her five years ago. I'd break that rule for her.

"You think this chi—woman is going to let you help her after you blasted her in your review?"

"Yup."

"Well, you let me know how that goes. My other line is ringing, I need to bolt."

"Later, man."

We hung up, and I paced my room. Would she call me and let me help her? She was a prideful woman, but I was pretty confident my phone would ring. The fact that she'd called my office and pretended to be my doctor's assistant told me she wanted the role. Now I needed her to bring that desire to her performance.

CHAPTER 4

Andi

My apartment greeted me with the comfort I needed. I grabbed a Diet Coke from the fridge. Screw him and his goddamn review. I didn't need him to assist me. I picked up my script.

Katie: *Jake, you're the one I want, the one I need. So many years have passed.*
<Katie lowers eyes>
<Jake lifts her chin with his index finger>
Jake: *I'm never letting you go again.*
<Jake kisses Katie with heated passion>

Of course heated passion. I set down the script. There was that word again . . . fucking passion. My phone buzzed. It was Gina.

"Hey." My voice was hollow and soft.

"What's wrong? I got your message. So this guy is hot? Details please!" At least one of us was excited.

I rested my head on the fluffy pillow on the couch. "I don't know if I'd classify him as just hot. He surpasses hot. Put it this way—if he wasn't the man from hell, I'd be trying to get him in bed. Actually, remember the guy from the diner?"

Gina let out an exaggerated sigh. "Yeah. He was fantastic."

"Yeah, well, that was him."

"Get out! Oh my God! So what happened? Did you lay into him?"

She's excited all right. "Yeah, I guess. He flipped it on me, G. Told me that I wasn't passionate. We had words, and I left, but not before I hit the table with my leg, because of course I couldn't have a graceful exit." Defeat overwhelmed me. "Then he kissed me."

"What? Wait, where? Why? You let him . . . he kissed you? Was it good?" The confusion surrounded by joy in her voice didn't help my situation.

"Gina, please, focus."

"Sorry, but geez. Okay, go on."

"I was leaving the restaurant, and he followed me out to the sidewalk. We were arguing, and he grabbed me and kissed me." My pulse quickened at the memory.

"Holy shit! So . . . how did he taste?"

I clutched a pillow to my chest, trying to contain my heart. I was sure it was going to come barreling out of my ribcage any minute. "'How did he taste?'" Those words squeaked out of me.

"You have to admit the man looks delicious. Like a warm truffle that'll melt in your mouth and coat your tongue in sweet sensuality."

"Oh my God!" I sighed. "Fine, I'll admit it. It was the best kiss I've ever had. I felt it everywhere, and I mean everywhere. The roots of my eyelashes felt it." I felt my face flush with lust. When our lips met, it was as if they'd belonged together. The comfort and familiarity that came with something that should have felt so foreign made me wonder what the hell had happened to my resolve.

"This is so great!" She sounded like a giddy schoolgirl getting the latest gossip.

"Great? You think this is great?" I shook my head. "G, how is this great? I mean, this man is just . . . ugh! I mean . . . UGH!"

Gina let out a full-blown laugh. "Well, someone has got your panties in a dampened twist. Look, Andi, you never know. Maybe this is all meant to be. Could it be possible that fate has brought you two together?"

"Fate? Are you kidding me? Whose side are you on?" My mind was in a haze as though I was floating and looking down at this situation rather than experiencing it.

"Yours. Always yours," she said, "but think about it. What are the odds of him reviewing so many of your shows? You aren't on Broadway."

"Yes, thank you for the reminder." I looked at the pages lying next to me. "Will you come over and run lines with me?"

"Of course I will, but answer something for me first." Her timid yet stern voice rang through the phone.

"Fine. What?"

"If he wasn't Bentley Chambers the hard-ass critic and just Bentley Chambers the man, how would you feel? Imagine us walking into a club and seeing him leaning against the bar. Would you feel the same way?"

A chill went down my spine as I remembered his face covered in dark scruff, his styled but messy hair, a jawline that was so lickable it made my tongue twitch, and eyes that infiltrated my soul. Even in a leather jacket, his body had looked toned and tight. I sighed at the memory.

"Andi?"

"Yeah?" The word came out as a whisper as I imagined my hands on his back.

"Well?" Gina giggled.

"I'd want everything he offered and more. But he's not just some random guy. He told me I lacked passion, that I didn't even know what it was and he could show me. Who says that?"

"I'll tell you who—a sexy-ass man with confidence. I'll be over in a little bit."

She hung up, and my mind replayed the kiss I'd shared with Bentley. I thought about the difference between that kiss and those I'd shared with Justin. There was no comparison. I needed a man who could awaken my body and make me wet with just the thought of him. I needed a man who could make me feel things no one ever had. And I knew who that man was . . . Bentley. Dammit.

Gina showed up about an hour later. We tried to run lines, but it really didn't work. When it came to the hugs and the tender words, all we did was laugh. That didn't help my cause, so we popped in *The Notebook* and watched a kiss that made me move toward my television. Their kiss . . . I could actually feel it and the rain that covered them. That was what my kisses needed to be like. That was what Bentley meant.

My best friend moaned slightly, and I could tell she felt it too. I turned my head toward Gina, who was still fixated on the movie.

"G?" I tapped her shoulder.

"Yeah." She sighed. "What?"

"That's the kiss, right? The one you can actually feel?"

"Hell yeah. Makes my mouth water, and I swear my thighs are throbbing." She crossed her legs and whimpered.

"Okay, well, on that note, I think I'll call Justin and see if he can run lines with me."

"Yeah, that's a good idea. He's so cute." She snickered.

"What am I going to do if he isn't available? I've practiced kissing the back of my hand more times than I'd like to admit."

Gina scrunched up her nose. "I'm surprised you admitted it at all. What are your other options?"

The business card I'd put in my purse popped into my head. "No way could I call him."

"Who?"

I squeezed my eyes closed, not realizing I'd spoken out loud. "Bentley." I peeked at Gina, who was speechless and staring at me as if I had three heads. "He told me he'd help me. How about that? Blasted me in the newspaper and then wants to help me perfect my role."

"That would be awesome." Gina's face lit with hope.

"You've got to be kidding." I headed into the kitchen for some wine. I opened the refrigerator and grabbed a bottle of chardonnay. "Want a glass?"

"No, I need to get home. Andi, think about it. If he

works with you and you still aren't up to par, it's like he failed. There is no way a guy like that will admit in black and white that your performance is lacking after he worked with you on perfecting it." She stood as I poured the largest glass of wine I could. "Sweetie, you should do this. We know he's gorgeous, so win-win, right? I mean, at this point, what do you have to lose?" She shrugged, and I lost a bit of my resolve.

We said our good-byes, and I told her I'd call her in the morning. I stared at my purse, knowing his number was in there. I shook my head and took my wine to my bedroom. I set the glass on the nightstand and looked at the picture of a marquee on Broadway. It read, "Starring Andrea Jordan." Gina had had it made for me when I was in my first off-Broadway play six years earlier. I'd made it to the big stage once when I landed a small part in a low-budget comedy, but the funding was cut, and the show never came to fruition. I padded to my bathroom and stared at my reflection. I really needed to get this part right, or no one would ever cast me in a role that was worth having. I put my long brown hair in a ponytail and got ready for bed.

I slept later than I had in a long time, but I didn't have any place to be since the show was shut down for two weeks. I stretched and rolled off my very comfortable mattress. I briefly considered staying in bed, but I had work to do.

I turned on the shower and brushed my teeth while the water warmed up. Once inside the steamy enclosure, I relished the streams from the shower head. I stared at the beige tiled wall then looked at my beige shower curtain. I was starting to see a pattern. Maybe I was just bland and blah when I needed to be red and fiery. *That's it. Decision made.* I hopped out of the shower, dried my hair, carefully applied some makeup, and grabbed my purse.

Coffee. That was what I needed—strong coffee. I tossed my purse on the couch and made my way to the kitchen. While I leaned against the counter, waiting for it to brew, I stared at my leather bag. The need to call him hadn't escaped me, but the courage did. Just giving him the satisfaction was making me feel ill, but a girl's gotta do what a girl's gotta do. I ran into my room to get my phone. Then in one quick motion, I snatched the business card from my purse and flipped the card over. I dialed before I lost my nerve or came to my senses.

One ring . . . two rings . . .

"Chambers." His voice was deep and raspy.

Shit. I may have woken him. *Oh well, too bad.* After a calming breath, my voice emerged. "Mr. Chambers, it's Andrea Jordan." I closed my eyes and prayed for him not to be an ass.

"Ahhh . . . good morning, Ms. Jordan. I had a feeling I'd be hearing from you . . . and so soon too." He chuckled. "Please call me Bentley. All my friends do."

Yup . . . an ass. My heart raced when he said his name, and I smiled when he said mine. What the hell was wrong with me? "Good morning. I wanted to discuss your offer."

The beep on my coffee maker alerted me that caffeine was ready to be consumed. The aroma of fresh-brewed coffee was one of my favorites, so I decided I needed some stat!

"By offer, I assume you'd like to run your lines with me?" His arrogance seeped through the phone, making me second-guess my decision.

THE CRITIC

With a fresh cup of coffee in hand, I sat at the kitchen table. "I know my lines"—*dickhead*—"but yes." Just admitting that made me cringe.

"You're a smart woman and beautiful too."

The grin that grew across my face was completely involuntary. "Well, thank you, but compliments will get you nowhere. This is business. When are you available?"

"My schedule is free all week, as I assume yours is. There's no time like the present. Would you like me to come to you, or would you like to come here?"

I glanced around the room and decided here would be the wiser choice. "My apartment will be fine. I'll text you the address, but I have rehearsal now. I'll be available after two."

"See you then, Ms. Jordan."

My phone beeped a few times, indicating our call had ended. I sipped my coffee and relished the warmth as I thought about what would happen when he arrived. I decided to clean up my apartment, even though it was spotless. Then I went to the theater to work on the role that could change my life.

Lucy and Greg, the two understudies, were there as well. My heart raced when I saw them, but apparently they were going to be rehearsing as well. It made sense that she would be preparing for the audition too, but it unnerved me.

She wasn't a bad actress. Actually, she was pretty good, and she'd improved since the last show she'd played in. I tried not to let that bother me. I knew I was a fine actress—I just needed to be better.

Once rehearsal was over, I headed home. Bentley would be at my place within the hour.

The buzzer on my apartment door rang.

"Yes?" I said.

"It's Bentley."

"Come on up." I unlocked the deadbolt and ran to the bathroom to check myself. I didn't look half bad. My hair was naturally wavy, and my makeup was understated yet covered any dark circles.

A knock on the door made my heart stop. How was I going to handle seeing him? After I stopped fidgeting, I opened the door and my eyes went wide. Just gorgeous. The man was perfection from head to toe.

"Hi." I stepped aside and opened the door wider.

"Hello, Ms. Jordan." Bentley breezed past me as if he'd been there a dozen times. He was carrying an umbrella and a black backpack.

I wondered what his bag held. *I hope he hadn't plan on spending the night.* He wore light-colored jeans and his worn leather jacket, which he removed. His navy Henley made his eyes stand out and my legs clench. His hair looked as though he had just run his hands through it.

"Would you like a cup of coffee?" I may as well have been gracious, and Lord knew I needed a few more cups.

"No, thank you. I had some earlier." He walked around the couch and sat down. "Nice place you have here."

I nodded and grabbed my cup from the kitchen. "Thank you."

The script was lying on the coffee table. He picked it up. "May I?"

"Sure. I went through a few scenes with my girlfriend Gina last night."

His eyebrows rose high as he looked at me. "You have a girlfriend? Are you . . . ?" He lowered his head, apparently waiting for me to confirm I was a lesbian.

I couldn't help but laugh. "She's my best friend, not my lover. Not that I have a lover. I mean . . ." *Holy shit, what am I doing?* I sat next to him and took the script. "So I know according to you I failed miserably on Saturday night, but was there a particular scene that made you throw me to the dogs?" This play was full of love scenes, and I couldn't imagine which one he'd hated, since I thought they were all good.

"No, there isn't a particular scene, just your overall performance. I didn't throw you to the dogs, as you so eloquently put it. I just didn't connect with it. If I could have the script back, we can go through it in its entirety."

"Its entirety?" Just then I realized my breath must smell like coffee. I reached into my purse and grabbed a mint. I offered him one.

He smirked and popped it in his mouth. "I have all week. Before we get down to business, I want to know a little about you." He tossed his arm on the back of the couch, making himself at home.

That threw me off guard. "Why?" My life was so boring. There really wasn't much to tell.

"It will help me understand you." He leaned back and raised his brows, waiting for me to begin.

I blew out a breath that made my bangs fly up. Why he needed to know about my life was beyond me, but if telling him about myself would move along what was sure to be a grueling process, I'd tell him my fucking life story.

"Fine. I've wanted to star in a Broadway production since I can remember. I was in every school play, and I enrolled in every workshop I could find. I used to buy old scripts just to study them and act out the parts." Talking about the frayed, crinkled papers I loved made my face light up. "I've studied theater history, Shakespeare. I've had countless drama and acting classes. I even studied improv. I've been busting my ass trying to perfect my craft."

I heard my voice turn more boisterous with a touch of sarcasm. "Then a critic from New York City reviewed a play I was in and blasted me in his paper, stating that I lacked . . ." My hand went to my chin and my eyes to the ceiling. "Let's see, what did he say?" I threw my hand in the air to get the light bulb that just popped up. "Ah yes . . . I lacked 'the ability to connect with a character to make it so believable that the audience gets lost in the performance.' So I continued to bust my ass and then . . . and then . . . finally . . ."My arms flailed a mile a minute while my pulse raced. "I finally landed the part of Katie." My heart was pounding so hard, I was sure it was going to escape through my shirt and land at his feet for him to stomp on. "This was my breakout role. Everyone told me this would be *the one,* that I was meant to play this character, as if it had been written with me in mind."

I stood and looked at him, ignoring his deep blue eyes and the slight flare of his nostrils. "So there it was in my hands and my soul. My chance was here, right? I could taste it, mouthwatering and delicious, and then you happened. Again!" My face tingled as my chin quivered and tears began to form. I walked into the kitchen.

THE CRITIC

My hands rested on the countertop in front of the sink, and I took a deep, shaky breath. The sound of his footsteps as he came up behind me put me on full alert, so I grabbed a glass out of the dish drainer and filled it with water. I took a sip and set down the glass. I couldn't do this, not with him.

"Andrea. . . ." His hands landed on my shoulders, which I rolled to get them off me.

I went into the family room and sat on the sofa, and he followed. My apartment felt the size of a shoebox.

"I can't apologize for my reviews. You understand that right?" he said. "I can't write a great review when I don't witness a great performance. I know you have it in you. Why do you think I came all this way to see you? I anticipated being astonished. I'd heard all about you and this role, and yes, it was slated to be your true breakout role. I'm not saying it won't be, but that didn't happen on Saturday. I wanted it too, maybe for my own selfish reasons, but—"

"Really, Mr. Chambers? You wanted it to?" I didn't want to take in his beautiful eyes glaring at me, but I couldn't help myself.

"Look, it's my job to leave critiques of the plays I attend. I have to write with honesty, or my reviews won't be worth the paper they're printed on. Understand?" His brows furrowed.

I turned away to avoid him because even though I was upset, he still affected me. "Yes, of course I understand, and you keep reminding me what a horrible actress I am, so why are you here exactly? Maybe you just shouldn't go to the shows I'm in." I spun around and saw his expression turn grim as he lowered his head. "I'm serious, Bentley. If I'm that bad of an actress, then why torture yourself? You came to Jersey, for Christ's sake, to see a way, way, way off-Broadway play, and for what? So you can write another negative review? Does it make you feel better doing that?" I shook my head. "This was a bad idea. I don't feel like running lines anymore. Please leave."

He placed his hand on mine. "Andrea—"

I stood and went to the door. The hand he'd just touched sent a shiver through me as I turned the handle. I opened the door and waited for him to get up, which he did. He faced me, and I tried to keep my composure. As much as I hated to admit it, he made me feel things I'd never felt before, and it wasn't all anger. But at the moment, I was sad and completely embarrassed, and he needed to go.

"Good-bye." I swung my hand toward the hallway.

Instead of leaving, he brought his hand to my cheek and ran the backside of his knuckles from the top of my cheekbone to my chin. "I come to see your shows because I know you have it in you to be fabulous, and you're the most beautiful woman I've ever seen. There's something about you. I can feel it, and to be quite honest, I'd hoped that we'd meet someday and you'd feel it too. When you came to the restaurant, I was surprised and thrilled." He stared at me as I tried not to flinch. "Call me if you change your mind."

He walked out and left me wanting more. I closed the door and leaned my right shoulder against it, chastising myself for being weak around him.

My couch cushion greeted me as I rested my head on the rolled cotton arm. Something caught my eye— Bentley's backpack. Dammit. My fingers itched to unzip it, but I didn't. I stared at my ceiling and wondered if he

63

was right and I wasn't as good as I thought. What I didn't understand was why I'd be cast in roles if I didn't deserve them. I shook my head and closed my eyes. This was getting me nowhere except frustrated.

I drifted off and thought of Bentley and his piercing, gentle eyes. The feel of his hand in my hair, pulling me to him. Our lips colliding and our tongues dancing while his scruff grazed my face. Hearing him moan with pleasure and grinding against me.

The sound of my phone startled me—I'd forgotten where I was. When I realized I was home alone, I felt a pang of disappointment. Those thoughts needed to stop. I hit the answer button. "Hello."

"Andrea, this is Bentley. I'm sorry to bother you, and I'm sure I'm the last person you want to hear from, but I left my backpack at your place. My hotel key is in there, along with my wallet. Can I please come back over and pick it up? I promise I won't stay."

I let out a silent breath. "Yeah." I couldn't bring myself to say any more. The words we'd had before he left were still making my head spin.

"I'm right around the corner. I'll be there in a few minutes." His voice was quiet and very different from the tone he'd used in my apartment. He was no longer the gruff, pompous man. He sounded sweet and almost remorseful, but that could have just been wishful thinking on my part.

"Fine." I clicked the phone off and grabbed his backpack. I checked my hair in the mirror next to my door and fixed the errant strands. When I opened the door, he was standing in the hall with his hand in the air, ready to knock. "I heard you coming."

He looked at me with a sad expression.

"Here you go." I shoved his bag at his chest. "Bye." As I went to close the door, he stopped it with his free hand.

"Can we talk?" His face was impassive and calm. Those damn blue eyes seemed to see through me.

The defeat I felt after every conversation with him drained me; I didn't know if I wanted to do it again. Yes, my heart beat differently for him, but I didn't want it to. My entire body felt as if it could collapse into a puddle. "Really, what more is there to talk about?" I leaned my head on the edge of the opened door, and a sigh may have escaped me.

"Let me in," he appealed, his voice not much louder than a whisper. He dropped his head before lifting his gaze to mine again. "Please, Andrea."

I moved out of the doorway and let him pass. He stood in front of my couch, set his bag down, and picked up the copy of the *Edge*. He held it and forcibly straightened his arm. "Do you see this?" His face softened, which didn't match his stern voice.

"Of course." I tried to get the paper out of his hand, but he held it above his head.

"This . . . this . . ." He shook the paper. "This review does not define you. Do you understand me?" His voice grew louder as I became more annoyed.

"Yeah, whatever. I want it back." I held out my hand and kept my feet planted on my carpet. "Seriously, Mr. Chambers, give it to me!"

"What the fuck is this 'Mr. Chambers' shit? Quite possibly, if you took some of the emotion you're feeling right now and put it in your work, you'd be a brilliant actress."

"Fuck you and your emotional brilliance. Give me my goddamn paper!" I felt my blood pressure spike and prayed I didn't erupt like a volcano.

His eyes darted around the room until he found my script. He put the newspaper under his arm and flipped through the script as if he was looking for something specific. He stopped flipping pages and held it out to me. "Read that."

"Go to hell." I crossed my arms to prevent them from shaking.

"Read it!"

"No!"

He shoved it closer to me, making the paper graze my chest, and said in the sternest voice I'd heard since my father's, "Yes."

I grabbed it and looked at the scene he'd selected. Perfect—the one he hated. *I think*. Fuck, he hated everything.

"Andrea!" His eyes narrowed.

His voice grated on my last nerve. "Where?"

"From the top."

My blood boiled. Why should I go along with this? I closed the script and tossed it at him; I didn't need to read something I'd memorized weeks ago. He caught it against his chest, making the newspaper fall.

I shook my arms and tried to get into character. I closed my eyes and took a cleansing breath. The scene was quiet and heartfelt. Katie had been afraid Jake had decided to move on, and she didn't want to lose him. I silently said to myself, 'Don't blow this, Andi."

With a quiet voice, I said, "Jake, it's been so many years." I walked forward as the blocking in my script dictated. I looked at Bentley's eyes then the paper on the ground. "What makes you think that I'm available, that I still want you?"

Bentley read Jake's line, making my eyes go wide.

"You're the only one for me." I placed my hand on his chest as the script dictated. "Can't you feel that?"

He placed his hand over mine, which Justin never did. Bentley's heart pounded strong and fast. My palm twitched.

"What are you doing, Bentley?" I looked into his eyes, trying to figure out his plan. Feeling his heartbeat did something unexpected to me. It was hard to pinpoint the emotion flowing through my body, but the only thing I could do was ignore it. No way could I let myself get wrapped up in him.

"Keep going." His voice was demanding, bringing me back to despising him.

My insides were on fire. Through a tense jaw, I said, "Yes, Jake, I can, but that doesn't mean anything!" I went to pull my hand away, and he held it there.

He shoved the newspaper with his foot, reminding me what an ass he was. Which was why I needed to crush the odd feelings growing inside me.

"It means everything." His voice tempered as if he were speaking as himself and not Jake.

I wouldn't fall for that. "It means nothing!" I ripped my hand away from his muscular chest.

"Kiss me."

"No!" I turned away from him.

"Katie, kiss me now." He grabbed the tops of my arms and spun me to face him. "Kiss me, dammit. Now!" That line was all his.

THE CRITIC

"I can't, and I won't." If he could ad lib, so could I.

He stared at me. "I said kiss me."

His voice was serious, and I was torn between feeling distraught and turned on. I should have been upset with myself for wavering, but instead, I decided I was frustrated.

I lunged forward and kissed him as hard as I could. The anger I felt poured out of me as our lips connected. I shoved my tongue in his mouth and pulled on his hair, lowering his face to mine. He grabbed my waist and hoisted me up so my legs wrapped around his hips. His lips went to my neck, and my head dropped back, giving him ample access. He licked from my collarbone to my ear, and his soft beard made me shiver. A groan of pleasure escaped me as my pulse quickened. Before I knew it, my feet were planted on the carpet. My world had tilted or maybe fallen off its axis.

"See the difference?" His voice became calm, making me anything but.

"What the hell was that?" I wiped my lips with the back of my hand to prove that I wasn't falling for it . . . for him. But I knew I had.

"That was perfect. Bring your feelings out, Andrea. Acting isn't just getting the words right or evoking whatever feeling you think is on that paper, and you should know that. You need to dig deeper. Let your feelings shine through. If being pissed off at me brings out the emotion I just felt, then take that to the stage. Don't hold back because you think you might do it wrong or someone else would do it better or that's what the director wanted. Acting 101: Be yourself and let your emotions shine through. You've been so caught up in doing it the right way and not blowing this shot at success that you've closed yourself up and done it all wrong." He picked up his bag and looked at me. "You kiss Justin like that, and you'll captivate the audience just like you did me. I'll call you tomorrow. Good night."

Bentley

I shut the door as my heart pounded and my mind raced. What the fuck? I'd never wanted to make anyone mine as much as I did that woman. The urge to take Andrea and ravish her body consumed my thoughts. I knew the words that had spewed from my mouth weren't what she'd wanted to hear, but she needed to hear them. I cursed myself for taking the train to Jersey. I wished I had my car so I could go for a long drive. Instead, I grabbed my cell and called a cab.

Once I was in my room, I grabbed the crystal bottle of scotch and poured a generous drink. I sat on the recliner and thought of her perfectly formed lips and how they'd tasted pressed against mine. They were as soft as a rose petal.

I picked up the program from *Together Again* and looked at her picture. Her eyes came alive as I stared at her, and I willed her entire being to follow suit. I adjusted my cock in my jeans as it pressed against my zipper. Buried deep—that was what I wanted—in her warm, slick pussy. Would she ever let me breach the wall with my name on it that she'd definitely erected? Would she ever allow me to love her and worship her body as I'd dreamt of doing?

My goal had been to prove to her that she exuded

passion and to give her the outlet to express it, but I'd never realized that she had done that to me. I was the one who needed the outlet, and she was it. I downed the rest of my drink and headed for the bathroom. The thought of jerking off to her picture was foremost on my mind, but that wouldn't be enough. So I settled for a cold shower to calm my shit down. I wanted the real deal, not just the image of her face and my palm. I needed to get closer to her, I needed her to trust me, but first and foremost, I needed her to succeed. She had to find herself before I could expect her to give herself to me.

After attempting to rid my thoughts of Andrea, I settled in bed. I grabbed my phone to see if she'd called, but she hadn't. Not that I'd really expected her to. My hand seemed to have a mind of its own as it typed out a text.

Bentley: You awake?

I stared at the screen, praying she'd respond. My need to talk to her was overwhelming, as was my fear of scaring her away.

Andi: No.

Bentley: Funny.

Andi: What do you want?

I relaxed a bit knowing I had her attention. All I really wanted was for her to think of me before she went to sleep.

Bentley: That's a loaded question.

Andi: I'm really tired, and I'm not in the mood for games.

Bentley: What are you in the mood for?

I chuckled, knowing what I was in the mood for and knowing that she was probably rolling her eyes and becoming angrier by the second.

Andi: Good night, Bentley.

Bentley: Wait.

Andi: What do you want?

Bentley: That kiss.

Andi: What about it?

Bentley: Did you like it?

I almost didn't hit send, but I wanted to know. I wanted her to think of it.

Andi: It was okay, I guess.

The fuck it was. That kiss had been incredible, and she knew it. She wanted to play? Well, so could I.

Bentley: That's what I thought too.

Andi: Good then we're on the same page.

Not exactly what I'd wanted her to say, but I hadn't expected her to give me an inch. Little did she know I wanted to give her a lot more than that.

Andi: Good night, Bentley.

Bentley: Sweet dreams, Andrea.

Tomorrow. I'd prove to her that she not only needed me but that she wanted me. She could try to say that when we'd kissed, it hadn't felt as if we were meant to be, but one day she'd admit it.

CHAPTER 5

Andi

I woke up and decided to go for a longer run than I normally did. Five miles in the fresh air should help clear my clouded brain. Sleep had evaded me for most of the night after his weird texts. All I could think of was Bentley and how he made me feel as if I were Mount Vesuvius. The way he spoke and kissed me . . . I shook my head to get rid of the images, but that didn't work. My mind went back to the previous night. The way he'd just left and made me want more of him . . . well, that was rude, but I shouldn't have been surprised.

The trees swayed as I ran through the crowded city park. My earbuds blocked out the sounds of traffic. I ran to my favorite instrumental playlist, which I listened to as I practiced my lines. Now I needed it to clear my head—too bad it didn't work.

When I'd heard Bentley as Jake last night, I knew I'd never forget it. Maybe he should have been an actor. My heart faltered a little when I had the fleeting thought that maybe I shouldn't. *Nope, get that out of your head.*

THE CRITIC

I looked at my watch and saw that I had run over three and a half miles already. I was so lost in my thoughts, I hadn't noticed running farther than I'd wanted to before I turned around and ran home. Fantastic, I'd just tacked on another mile. I needed to take a break, so I ran to the park bench near the statue of a man carved out of an old oak tree that had been dying. I stared at the intricacy of the carving. The shaded areas under his eyes caught my attention. I wondered what the artist's feelings had been when he'd created this. I walked around the entire statue, trying to figure out the artist's motivation. Naturally, Bentley came to mind, the way he pushed me and motivated me. Had I been missing that all along? Was it possible to miss something you'd never had or even realized was missing? All I knew was that he got under my skin. I grabbed my water bottle from the holster around my waist and took a sip before running back home.

Memories of the night before replayed in my head. Would I ever forget the way his lips had made mine feel or the way he brought something out of me? My steps grew faster. I couldn't wait to get home and talk to Gina.

I sent Gina a text telling her I wanted to talk to her. I stripped off my clothes and hopped in the shower. I needed to get cleaned up and talk to G. Thank God I had her in my life. She was the least judgmental person, and she always had my best interests at heart. She was like a sister to me, and her take on what had happened between Bentley and me was important.

Once I was dried and ready to go, I grabbed my phone. Two text messages: one from Gina and the other from Bentley. I stared at the green bar and wondered which to read first. I had to go with my girl.

Gina: Hey. Lunch. Twelve thirty at Tornatto's? I'll pick you up.

Andi: I'll take a cab and meet you there.

I didn't want her to go out of her way since she lived closer to the restaurant.

Gina: Okay if you're sure, but I'll drive you home. I can't wait to see you.

I smiled at that text. It was just about noon, so I needed to get moving after I read my other message. I swiped the green bar to the right.

Bentley: Hi. I'd like to see you. If you're not busy tonight, can I come over?

My heart raced at the thought of having him here again. I didn't know what was with him, but I was starting to feel like a pet project. Then my eyes went to the spot where we'd had our moment, and my decision was made.

Andi: Yes.

Bentley: Great. On my way to a meeting. I'll call you later to set up a time.

Andi: Fine.

With my purse in hand, I left to meet my friend. What would she think of all this?

⸎

Gina waved to me from a table in the rear of the restaurant. She was so pretty. I needed to figure out a way to get her and Seth together. They knew each other of course, but both were shy about hooking up.

"Hi!" I pulled her into a hug.

"Wow! What's with you? Is everything okay? Is it Mr.

Chambers?"

A loud sigh escaped me as we both sat. "Something happened last night."

Before I could say anything, the waiter approached to take our drink orders. G ordered a soda, and I ordered a glass of chardonnay.

"Okay, if you're drinking wine in the middle of the day, something had to have happened." She put her index finger in the air and called to the waiter, "Sir? I'd like a glass of merlot instead please."

The waiter nodded.

She leaned forward. "Okay, spill it."

"Well, Bentley came over yesterday."

Gina's eyes widened. "Excuse me? Bentley?" Her lips quirked into a snarky grin. "Hmm."

I smiled from just hearing her say his name. "Yes, Bentley." The temperature in my cheeks rose as I thought of him.

"Oh my god! You didn't . . . did you? Was he good?" She bounced up and down in her chair as if her ass were on fire. Her voice grew louder as she continued her inquisition. "Was he big?"

My nose crinkled, and I tossed my cloth napkin at her. "I did not sleep with him if that's what you're thinking. Geez, G, calm down."

The waiter set down our wine and grinned at me. "Ready to order?"

I let out a huff and shot Gina a look before she dove behind her menu. I was sure she was laughing. "Yes, I'll have the grilled chicken Caesar salad please."

He turned to Gina, who cleared her throat and smiled

as if nothing had just happened. "I'll have the pasta marinara please." She handed him the menu, and he took mine before he walked away.

"Honestly!" I rolled my eyes.

She laughed. "What? He's smokin' hot, and by the look on your face, I know more went down than just a hug."

"Well, yeah. If I tell you what happened, can you try not to shout it across the restaurant?" My brows rose, and I waited for her reply. I knew she was ready to come out of her skin in anticipation.

"Yes, sorry." She giggled some more and handed me my napkin.

"So he came over yesterday then forgot his backpack, so he needed to come back."

Her head tilted. "He forgot his bag? Intentionally?"

My brows lowered. "I don't think so." I shook my head and shifted in my chair. "Anyway, that's not the point. When he was at my place, I was so upset with him that I just wanted him to leave. We had argued before he left the first time." I took a sip of my wine. "After he came back, we had a few more heated words about his review, and he wanted me to go over my lines with him. He picked the scene where Jake tells Katie to kiss him."

Gina placed her hand on her chest, and her body sagged a bit. "I love, love, love that scene. It's so sweet and sexy."

"Sweet. Well, it wasn't last night." I tried to quash the thoughts flooding my memory.

"It wasn't? What was it?"

The waiter brought our meals and smirked at us. Boy, he'd been getting an earful.

THE CRITIC

After he'd left, I said, "Intense. Bentley made the scene so different from the one you've seen that it scares me."

"Why?" Gina's scowled as her cheeks lost a bit of color. "Did he make you do things you didn't want to do?"

"No, not at all. I was scared because he made me feel things. He brought emotions out of me." I shrugged. "I've never felt them before. Have I been doing this all wrong?" At that point, I wasn't sure if I was talking about acting or my life.

Gina's eyes went wide, and she shifted in her chair as her smile grew. I was about to turn around to see what she was looking at, but there was no need.

"Intense emotions are a wonderful thing. You should embrace them." His husky voice made the tiny hairs stand up on my neck.

My mouth dropped open as I looked up to see Bentley standing next to me.

He stretched his hand toward Gina. "Bentley Chambers."

"Gina Russo." She eyed him up and down. "So you're him." Her lips curled into a shy, crooked smile as she regained color in her face. "It's a pleasure."

I just stared at my friend in disbelief. There it was, her full-watt "let me be in a toothpaste commercial" smile. Wow, she was really turning on the charm.

He released her hand. "Yes, apparently I'm him." He glanced at me then refocused on Gina. "And the pleasure's all mine, Ms. Russo."

"Please call me Gina."

What the hell was going on? One look at this man,

and Gina had turned into a blushing schoolgirl.

"My apologies for the interruption, but when I saw you, I wanted to say hello. I didn't mean to eavesdrop." Bentley smiled.

"Would you like to join us?" Gina motioned toward the empty chair next to me, and my jaw dropped in shock.

"Thank you, but I'm waiting for my brother, Brett. He's in from the city, and this is his favorite place." He looked at me. "Just in case you thought I was following you." He turned back toward Gina. "Maybe another time, Gina."

She nodded.

"Andrea, I'm glad I ran into you. I'll bring dinner over around seven. How's that sound?" His voice was friendly, as if we hung out and shared meals all the time.

"That's fine, but you don't need to bring dinner." Being cool and nonchalant wasn't in the cards for me, since I couldn't stop staring at his lips when he spoke. The memory of their softness on mine replayed over and over in my head.

He bent down to my ear and whispered, "I'll bring dinner. You'll need your energy." He softly kissed me behind my ear and stood, leaving me wanting more. The warmth of his breath and the scent of his cologne made my spine tingle. "Have a nice lunch, ladies." And just like that, he was gone.

"Holy shit." Gina took a sip of her wine and licked her lips. "He's stunning. I hate to say this, but he really doesn't seem like a jerk."

I watched him walk away. His body was just perfect. I sighed. "Yeah, I know. Although I wish he was." The tartness of my wine lingered on my tongue as I finished the glass.

"So why do you think he's doing this?" Gina glanced at me before eating.

The sauce's aroma drifted across the table and made me sorry I'd ordered a salad. "I don't know exactly. He says that I'm better than how I performed the other night, and let me tell you, when he kissed me, it felt phenomenal."

"Look, if this guy isn't a nasty-ass ogre, which he obviously isn't, and he truly wants to help, then let him. If you think that you guys can have more than a working relationship, and he definitely acts as if he's interested, then what do you have to lose?"

After we finished eating, I pushed the remainder of my salad aside. "I know. It scares me. He doesn't even live here."

Gina shook her head as she polished off her wine. "Doesn't matter. Once you get to Broadway, you'll be living near him, and it's not like Jersey is far away. Stop making excuses."

"Are you ready to get out of here?" I grabbed my purse.

"Yeah, let's get our bill." Gina signaled for the waiter to come over.

When he reached us, he informed us that Mr. Chambers had taken care of our tab and tip. From his smile, I bet his tip was huge. I closed my eyes and pictured Bentley's hands on my body. I shook it off and looked at my friend.

"See. He is a nice guy." Gina batted her beautiful eyes and smiled.

At that point, I had no idea what to think. "Yeah, I suppose we should go thank him." I turned to look for him and saw him sitting with an extremely handsome man I assumed was Brett.

As we walked toward his table, Gina grabbed the back of my blouse, making me stop in my tracks. "Andi, that guy he's with is gorgeous. Do I look okay?" She pressed her lips together. "Is my lipstick still on?"

I loved Gina. "Yes, you look beautiful. Come on."

When we were near their table, Bentley looked up then stood. "Andrea and Gina, I'd like you to meet my brother, Brett. Brett, this is Andrea and Gina."

He stood and shook our hands. "It's a pleasure to meet you both. Andrea, I've heard a lot about you."

My bright smile faltered, and my pulse quickened. "You can call me Andi. I hope you've heard all good things." I glared at Bentley, who let out a low laugh before covering his mouth as if he were stifling a cough.

Brett beamed. "Of course. Would there be anything else?" He winked and sat down, as did Bentley. Apparently both brothers had sexiness down to a science.

"We just wanted to come over and thank you for lunch. You didn't have to do that." Every time I talked to Bentley, our eyes locked, and I melted a little more, as if I were an iceberg that had just landed on a tropical island.

"My pleasure." His smile was captivating.

The expression on Gina's face told me she was enchanted. The way this man made me feel with just his voice or the look in his eyes was so foreign to me. I wasn't sure how to deal with it, except to avoid it.

"We're going to go. Thanks again." I looked at Brett. "Great meeting you."

Brett nodded. Gina gave a quick wave, and we were on our way. We made it out to the crisp air, and I relished the feeling.

"Wow, Bentley's super sweet," she said.

I rolled my eyes. As much as I hated to admit it, there was no denying it. "Yeah, I know."

We were just about to get in the car when I heard my name. I turned to see Bentley walking briskly in our direction. Gina got in her car, and I was left alone with him.

"Hey." His breaths were short after he'd hurried across the paved lot.

"Yeah?"

"Is Chinese okay for dinner?"

The look on his face was different—hopeful maybe? He was definitely keeping me off-balance, and I wasn't used to that.

"Yeah, sure, that'd be great. Thank you."

"Perfect." He turned to walk away but stopped and stalked back toward me.

I stepped backward until my ass hit the car door. With one hand on the door frame and one cupping the side of my neck, he brought his lips as close to mine as possible without touching them. His nose grazed my cheek, making my eyes flutter closed.

His warm breath caressed my lips as he whispered, "See you tonight."

He left me against the cool metal, yet I was warm from the inside out. My attraction to him had become fierce, and I needed to figure out how to handle it. Once I got in the car, we headed toward my apartment.

Gina, who was a music fanatic, lowered the radio's volume. "So what was that?"

"I think he just likes to drive me insane." I laughed insincerely, hoping to stop her thoughts before they met mine.

"Hmmm. I think he just likes you . . . like a lot!"

"Is it wrong that I'm attracted to a man I hated just a few days ago?" I looked out the window at the green trees. "This is the last thing I wanted."

"Yeah, I get that. Look, Andi, there isn't anything wrong with liking him. He's obviously into you. But you need to figure out where you want to go from here. I can't do that for you." Gina turned into my apartment complex.

"I know. Maybe I'll see how tonight goes and take it from there." I closed my eyes and shook my head. "It figures that I'd fall for him. This is all kinds of wrong . . . right?"

"Does it feel wrong?" Gina put the car in park. "Look, things happen for a reason. You said yourself that he doesn't review plays in Jersey, and he came here. Ask him why. I think knowing what his intentions are will make all the difference."

"Yeah, maybe. Thanks, G." I gave her a kiss on the cheek and opened my door.

"Hey, and find out if Brett is taken."

I laughed. "Okay. But I did have plans for you and Seth."

Gina shrugged. "Yeah, him too."

She winked, and I shut the door. I watched her pull

away before I went inside.

Mack had sent a text cancelling rehearsal for today, so I read for a couple of hours and then decided to take a bath before Bentley came over. I turned on the water, sprinkled in lavender bath salts, and settled in. I stared at the tiled wall, wondering why this was happening. Could I let him into my life? Did he even want to be there, or was this some way of proving a point? *Maybe I should talk to him.* I had way too many thoughts running through my head, and it hadn't escaped me that my career wasn't the first one. Bentley Chambers had taken over that spot in my brain, and that was a first. No one had ever come close to being my first thought, not even myself. I'd closed myself off while trying to perfect my craft, but now all I thought of was a dark-haired, perplexing man.

I lifted my leg to rub the now-soft water on it. As I watched iridescent bubbles roll toward my knee, I thought of Bentley and his fingers being there instead. How would they feel? Would they be as they had been when he'd caressed my cheek? Or like his soft lips? I shook my head. I needed to put things in perspective and get back to reality which was . . . I needed to get my shit together.

I stepped out of the tub, wrapped myself in a perfectly soft light blue towel, and applied lotion to my body. I was taking more time than normal getting ready. I was actually primping for a man—a man who had been the bane to my existence a few short days ago. I stared at my reflection and hoped that the woman looking back at me would have a revelation as to why my heart fluttered when I was near him.

Once I was dried and dressed, I grabbed a Diet Coke and sat on my sofa with the script. I read the section that

I wanted to work on before I stood in my living room and recited the words in various ways. But each way sounded like the last. I felt as if they were just words, and they needed to be so much more. I shook my arms and feet to regroup. I closed my eyes and pictured Bentley, rather than Justin, playing the role of Jake, and I said the lines again. This time, my heart thumped wildly.

Jake, you have to know that I'd never forget you or forget how I wanted you, no matter how many years have passed. My life was incomplete until you. Seeing your face makes me want to live and breathe. You are my heart and my love. I stretched out my hand to touch the invisible face in front of me. *Please stay this time. I can't face heartbreak again; I won't recover. I won't want to.*

Buzzing startled me. It was just after seven. I opened the door after clicking open the one outside. I knew it had to be Bentley, so I just stood in the doorway, waiting for him. As he took the corner to come to my apartment, I stared at him. He stopped dead in his tracks. His deep denim jeans rested perfectly on his hips, and his black T-shirt made my mouth water. The same bag was slung over his muscular shoulder. He was perfect.

"Hey there." He lifted a brown paper bag. "I hope you're hungry." He grinned as he looked past me into the apartment.

I smiled and stepped aside to let him in. Was I hungry? My stomach growled, indicating that I was. "I suppose I could eat."

Bentley chuckled. "All I've seen you eat is salad, so I bought a bit of everything."

The thought of him taking note of what I'd eaten, even if it was just one meal, made my head cock to the side as if I were a puppy whose owner had asked him if he wanted a treat. I shook my head, getting back to the task at hand: saving my career without acting like a giddy fool.

"Would you like a beer or wine?" I asked.

"Beer would be great, thank you."

He set the bag on the kitchen table while I snatched a beer for him and a glass of wine for me. Then I went to grab a couple plates and forks.

"Really, Andrea? Silverware? I have these." He held out chopsticks.

"Um . . . I'm not that proficient at eating with skinny wooden sticks."

He laughed as he removed several cartons from the bag. I sat at the table and watched him open them one by one.

"Okay." He clapped then rubbed his hands together. "We have sesame chicken, kung pao shrimp, Mongolian beef, vegetable fried rice, white rice, pork lo mein, egg rolls, and of course, fortune cookies." Bentley smiled and sat as I looked at all the food. "Please don't tell me you're a vegetarian."

"No." I smiled at him. "There's just so much food here."

He handed me chopsticks. "Yeah, and it's all good stuff, so dig in." Using his chopsticks, he masterfully scooped some fried rice onto his plate, along with a little of everything else. I grabbed my fork, and he shot me a look. "Always conventional, aren't you?" He smirked and ate some chicken.

"That's not true. I just don't know how to use these."

Why did he always make me feel as though he was

testing me? To prove him wrong, I held the sticks while looking at the way he did it. I tried to grab a shrimp out of a carton, but it slid right off my chopsticks. I thought of using the stick as a spear, but that wouldn't have worked either. I moved on to the chicken, hoping it would be easier to grab; it wasn't.

"Seriously, this makes no sense." I set the sticks down and reached for my fork.

His hand touched mine. "Here."

Using his chopsticks, he held the piece of chicken I'd unsuccessfully tried to get to my mouth. He raised his brows, so I tentatively opened my mouth and let him place it on my tongue. I closed my lips around the sticks, and he pulled them out slowly. I moaned in delight, and his expression turned darker.

Bentley smiled. "It's really good, right?"

I nodded and savored the morsel before swallowing. "Yeah, but at this rate, we'll be here until morning."

"Sounds like a good plan to me." Bentley winked, making me blush. "Here, hold them like this."

He set his down and positioned the sticks between my fingers. His hand was much larger than mine, and as I watched it, I pictured it on my body. The man was going to drive me insane. Once the chopsticks were in position, I stared at my hand, trying my best not to move so they wouldn't slip.

"Now what?" I asked.

He laughed. "Well, now you need to move them. Think of them as an extension of your fingers or like an alligator's mouth—like this." His chopsticks moved effortlessly, the ends coming together in a tapping motion.

"Okay." I pointed them into the box of chicken and tried to close them around a tiny morsel. "Aha! I got it!" I slowly pulled the sticks out of the box, and the chicken fell. My shoulders slumped. I glanced at Bentley and saw him watching me. My spine straightened, and I focused and tried again. I stifled a laugh as I imagined tiny air traffic controllers standing on my tongue, moving their miniature orange flashlights to guide the poor piece of food into my mouth. When it finally made it past my lips, I beamed and slowly chewed. I relished that chicken as if it were filet mignon. "Ha! I did it!"

Bentley nodded. "Very good. See, I knew you could do it." He ate his rice, and I just stared at him. "Okay, rice is a tad more difficult, but I bet by the next time we have Chinese, you'll be able to eat miso soup with these bad boys."

"Really? Soup?" I shook my head, and we both laughed.

"Hey, I have confidence in you. I believe in you, and I think you can do anything you set your mind to."

"You do?"

My tone made his brows draw together. "Of course I do. Don't you?"

"I suppose so. I've just been questioning myself lately." I smiled as I successfully picked up a shrimp.

His eyes met mine, and he smirked. "The shrimp is really good."

"It's all delicious. Thank you for bringing it over." I used the sticks as a scoop for the rice.

He clicked the chopsticks together. "It's even better using these."

I giggled. "I suppose." I continued enjoying my meal

and, oddly, his company.

He pushed his plate aside and rubbed his stomach. I couldn't help staring at the circles his hand was making.

"Andrea?"

"Yeah?" My voice trailed off, and I wondered if he had a six- or an eight-pack under that shirt.

All of a sudden, there was a hand waving in front of my face. "Earth to Andrea . . ."

My eyes sprang up to his. "I'm sorry, what?" Heat rose in my cheeks.

"I said, don't you have confidence in yourself?"

"Oh. Yeah, I do when it comes to some things." I needed to change the subject and alleviate my embarrassment. "What about you? Is there anything you can't do?"

He looked toward the ceiling in thought then at me. "Nope. I can pretty much do it all." His smile was brilliant and contagious. "Okay, Ms. Jordan, which fortune cookie do you want?"

His hand held two out to me, and I took the one closest to me. I opened the clear wrapper and looked at Bentley. "Aren't you going to open yours?"

He picked his up, and we cracked them open at the same time.

I read mine and let out a sarcastic laugh. "Figures." I shook my head and put the fortune down.

"Tsk tsk, you can't do that. What does it say?" His eyes were playful and almost dancing, waiting for me to speak.

In a huff, I picked up the small piece of paper and read it. "'In order to soar, you must learn how to fly.'" I looked at Bentley. "What does yours say?"

His expression was serious. He looked as if he agreed with my fortune or at least was pondering it. He cleared his throat. "Mine says, 'Intuition will guide you to success.'" He smiled then shrugged.

"Of course it does. It's perfect. Did you write them?" Honestly, what the hell?

"Come on, they are just prepackaged fortunes." He winked, walked into the family room, and turned toward me. "You coming or what?"

"Yeah." I tossed the fortune on the table and joined him on the couch.

Bentley

Holy shit, I'd never think about chopsticks the same way. The image of her sliding her lips down them . . . I've never wanted to be two skinny sticks so much in my life.

"So tell me about Brett, other than that he lives in the city." She smiled.

My heart clenched at the sight of her smile, but talking about my brother wasn't what I had in mind. "Ahh . . . Brett. He's my younger brother. I don't get to see him too often." I shrugged. "Our jobs keep us too busy. He's the co-owner of a nightclub, The White Orchid. His best friend, Alex, owns it, but Brett and another guy bought in. Now they all co-share."

"That's cool. Does he have a girlfriend?"

I felt each of my facial muscles fall at her question.

"You're interested in Brett?" I shook my head. "Unreal. That guy is truly unreal. Even when we were kids, he'd get all the girls."

"No, no, I'm not. I was asking for Gina, not for myself." She sounded panicked.

I exhaled in relief. "His life is difficult right now. He had a girlfriend and apparently loved her, but he didn't handle a situation correctly. Now it's complicated." My heart was broken for my brother, and I was positive I didn't do a great job of hiding that.

"Complicated? Okay, then I'll let G know he's off the market." She stood, and I couldn't tear my eyes from her perfect body. "Would you like another beer?"

"Yeah, thanks." Maybe a cold beverage would extinguish the fire raging inside me. She grabbed more drinks as I made myself comfortable on her sofa. "So you're asking about Brett for Gina, not you?" My heart raced, and I felt sweat forming on the back of my neck. Maybe she wasn't attracted to me.

CHAPTER 6

Andi

I answered him from inside the refrigerator. "No, not for me. G asked me to ask you about him."

I looked at the gorgeous man in my family room. I'd almost forgotten why I hadn't always liked him until he picked up the paper and looked at his review. Did he feel badly about the way he'd slammed me? I watched his features change from relaxed to tense while I went from happy to sad. Why had I left that paper there? Oh yeah, as a reminder of how much his words had cut me. With glassy eyes, I made my way to the sofa.

"Here you go." I handed him his beer and sat next to him. "Are you refreshing your memory?"

"No, it's just . . . I don't know." His head fell a little as he looked at me from the corner of his eye.

I unintentionally sniffed and took a sip of my wine before setting my glass on the table. "I have a question." I stood. "Hang on. I'll be right back." I went to my room and grabbed older copies of the *Edge*. I sat back down beside him and opened one of the older papers. I saw him flinch when he realized what I was holding. "Let's see . . . oh, here it is. 'Andrea Jordan's performance lacked finesse, and although her appearance was worthy of the stage, her performance wasn't.'" I set the paper down and picked up the next one. I glanced at him. His eyes were on me, and his lips were in a tight line. "Okay, here we go—"

"Why are you . . . ? Please don't . . ." He sounded desperate and a bit scared.

My hand went up, indicating that he needed to let me finish. He recoiled a bit, and I continued to read his words to him. "'Ms. Jordan's opening night performance was lackluster. I had high hopes when I walked into the theater. The buzz around the city was palpable. Then the curtain rose. Let's say I'd be surprised if it rose again tomorrow. Ms. Jordan was—'"

Bentley snatched the paper from my hand. "I know what I wrote. You said you have a question. Do you have one, or are you just going to read to me?"

"Yeah, I do actually. I'd like to know why?" My hand wiped the lone tear that had seeped from my eye. "Why do you come to my shows if you don't like the way I perform? I don't understand." Another tear escaped. "Help me understand. I mean, I get that you don't like the way I act—that's here in black and white—but why do you waste your time? Why are you here now?"

His fingers raked through his hair. "Do you keep all your reviews? I've seen you get good ones too. Where are they?"

"I have them as well. Not everyone thinks I suck, you know." I had them in a box under my bed, but for some reason, I didn't think about them as much.

"What do those reviews say? Do they say you're

going to get nominated for an award or that you're the next big star?"

Was he trying to make me feel worse? I shook my head. "No, they just said that I performed well and I was a good actress."

He nodded. "And that's what you want to hear? Are you okay with being called a good actress when you could be a great one?" He took my hand and looked me in the eye. "I don't want you to be upset, but shit, Andrea, when are you going to go for it? I watch you on stage and see you light up, but then it just turns into words and deliberate movements and planned actions. You're so much better than what you're giving the audience." Bentley placed his hand on the side of my face. "I think you can be amazing. Do you hear me? I said amazing, not good or mediocre. That's why I go to your shows. I'm waiting for greatness, because I know you have it in you. I just don't know what you're waiting for."

"Bentley," I whispered, but my want for him was loud and clear.

"What do you need? Tell me."

His stare made me melt, and I was sure there was a puddle pooling at my feet. "You." I lowered my head before raising it again. "I need you. I don't want to, but I do." My chest ached at my words. Admitting that I needed someone other than myself was new to me. But I did, and I couldn't lie—not to him and not to me.

"I told you I'm here for you. I'll help you, but you need to help yourself too. It's about time, isn't it? I'll ask again, what are you waiting for? You want this, right? To be on Broadway under the bright lights with your name on the marquee? You say you need me, but what for? A good review? Because a critic doesn't slingshot you into stardom. You need to control the pull and release. The slingshot can only go as far back as you decide to draw it."

Stunned, I looked down at his fingers, which were now interwoven with mine. Once I was able to breathe again, I just nodded. He pulled me to him and hugged me.

"Bentley, I don't know what to do. I'm so confused." I got up and paced then looked back at him.

He stood in front of me. I rested my forehead on his hard chest as his strong arms came around me. He placed a soft kiss on the top of my head.

"Confused?" His voice was steeped in genuine concern. "Look at me."

I bit my lip and looked at his deep blue eyes and realized I could fall for him . . . hard.

"I've always strived to be the best at anything I did. I've worked hard to perfect my craft so I wouldn't fail. The thought of failing? It's scary." I shrugged. "I thought I was finally getting there, and my fear had subsided. I was starting to be proud of my work and then . . ." My arms crossed in front of me as I tried to hold back tears.

"And then here comes an asshole who made you doubt yourself, and he did it in black and white." His voice was low.

"Yeah, and for everyone to see. I could lose my job now. I don't have anything if I don't have my work. I'm nothing if I can't act. You don't know everything I've sacrificed to be here. I've lost everyone I've ever cared about. If it weren't for Gina, I'd be alone." My voice weakened. "If it weren't for Gina, I'd never say or hear the words 'I love you.'"

His eyes pierced mine. I couldn't tell if he understood what I was trying to say or if he just felt sorry for me. That was one thing I didn't want from him: pity.

He linked his hands behind his neck and looked toward the ceiling as if searching for the perfect words. Given his profession, he should have had them already. "I don't want you to be alone or feel as if you have only one person who cares. You have me. I'm on your side. Yes, I realize my reviews brought us together and you were ready to rip my head off because of them, but as odd as it may sound, I was happy when you showed up ready to fight me. You have so much fire in you. You're a strong, gorgeous woman, and I want to get to know you if you'll let me. Will you let me?" The back of his hand trailed from my cheekbone to the small of my neck.

He looked at my lips before he bent to kiss me. It was a soft, swift kiss, nothing that indicated he had feelings for me other than friendship.

"Sit with me?" His eyes pleaded for compliance.

"Yes." He wanted to get to know me? I kept asking myself how that had happened.

"Why are you alone? Don't you have family?" He put his hand on my knee and stroked it with his thumb.

I hadn't planned on telling him about my past, but none of this was planned. My sigh was long and had a twinge of sadness at the end. "My family . . ." I quirked my lips and felt them curl downward. "My parents are very prominent in their community. They live the country club life. They're affluent and expect nothing but the best? Well, I didn't follow in their footsteps.

They're Ivy Leaguers, and I went to community college. I wanted to go to Julliard, not Brown, but since that wasn't in the cards, I did what I needed to."

"Did you audition for Julliard?"

Bentley's voice had a soft tone that made me feel worse. I still wondered what my career could have been like if I'd studied at a prestigious school for the arts and taken classes with those who shared my passion. When Bentley, or anyone really, asked me if I had auditioned, my heart broke a little.

"No, I didn't. My parents wouldn't help me pay for it or co-sign a loan, and I knew I wouldn't get a scholarship." I shrugged. "My parents offered me full tuition to the Ivy school of my choice, but I didn't want that. We had words, and I left." A hot tear ran down my cheek, and I swept it away. "So after a one-year stint at community college, I decided to try New York City on for size, but as you know, thousands of people have the same idea. The rent was too high, and I didn't know anyone to room with. I decided to move to Jersey and commute for auditions. Then, if I landed a long-standing gig, I'd move." I let out a sarcastic chuckle. "That was six years ago. But I've kept busting my ass, and that's what I intend to keep doing." My voice became stronger. "I love the rush of the stage. I was born to act—that much I know."

"I'm sorry my critique hurt you, but I was born to write," he said. "I didn't mean for my words to make you doubt yourself. I wanted you to become stronger." He pulled me to him and held me. "You can still make it. I have so much faith in you. I see your potential."

"Really? Why? I mean, what makes you all of a sudden think I have potential?" I caught the sarcasm in my words, but I couldn't hold it back.

"It's not all of a sudden. Don't you understand that?" He leaned back on the sofa but kept my hand in his. "You're talented and one of the most stunning women I've ever seen."

"Do you really think I'm talented?"

"And stunning. Hasn't anyone ever told you that?"

"Yes." I knew how that sounded. My looks had never been my concern, but I didn't want to be known for my looks. "But I'm old now. I mean, in actress years."

Bentley roared with laughter, breaking the tension. "Is that like dog years? Don't get me wrong, I completely understand what you mean, but that's not true."

I forced a grin and let out a quiet sigh.

"So should we run more lines?" he asked.

"That would be nice. I mean, if you want to."

"Of course I do." He smiled.

"Great, but I want to work on a different scene tonight." There was a pivotal scene between Jake and Katie which was devoid of any physical contact. I found this part of the show played a pivotal role in their reconciliation.

"It's up to you. Whatever you feel like you want to rehearse. I'm here for you."

I handed him a copy of the script. "Act two, scene seven."

Bentley nodded and worked with me until I was tired of hearing my own voice. I could have listened to him all night, but if I didn't have this section mastered by now, I never would.

THE CRITIC

I flopped onto my couch and propped my feet on the table. Bentley sat in the chair next to the couch and laid the script on the coffee table.

"You can go if you'd like." *Please don't leave.* "Or we can watch a movie."

It dawned on me that I only had a few more days left with him. That thought shouldn't have made me sad, but it did. Bentley had definitely begun to occupy a large part of my heart, and I enjoyed having him with me. Oddly, I relied on his honesty. I'd never thought I'd miss him, but now I knew I would, and that thought depressed me more than I'd ever thought it could.

"I'd like to stay. A movie sounds like a great plan!" Bentley perked up and rubbed his hands together. "Where's my backpack?"

And just like that, the tension and the sadness I'd felt dissipated. My lips curled upward. "It's by the door. Do you carry that around everywhere?"

He laughed and grabbed it. "Yup." As he sat back down, he smiled as if he were opening a present. He unzipped it and pulled out a few DVDs, a box of Cracker Jacks, a pack of M&Ms, and a penny. He shrugged with a snarky grin. "For good luck."

My mind went back to that day. I still couldn't believe that had been him. What would have happened if I hadn't rushed out of the store for dress rehearsal? Would we have met, maybe gone to dinner?

I shook my head to get back to the here and now. "Do you always carry movies and snacks with you? And for the record, I can't believe you remember that store."

"As a matter of fact, I do. I actually have some juice boxes and water bottles in here too if you get thirsty."

"What are you, twelve?"

"Ha-ha. No. But when you spend the majority of your time in the dark and alone, you get thirsty."

My eyebrows rose, and I tried to stifle a laugh. "What do you do alone in the dark that makes you thirsty?" My eyes automatically went to his crotch then to his face.

I grabbed the package of popcorn and walked into my kitchen. "Want a fresh beer?"

"But what about my juice box?"

I looked at him over my shoulder. "I prefer my wine box."

I tossed the popcorn in the microwave, and when I turned around, Bentley was in front of me. His hands went to my hips, and my eyes trailed from his muscular chest to his eyes.

"Andrea, I don't know what's going on with us or if you're feeling what I am, but I'm glad I'm here, and I wanted to tell you that. I've wanted this since I first saw you."

My mouth opened. I attempted to move, but his grip became firmer, rooting me in place.

"Other than the disgust you felt when we first met, do you feel a connection between us?"

His smell became intoxicating, and I wanted to remember this moment. His eyes searched mine. My heart raced with my want to answer him, but I was afraid.

I needed to know, so I asked, "What are you feeling?"

"This." He cupped my face and trailed kisses along my jawline.

THE CRITIC

My head dropped back, and a soft breath escaped me. I felt his tongue on my neck, and my thong became saturated with my arousal. His lips found mine, and the sensation between my legs consumed the rest of my body. Our tongues danced, and our bodies came together as my arms reached around his back. The way his muscles flexed with each breath made me weak in the knees. If I wasn't near the counter, I would have crumbled. He broke the kiss, and I let out a frustrated groan. His hands were still cupping my face, and mine were on his wrists.

"Bentley . . ." Words had escaped me as my mind tried to rationalize what was going on.

His eyes searched mine. "So, do you?"

"I don't know how to feel right now." I bit my lip as his shoulders slackened in defeat, making me feel like shit.

His forehead pressed against mine. "Typical, Andrea." He shook his head and put his hands in his front pockets.

"What's that supposed to mean?" I leaned back and looked into his eyes, trying to gauge what he meant by that comment. The microwave beeped, giving me a chance to turn away from him. I grabbed a bowl and poured the popcorn in it.

"It means that you're always worried about how you're supposed to feel rather than just feeling it."

My nerves were beginning to spike, as was my blood pressure. I felt his warmth behind me, and it was unsettling.

"When you rehearse, you worry about how to speak and move. Just do it; don't think about it. Can you ever fucking let go of what you think people want and just be you? Or is that why you like being an actress? So all of your words and motions are scripted? Life isn't a script. You need to live it."

His words cut right through my heart like blades. I spun around, almost knocking our buttery snack on the floor. "You don't think I live? My life isn't a script. Weren't you listening?" I pushed him as hard as I could, forcing him to step back. He tightened his brows as my voice rose. "If I'd followed the path my parents wanted, I wouldn't be here right now . . . standing in my kitchen and arguing with a man I can't stop thinking about. So you want to talk about living? That's what I'm trying to do. Then you come in here all high, mighty, and sexy, thinking you know it all. Well, you don't." My breathing was becoming erratic while my thoughts were bordering on erotic. "You want to know what I feel for you?"

Bentley looked at me blankly and nodded once.

"I want you. I'm so mad at myself for that, but you've invaded my heart and . . ."

His wide eyes stared at mine as he stepped forward. "Go on."

I shook my head. My blood was pumping at NASCAR speed around my heart. "You aren't what I expected. This"—my hand waved between us—"isn't what I expected. Wanting you wasn't what I anticipated."

He grabbed my waist. "I want you too, so much that I can't stop myself from doing this."

He lifted me and set me on my Formica counter as he stood between my legs. His lips crashed on mine. They were forceful, soft, and everything I desired. His hands swept into my hair, grabbing it to pull me closer. Our teeth clashed as my legs wrapped around his waist. Another low groan emerged from his throat. We feasted on each other as if we were starving. Our chests were touching, and my nipples hardened and tingled with anticipation. My arms rested on his shoulders as my fingers threaded through his dark hair.

His breathing was ragged as his lips found the curve of my neck. "I need you."

I nodded and cleared my mind of all reasons why we shouldn't do this. He carried me down the short hallway, and I pointed at my bedroom door. As he laid me on the comforter, his hips pressed against mine. His eyes, darkened with desire, made me shiver. He lifted my shirt and palmed my breast. My hands ran down his back to the curve of his perfectly rounded ass. I felt his hardened excitement between my legs as we grinded together.

"Bentley . . . ahhh . . . should we . . . ? My God, you're . . ." I couldn't form a sentence that made any sense. I felt as if I'd never spoken a word in my life.

He moved his hand off me, and I immediately missed its warmth. He propped himself on his elbows and looked at me. "I don't want to rush us. If you're not ready, we can wait."

Us. Could we be an *us?* "Don't stop. Please. It's been so long since I've felt this way."

His deep eyes bored into mine as I lifted my arms above my head as a signal to take off my shirt, which he did with ease. He stared at my breasts, enhanced by my black lace push-up bra. "You're beautiful. I knew you would be, but shit, I never thought I'd be here with you like this."

My fingers found the hem of his shirt, and I relished the feel of his taut muscles. He was pure perfection.

With one arm, he ripped his shirt off over his head. He lowered the straps on my bra, and I sat up enough for him to unfasten it. Then he tossed it on the floor. His tongue circled my nipple as his teeth gently grazed it. His lips continued down my stomach to the top of my jeans. He unbuttoned them and knelt between my legs, staring at me. He waggled his brows and pulled my jeans down before tossing them on the floor.

I think he actually growled as he brought his nose to my black lace thong. His fingers grazed my most delicate area as he stripped off the last piece of clothing I had on. He slid his finger into me while working my clit with his tongue. The scruff on his chiseled jaw brushed against my oversensitive skin, unleashing a groan from inside me.

When I opened my eyes, his were closed. He continued making me feel things and awakening parts of me that had been dormant for so long, including my heart. He moved up my body, kissing his way to my neck. I unbuttoned his pants and slid them over his perfect ass. He grabbed a condom out of his pocket before I pitched the jeans aside. His black boxers were next. With deft fingers, he sheathed himself and positioned his tip at my entrance. All I could do was smile, and that was the green light. He slowly entered me, making my knees fall aside. Our chests rubbed together as we moved in unison.

"Andrea, you feel better than I could have imagined. You're incredible."

My back arched as I nodded. He held my hands above my head, interweaving his fingers with mine. That wasn't what I had expected at all. This didn't feel like sex. I mean, it was sex, but it was gentle lovemaking, and my heart swelled at the thought of this being the start of something fantastic.

His pace increased, as did the tension in his hands. Our fingers molded around each other's, and I was sure I was going to melt into my sheets. I leaned up as far as I could to reach his neck with my tongue. His skin was salty with sweat, and my desire for him was heady.

"Babe, I can't hold back."

The depth of his voice made my insides clench as I moved my hips faster to meet his movements. "Then don't. Give me what you got. I want all of you, Bentley. Let me feel all of you."

He rolled his hips to hit a spot that sent me into a dizzying orgasm.

"Oh my God!" I cried.

He grunted, and I looked up just in time to see his face contort as he came.

Once he was satisfied, he let go of my hands and brought his to the sides of my face. "Open your eyes."

Unaware I had closed them, I lifted my lids. He lowered his head to mine and kissed me.

"Are you okay?" he asked.

His tender demeanor made me realize this was right. We were right.

"Mmm hmmm. I'm better than okay."

Bentley smiled as he slowly rolled off me to dispose of his condom in the bathroom attached to my bedroom. My view had never been better. To think I'd once thought that Bentley Chambers was an old man with a comb-over made me giggle. He walked toward me, and I appreciated the view. The man was built everywhere. I slid under the covers and propped my head on my pillow.

"What's so funny?" He lifted the cotton duvet and slid in next to me.

"Nothing. I was just thinking about when I didn't know what you looked like. I had you pegged for an old man who was balding." I had a fleeting thought of Melissa, the hostess with the mostess, but decided she wasn't worth wasting thoughts on.

His arm went under my shoulders as my head rested on his chest. "I don't want this to be just one night, but I leave soon."

My fingers traced the definition of his ab muscles. "Yeah, I know you do—back to the big bad city." My heart felt heavy. I nestled into the soft spot under his shoulder and closed my eyes.

Bentley

"It's not far, and I want to get to know you and for you to know me. I'm not a bad man." I lowered the sheet she had pulled over her amazing breasts and positioned us so we were facing one another.

My fingertips made calculated movements over her nipples, and they reacted, turning into tantalizing buds I craved to have in my mouth. I lowered my head, and she arched her back, giving me ample access to lick them. My tongue grazed one then the other.

"You're beautiful." I kissed the tip of her nose while pulling her into my embrace. The scent of her hair caressed me as if gentle hands were massaging every cell in my body. I finally had the one I'd always wanted in my arms.

She giggled, which totally threw me.

"Did I miss something?"

She rolled away from me, making her ass rub me. My cock woke up and pressed against her flawless backside.

"It's just funny, isn't it? I mean, a few days ago, I figured you were a senior citizen that'd need a prescription to combat erectile dysfunction." She giggled again. "Who would've known that you're this hot, sexy man that I could . . ." She wiggled her hips on my full-fledged erection. "That could make me feel the way you did . . . the way you do."

"And which way is that? How do I make you feel, Andrea?"

She sighed. "Adored. And please, call me Andi."

I rolled her toward me so I could see her face. "Andi, huh?"

"Yeah, I really don't like Andrea, and it's been driving me crazy." She snickered.

"Hmmm . . . okay. Andi it is."

"Stay with me tonight?" She smiled as she ran her finger along the scruff on my cheek.

I moved my lips to the edge of her ear and let out a soft breath, making her skin prickle and breasts press against my chest. I whispered, "Yeah."

CHAPTER 7

Andi

The sun peeked through my blinds as I felt an unfamiliar warmth next to me. I turned my head. Bentley was sleeping, his hair perfectly messy and his scruff a little thicker but still sexy as hell. His right eye slowly opened, and he smiled.

"Good morning, Ms. Jordan." He kissed my forehead then my nose, and then his lips gently grazed mine.

I licked my lips. "Good morning yourself, Mr. Chambers. Would you like some breakfast? I could make us something." I nestled closer to him.

"I wish I could, but I have a meeting today. I need to head back to the city."

His words saddened me, and I felt his loss already. He slung his legs over the side of the bed, slid on his boxers, then put on the rest of his clothes. Before I knew it, his perfect body was covered. He walked into my bathroom.

I was so disappointed—I had no idea he'd be leaving this morning. Why I felt as if New York City were a thousand miles away from Jersey was beyond me, but I felt as if he may as well have been leaving for California. I'd thought he'd be here longer.

I got up, threw on my running clothes, grabbed a hair tie off my dresser, and threw my hair in a ponytail. My reflection was bleak as I looked at the pictures stuck in the wooden mirror frame: me and Gina, my parents, and me holding my first script. The worst was the newspaper clipping taped to the bottom right-hand corner. I looked at that title every day and told myself it wasn't about me—"Acting isn't for the faint of heart."

Before I knew it, Bentley was behind me, wrapping his arms around my waist. He rested his chin on my shoulder, and his beard tickled my cheek. We looked at each other in the mirror, and his eyes landed on the newspaper clipping.

"Do you have reminders all over the place?" His chest vibrated against my back as he spoke.

"Reminders?" My voice fluctuated as I tried to reel in my emotions.

"Yeah, this article, the reviews you keep, and the picture of the marquee with your name on it. Not to mention the numerous theater programs scattered all over."

I shrugged out of his embrace and sat on the edge of the bed. My feet shifted on the carpet.

He walked over and knelt between my legs. His hands settled on my thighs. "Andi?"

"Don't, Bentley. I know what you're thinking, so you don't need to say it. You need to go anyway, and I need to go on my run." I tried to stand, but his hands were like weights on my legs.

"I know what you're doing." His eyes were fixed on mine, waiting for me to confirm whatever he was thinking.

"Really? What's that?" I crossed my arms.

"You're pushing me away."

"Why would I do that?"

"Because you showed me that you're vulnerable, and you're afraid."

My head lowered. He was correct, but having someone see that side of me wasn't in my repertoire. I was a bit anxious.

His index finger went under my chin, and he raised my head. "This isn't a one-night thing for me, Andi. I want to come back tonight if that's okay. We never did watch our movie."

"You do?" I didn't know why I felt the need to constantly question him. Maybe it was because out of everyone I knew, he was the one who had inserted doubt into my life.

"Of course I do. Don't you want me to? We also need to run more lines." He winked, and my lips curled into a smile. His lips mirrored mine. "Is that a yes?"

"Yes. I'd like that."

"Perfect, then I'll see you later. I have to meet my mother, but I'll be back." He placed a chaste kiss on my lips and left.

I went into the bathroom to brush my teeth. I needed to get outside and start my run before I went to rehearsal. I grabbed my phone, my headphones, and a small bottle of water, placed them in a running holster around my waist, and headed outside. Running normally cleared my head, but today my brain was too full of scattered thoughts. I needed to talk to Gina about last night. I could only imagine what she'd think. Once I hit my stride, I felt so much better, and I couldn't wait to get home. I'd never run so fast.

Once home, I stripped out of my sweaty clothes and got in the shower. The past day played through my mind. I couldn't believe all that had happened, and I wondered if being with Bentley was meant to be. What would've happened if I'd nailed my performance? I never would've met him. For once, I was glad he thought I sucked. I laughed as I shampooed my hair. What a ludicrous thought. But on some weird level, it was completely true. I rinsed off, stepped out of the shower, and dried off. My hair was naturally wavy, so I let it air dry. I threw on a pair of jeans that perfectly hugged my body and a cute white top.

I grabbed my phone to text Gina.

Andi: G, you're never going to believe what happened.

Gina: I bet I can guess.

Andi: Really?

Gina: You slept with him.

Oh my God!

Andi: Why would you think that?

Gina: Um . . . because I saw him and he's hot as fuck and if you didn't I would've thought something was wrong with you—like your vagina dried up!

Andi: OMG, you did not just say that!

Gina: Well?

Andi: Want to come over for coffee?

Gina: Am I right? Was he fantastic?

Andi: Come over, and I'll tell you all about it.

Gina: Fine, but I have an appointment at noon.

Andi: Okay. See you soon.

I walked into the kitchen and stared at the counter, remembering how hot Bentley was. The bowl of stale popcorn was proof that I hadn't dreamed up everything. It was real . . . he was real.

After I finished cleaning the kitchen, I sat on the sofa and reread my script. Justin texted me that he'd be at the theater early if I wanted to meet him there. I loved running lines with Bentley, but if this was going to work, I needed to rehearse with Justin. Kissing him would be even more like work now.

With a knock on my door, Gina walked in. "Hey, chick! Your neighbor was walking out and let me in." She tossed her purse on the chair and plopped down on the sofa. "So tell me. Was he as good as he looks?" I threw a pillow at her, making her laugh. "I knew it!" She tossed the pillow back. "Ha!"

I leaned against the back cushion. "It's so strange."

"The sex was strange?" Giddy didn't come close to describing the way Gina was acting. She was acting like a teenager hearing about sex for the first time.

"First of all, I didn't say we had sex." I extended my hand and studied my nails.

"You didn't have to. You look totally satisfied." Gina giggled.

My lips curled. "Well, I'm not exactly sure what that means, but yeah. Am I crazy? I mean, I really feel like

I'm losing it."

"Tell me what happened." She crossed her legs under her, waiting for me to give her details.

"Well, we started talking—I mean, really talking—and I told him about my parents and their plans for me. Oh, and Brett has some complicated relationship issue going on, so I'd stay away from that one." I shrugged.

Gina's lips quirked. "Figures. The good looking ones are always taken or fucked up."

The corners of my mouth dropped, and I felt the blood drain from my face. "Do you think? No. Do you? Oh my God, I never asked! Holy shit!" I felt my blood pressure rise, and I was sure I was going to have a heart attack. What if I wasn't the only one he was seeing? I mean, he was beautiful. How many others could there be? When did he have time? Were we all actresses? My brain shot scenarios around like a pinball machine.

Gina's eyes widened as she studied me. "What the hell just went through your head? You look sick."

"Bentley. I never asked him if he had a girlfriend. I thought about asking, but before I knew it, I was on the counter with my legs wrapped around him." My head dropped in my hands.

"You screwed him in your kitchen? Getting kinky, girlfriend!"

My head popped up. Gina was looking toward my kitchen, smirking.

"No! That's where it started, but what if he has someone? I'm so stupid. I should've asked."

Gina placed her hand on my leg, which was rapidly bouncing up and down. "Do you really think he does? I mean, come on. I think you're looking for something to be wrong here."

"I honestly don't know. I hope not. And I wouldn't intentionally screw this up." I grabbed my phone and texted the question that I should've asked last night. Sheer panic set in. I was officially jealous, and it was all his fault. I'd never felt this way before, and I wasn't sure how to handle it other than the way I handled everything else—head on.

Andi: Do you have a girlfriend?

I set the phone on the coffee table as if it were burning my hand.

Gina picked it up and looked at it. "Oh my God! I can't believe you just did that!"

"Why?"

She shook her head. "Um, I don't know . . . you basically just accused him of being a cheater." My phone dinged. Gina looked at it and handed me the phone. "Shit."

Bentley: Are you serious?

Well, that wasn't an answer. I looked at Gina. She was the one who looked sick now. My fingers frantically punched letters on my phone.

Andi: Yes.

Bentley: First of all, I don't cheat.

I closed my eyes. I should've listened to Gina. I was an idiot. I needed to regroup.

Andi: I didn't say you did.

Okay, I did, but I'd needed to be sure. Fuck. This was a mistake of epic proportions.

Bentley: Second, if I had a girlfriend, I wouldn't

have slept with you. Does that answer your question?

I felt like an ass . . . a dumbass. Why had I sent that text? I stared at my phone for a beat.

Andi: Yes.

Bentley: Good.

Andi: I'm sorry.

Nothing. No reply.

"See! This is why I haven't had a relationship in years." I tossed my phone aside.

"I think you need to relax and enjoy whatever's going on between you guys." Gina's head tilted. "What is going on?"

"To be honest, I have feelings for him, and I think he does for me too. I'm scared, and I'm getting distracted from my work. This isn't me, but he makes me question myself." For once in my life, I wasn't focused on my craft. I'd let my heart get involved. "Maybe I find his opinion so important because he's always thought I was lacking, but I'm so irritated with myself. He shouldn't even be a factor—the play should be—but it's too late for that now." I dropped my head in my hands and rubbed my temples before looking at Gina, who looked as stunned as I felt. "You do realize that if I lose this role or this play gets shut down, I'll have to find a 'real' job right? I don't' know of any shows looking for actresses that have to audition to keep their jobs. My savings is just about depleted, and I'm not going to ask my parents for anything out of my trust fund."

Gina walked into my kitchen and brought us each a Diet Coke. "Look, don't get ahead of yourself. It'll work out." She placed her hand on mine. "You're talking yourself out of something because you're scared. What's the sense of living if you don't let yourself feel?"

The bottle hissed as I unscrewed the top of my soda and let her words sink in. "Yeah, maybe. I don't like uncertainty, and between my career and my heart, that's all I have."

She sighed. "Don't keep fighting what life throws at you. Try to go with it."

Maybe she was right, but something felt off. I didn't know if it was because I'd spent the night in the arms of the man I'd once hated or the stupid text I'd sent him. My phone dinged. I couldn't have grabbed it fast enough.

Gina's brows rose at my haste. "Seriously, I've never seen you like this."

"Shut up." I took a breath and looked at my phone. To say I wasn't disappointed it was a text from Justin and not Bentley would have been a lie. I looked at her. "It's Justin."

Gina perked up. "Ooh, tell him I said he's hot." She laughed.

"Seriously? Go for Seth, but if you want me to tell him . . ."

She grabbed my arm. "Don't you dare!"

I smiled and read the text.

Justin: Hey, I'm on my way to the theater.

Andi: I'll be there soon.

Justin: Later.

"Everything will be fine. Don't worry about it." Gina got up and kissed me on the top of my head. "I'm going to head out for my appointment."

"Okay."

"I'll see you later. Let me know if you want to hang out after rehearsal. If you're getting together with Bentley, that's fine too."

"Yeah, okay," I said.

Gina walked out. As soon as the door clicked, I looked at my cell phone's blank screen. Unable to let it go, I sent him another message.

Andi: Are you still going to be able to come over later?

Nothing. Maybe he was just in a meeting and couldn't get back to me. At least, that was how I would rationalize it for now.

After a quick lunch, I headed to the theater. The air was warming up, and I loved that summer was just around the corner. At the stage door, I heard Bentley's deep voice and stopped dead in my tracks. I strained to hear what he was saying and who he was talking to. Heading toward his voice, I stopped backstage when I saw him, looking extremely handsome in his crisp gray shirt, talking to Mack in the front row of the theater. What the hell was happening? Why was he talking to my director, and where was Justin?

"What's going on?" Seth said from behind me and slung his arm around my shoulder, startling me.

"Not sure. I don't know what they would be talking about." My voice was barely above a whisper.

"Who is that with Mack?" he asked.

"That's Bentley Chambers." Just saying his name made my soul ache.

"Wait . . . that's . . . ?"

I quietly said, "The critic who wrote a contemptuous review about my performance."

We were acting like spies, peering around the curtain at the men in front of us.

"Huh. I figured he'd be older," he said.

"Yeah, me too."

Just then, Bentley's eyes caught mine, but they didn't light up. Rather, they glared at me. *Shit.* When they shifted to Seth, they really became stern.

"Oooh, I think you're in trouble." Seth nudged me with his elbow, and I let out an unenthusiastic laugh. "Wait, I thought you didn't know what he looked like? Did I miss something?"

"We have some catching up to do. Let's go to my dressing room and talk." I wasn't sure what details I would give Seth, but he'd get the gist without me having to tell him about my newfound sex life. I led us to the small room that had been set aside for me.

Seth shut the door and turned to me. "Okay, what's the scoop?"

"The short of it is, after I met with Mack about the future of this production because of Bentley's review, I decided I needed to meet the guy and give him a piece of my mind. But instead . . . let's just say, he isn't all bad."

"Andrea Jordan, have you fallen for the big bad critic?" Seth chuckled, and I wanted to cry. "Wait, you did?"

"It's really hard to explain. I don't understand it myself. I'm so nervous. If I can't pull off this audition, then I'm out of work, and who knows what will happen after that. So Bentley offered to work with me, and I accepted. One thing led to another and . . ." I shook my head. "It just got intense really fast. We went through the script together, and he evoked such emotion in me that even I could hear the difference in myself. How did I let this happen?"

Seth lowered his body so that we were face to face. "There isn't anything wrong with that. Was he able to help?"

"Yeah, he really did." The memory of our time rehearsing made me happy, but I was still so confused. What was he doing there? "I screwed it up, and now he's here talking to Mack. What do you think they're talking about? There's no way he would tell him I still sucked, right?" My "do you have a girlfriend" text flashed in my head.

"Andi, you're making me jumpy, and I'm not even acting in this play. Please just relax. I'm sure it'll be fine."

Pressure built in my eyes until tears slid down my cheeks. "What will I do if it isn't fine? This isn't a cheap place to live. I'll have to move or get a roommate." Pure panic was about to set in if I didn't calm down. I wasn't one to have panic attacks, but there was a first time for everything.

"If this dick does anything to hurt you, I'll critique his ass back to where he came from. Mack has the final say, and you need to relax. If he tells Mack you suck, then that doesn't say much about his teaching skills."

Seth's words made me feel better, but I still wished I hadn't texted him that question. What if he was so upset that he was telling Mack I was hopeless? Seth pulled me into a hug and held my head close to his chest. The rhythm of his heart was calming and exactly what I needed. After a few deep breaths, I started to feel better about the entire situation. Before I could say anything, the door swung open. Bentley was standing there with Mack, and they both stared at Seth and me.

"Sorry to intrude. I did knock, but you mustn't have heard it." Bentley's eyes darted between Seth and me. He walked toward us and whispered in my ear, "Maybe I should've asked about your boyfriend." His words were curt and condescending.

My eyes widened, and I looked at his, which were dark and full of anger. He glared at us. What was going on? My stomach knotted, and beads of sweat trickled down my spine. My anxiety was nauseating. Adrenaline coursed through me, making my hands quiver. I couldn't shake the feeling that I was about to lose everything—my job and him.

Mack cleared his throat, drawing my attention to him. "Andi, I've agreed to allow Mr. Chambers to observe today's audition. He won't be reviewing the show again, but he has provided funding to produce it, so I felt it right for him to be here."

My jaw dropped, and I shook my head. No . . . just no. *He's going to use his money to fund the very show he thought sucked? Wait. He didn't think the show sucked—just me. Does he think I can't pull it off? I came to rehearse, and now I'll be fighting for my job.* I stared at him for some indication of what he felt. Just a hint would have been sufficient, but he remained stoic. *Is he doing this for me or to have control of a situation?* I glanced at Seth, whose expression was full of disbelief. Seth placed his hand on my shoulder.

My thoughts rushed as my heart shattered. The pain in my chest was so intense I felt as if a thousand-pound boulder were resting on it and rendering me incapable of breathing. I straightened my spine, raised my head, and as proudly as I could, looked at Mack. "Is that so?"

I turned my focus to Bentley. He was leaning against my dressing table with his legs crossed at the ankles as if he had all the answers in the world. Asshole. How could he not know this would devastate me?

"I need to go check on the sets." Seth turned and stood in front of Bentley, which made Bentley stand straight up. Seth was a couple inches taller, but Bentley didn't look threatened. "Andi is one of my closest friends and one of the best actresses I've ever known."

Seth leaned in and whispered something I didn't hear. It must have irritated Bentley because his brows practically shot up to his hairline. I watched my friend leave, and I felt completely alone.

"It's about that time." Mack clapped. "Lucy is already on stage, so let's do this."

"I wasn't aware the auditions were today." My voice wavered.

"Andi, I said they'd be this week, and today is the day. You've rehearsed, just as Lucy has. She tells me she's ready. Are you?"

I lifted my chin. "Yes, sir. I am."

"Then let's get this show on the road." Mack walked out of the dressing room.

I looked at Bentley, who turned to follow. I needed to remind myself that I was good and the part was mine to lose. We followed Mack to the stage, where Lucy and I greeted each other with a hug. Mack and Bentley headed down into the house.

"Good luck, Andi." Her words sounded sweet, but I knew she wanted the role just as much as I did.

I looked at her. "Thank you. Good luck to you too."

Justin rushed up to me from the front stairs. "I'm so sorry, Andi. I got stuck in traffic." He pulled me into a hug and whispered, "You got this. Knock 'em dead." He turned to Lucy and gave her a small smile before he exited the stage.

We went through scenes from both act one and act two. I really let myself go and nailed it. Once we were done, Bentley and Mack spoke softly to each other. I felt totally vulnerable and a bit uneasy. I glanced at Lucy, who stood with a straight spine. Her still hands hung at her sides, and mine were beginning to tremble. Mack and Bentley came up on stage.

"Well, ladies, that was very good, and this was a difficult decision to make. One of you edged out the other by a small margin." Mack looked between us and said, "Congratulations . . ."

My world stood still as I focused on Mack's lips, watching their shape as I hoped he'd say my name.

"Lucy, you have earned the role of Katie." Mack looked at me. "I'm very sorry, Andi. The understudy part is yours if you'd like it."

My heart fell so hard I was sure he could hear it hit my feet. Before I could say "thank you for the opportunity," Lucy shouted something that rendered me speechless.

"Thank you so much, Bentley. I wouldn't have been able to do this without your help." She embraced him, and his hands curled around her back.

"Congratulations, Lucy." His voice didn't falter, and his eyes never met mine.

I needed to get my shit together. I slowly went to Mack. "Thank you for everything, but I think it's best that I bow out gracefully." I shook his hand and turned to Lucy, who was standing next to Bentley. "Congratulations. I'll have my stuff packed up in few minutes."

There. I'd done it. I'd kept it together after finding out that the man I'd just given my heart to made a habit of helping actresses. I wondered if he thought she was better in bed than me. I couldn't believe I'd fallen for his bullshit. I hurried to the small room that contained my belongings, ignoring Justin as I breezed past him. I tossed my stuff in my duffle bag and slammed the small locker shut. *Idiot.* That was all I could think. No, not Bentley. Me. *I'm the idiot.*

I had to go home, make a few calls, and check the trades for upcoming auditions. I wasn't going to back off my dream just because I'd fallen for the wrong guy. I tossed the duffle over my shoulder and left.

"Andi!" Bentley's voice bellowed through the empty corridor.

My feet betrayed me, and I stopped in my tracks. I spun on my heel, and he was right in front of me.

"Don't." I didn't have the energy to yell. I felt utterly defeated and let down . . . and alone.

"Please . . ." He reached for my arm, but I pulled away.

"How could you do what you did? I guess you believe in everyone, not just me. Was that just a line so you could fuck me? Or was I right and you have someone else? Maybe it's Lucy? I really thought you cared." I shook my head in disbelief.

"Really? I can't believe you just said that." His chest rose higher with each breath. "I do believe you can be great. I also believe this show could be great. That's why I decided to help you and suggested that my mom's theater guild provide the funding. It had nothing to do with us."

"This has everything to do with us. I trusted you with more than my career, and you completely disregarded me and what we shared. But I suppose you share a lot of yourself. When you told me you had reach, I didn't think you meant you reached into actresses' pants." A tear escaped, and I wiped it away.

"Andi, it wasn't like that. It was different with Lucy." He attempted to touch my arm again.

"Do not touch me!" I jerked back and stepped away. "You don't get to touch me. Not anymore." I couldn't suppress a chuckle. "Lucy was different? Why? Because she's younger? Better?" I raised my hand. "Never mind. I don't want to know."

"So you're going to give up on us because of this?" His eyes narrowed. "You are so off base."

"You just don't get it." I shook my head. "I thought your written words were painful, but your actions are so much worse than anything you could have ever printed. You told me I controlled my slingshot, right?"

His eyes dropped as he nodded once in acknowledgement.

"Well, you're right—I do. And I opt to pull it back as far as I can without your help. I know people in this industry too. The days of you helping me are over." I jabbed his muscular chest with my finger. "And as far as we're concerned, I'm done."

His eyes softened as he looked at me. I crossed my arms in an effort to keep my heart in my chest.

"You should really go celebrate with Lucy. I'm sure she'd love to thank you in private." I pushed open the metal door that led to the back lot. The thick, humid air made breathing more difficult than it already had been. It had taken everything I had not to completely fall apart in front of him.

Once I was tucked safely in my car, my tears flowed freely as I gasped for air. I did my best to regain my composure before I drove away from the theater. It dawned on me that I wasn't sure if I was more upset about leaving my job or Bentley.

The drive home seemed to take longer than normal. My mind replayed the past thirty minutes over and over, and all I could do was shake my head. Usually in a situation like this, I'd need to talk to Gina, but I just wanted to be alone.

Bentley

"Well, Mr. Chambers, I think we made the right decision." Mack smiled and shook my hand. "I'm sorry to lose Andi, but she'll land on her feet." He walked into his office and shut the door.

She'd walked away from me without hearing me out. I'd figured that by now, she'd think more of me than to believe I slept with every actress I met. I didn't know which way to turn. What the fuck had happened? My phone rang, and I answered without looking at the screen. "What!"

"Well, that isn't a very nice way to greet your mother."

My eyes squeezed closed as I cringed. "Sorry, Mom, I've had a bad day."

"Well, that really isn't an excuse, but I'm sorry to hear it. Would you like to talk about it?"

"No." Telling my mom about Andi and the show would be the worst thing I could do. She'd have me bring Andi flowers and give her an in-depth explanation, and I wasn't in the mood for that. Andi should have trusted that I didn't sleep around.

"Have you taken care of the theater endowment?" she asked.

"Yes, everything is all set. We had a minor glitch, but it'll work out."

"Glitch?" Her voice was full of concern.

"It's really fine and already taken care of. I'm sure the show will be wonderful."

"Sweetheart, you don't sound like yourself. Why don't you come home and we can talk about it?"

My mother always wanted to make things better, but I needed to handle this. I was sure she'd have vast amounts of wisdom to share, but I was so upset with Andi that wisdom was the last thing I sought.

"I'll see you soon, I promise," I said. "I have some business to take care of. Please tell the women in the guild that the director is very grateful. He'll be sending tickets to all of you for opening night."

"Fantastic, I'll tell them . . . Bentley, are you going to be okay?"

Just then, my phone beeped, and I saw it was Brett. I needed to talk to him. He would understand this situation and tell me what I needed to hear, not necessarily what I wanted to hear. "Mom, your number-two son is calling. I need to go, and yes, I'll be fine."

She laughed. "Tell him to call his mother every once in a while. Love you."

"Okay. Love you, Mom."

I hung up, answered Brett's call, and proceeded to tell him that he wasn't the only one who could fuck up a relationship and to call our mother.

CHAPTER 8

Andi

Curled in a ball on my bed, I was numb. The pressure in my entire body was too much for me. My brain felt muddled with thoughts of Bentley, but I needed to find a new energy source and get moving. Maybe I'd give myself a day to mope and start looking for work tomorrow. My eyes roamed over the picture of my name in lights, the theater programs I'd collected over the years, a picture of me and Seth from dress rehearsal, and a newspaper clipping stuck on the frame of my mirror. A sigh escaped me, along with a tear that I hoped would be the last one.

My phone beeped. I picked it up and stared at the screen.

Seth: I heard. Are you ok?

He was such a great guy. It was a shame we weren't attracted to each other. At one time, we'd joked about it and kissed, but it wasn't something either of us would have written home about. He was a great kisser, but it just didn't curl my toes or make me feel the way I should have, like when Bentley kissed me. Figured.

Andi: Not really, but I will be.

Seth: Can I come over?

Andi: Now's not a good time.

Part of me wanted him to, but I wasn't ready to get into what had happened between Bentley and me. I was glad Seth had texted because I was sure the sound of my voice would bring him over within minutes. I could lie to myself and say I wouldn't let Bentley's betrayal affect me, but my friends would see through my façade.

Seth: Did you talk to Gina?

Andi: No.

Seth: Can I?

Andi: I'll call her later or tomorrow and tell her everything. Thank you.

Seth: Will you call me too? I'm worried about you.

Andi: Yeah, I'll call.

Seth: Great. Don't get mad if I don't wait that long.

I felt as exhausted as if I'd just run the New York City Marathon. As I tried to process how this had happened to me, how I could have let him crush me this way, there was a knock on the door. I slowly swung my legs over the side of the bed, feeling as if I had weighted shoes on rather than bare feet. Another two knocks sounded. As I stood, my toes gripped my carpet, and my hand went to the side table for support.

More knocks.

In a soft, lazy voice, I told whoever was there that I

was coming, but I doubted they heard me. As I opened the door, my eyes found Bentley's. Too tired to do anything else, I asked, "What do you want?"

His right hand rested on the doorframe while his body leaned in just enough for me to smell him. "We need to talk."

"No, we don't. I'm tired and don't have anything to say."

I dragged my body, which had awakened with his presence but still felt weighed down, to the kitchen for a glass of water. My hand shook when I raised the glass to my mouth, and I felt him behind me, bringing back the memory of our night together. I stood stock still, keeping my back to him. His hands went to my shoulders, and my head lowered. Too weary to argue, I set the glass in the sink and turned to face him. His eyes lacked the sparkle I'd become accustomed to. They were deep, dark, and searing.

"I'd tell you I'm sorry if I thought that would help," he said.

My head shook. "Don't. It doesn't. Plus, I doubt you are. Please just go."

He ran his hands through his dark hair. I walked to the door and opened it.

"You really want me to leave? I'll be leaving tomorrow, so if you want to talk this out, now's the time. I'll only be coming back as necessary for the show." He crossed his arms, awaiting my reply.

A lump formed in my throat. Whatever this was between us was over before it had really started. I nodded. "Okay."

"Okay? Wow, Andi. You aren't the person I thought

you were at all. What happened to that feisty woman who found me in the restaurant to tell me off? Where'd she go? Where'd your fire go?"

"You extinguished it the moment you lied to me." I half shrugged. "Or maybe it never existed. Maybe your reviews were spot-on when you said I lacked passion. How ridiculous I must've seemed as I poured out my heart about my dreams and my parents and how hard it was for me to accept your help in the first place." I shook my head in disbelief. "Only to find out it wasn't just me you wanted to help. I thought I was special to you. I thought you were different."

"I am different. I did believe in you and your talent, and more importantly, in us. I still do, or I wouldn't be here."

"Save it. I don't want to hear it." I didn't want his bullshit explanations. I wanted him out.

"You're talented and deserve the spotlight." He turned to leave but not before looking back at me with piercing eyes. "I thought you wanted me too, that you wanted us."

"We aren't an 'us.' You still don't understand—I trusted you. Every word you told me, I believed. Enjoy the show. It really is a great story, and I'm sure with your continued assistance, Lucy will make sure the show will be filled with the passion it lacked."

Without a word, Bentley walked away. As the door closed, my tear ducts opened. I looked around the apartment; it felt as empty as I did. I sat on the sofa, wrapped my arms around a soft throw pillow, and tried to stop my heart from shattering into a million pieces. I rolled to my side as sobs wracked my body. I wondered if I'd ever get over him.

His words haunted my thoughts. "*I did believe in you.*" "*You're talented, Andi.*" "*I think you're beautiful.*" Were those things true or just lines he'd used to get what he wanted? And not just from me apparently. That was the thought I couldn't get rid of. How many were there? How did he even know Lucy?

I found myself pulling the soft blanket off the back of the couch. I wrapped my body in it before I drifted off to sleep.

A knock on my door made me sit upright. Had he come back? In a place deep in my heart, I wished he had, but when I opened the door, Seth was standing there with a pizza box and a bottle of my favorite wine.

"Holy shit, what happened? Are you okay?" He walked past me into my kitchen.

I followed and sat at my kitchen table. "You didn't need to come over. I would've called."

Seth turned to me. "Chambers came back to the theater looking like his dog just died, so I figured you weren't doing much better."

My voice cracked. "He did?" *Good.*

"Yeah. I don't know what happened, but I heard him tell Mack that he'd be back periodically to check in. I came to the conclusion that you'd probably told him to take a hike. Am I right?"

I nodded. "It was horrible."

Seth grabbed plates and glasses from my cupboard and set them on the table. "Talk to me, Andi."

I fiddled with a napkin. "There isn't much to say. I thought he was different, but he wasn't. He was exactly what I didn't need, which is the opposite of how I've felt the past few days."

Before Seth could reply, the door opened, and Gina flew in. "I'm so sorry I'm late. The bitch didn't like the way her eyes looked because she 'looked older.'" Gina tossed her bag on the sofa and removed her jacket in a huff. "She *was* older, and I made the mistake of saying that I'm a makeup artist, not a plastic surgeon. I'm telling you, these actresses can be a major pain in my ass! No offense, Andi, but I'm telling you, if I didn't get paid well for what I do, I swear I'd quit and get a job at a department store makeup counter where all I'd have to deal with are everyday women who appreciate me! *Ugh!*" She put her hands on her hips and looked to Seth and me. "Shit. What the fuck happened? You look horrible."

I looked at Seth, who was smirking. "I left a voicemail for Gina to come over too. I didn't tell her why." He shrugged apologetically.

"Seriously, will someone tell me what the hell is going on?" Gina sat down as Seth got her a plate and glass. "Andi?" She reached out to me.

I took a sip of wine. "Well, Bentley isn't who I thought he was."

She lowered her brows and deadpanned, "Who is he?"

A slight laugh escaped me. "No, I mean he did something. I found out about it at the re-audition, and now I'm out of a job."

Seth handed her a glass of wine as she said, "Shut the fuck up! You got fired?"

"Gina, please." Seth sat back down.

"I'm sorry, but I'm in the dark here. What happened?"

I didn't want to rehash the entire thing, so I just summed it up. "Bentley's involved with a theater guild, and they're going to fund the show."

"That's a good thing, right?" Gina furrowed her brows.

"Yes, that part is fine. But at the re-audition, Lucy got the part." I shrugged one shoulder. "But that's not the worst part."

"What's worse than that, and what does that have to do with Bentley?" Gina placed her hand on mine and gave it a gentle squeeze.

"After Lucy got the role, she thanked Bentley for his help." My wine was going down easier than it should have been. I kept refilling my glass.

"Holy shit! He's involved with Lucy?" Gina put her hand on her chest. "What the fuck?"

Seth shifted in his chair. "Okay, ladies, let's have some pizza. I'm starving." He smiled as he lifted the brown cardboard cover. "Looks good, right?"

The smells of tomato, cheese, and pepperoni were comforting. I took out a piece and placed it on my plate, but I just picked at the crust, placing small portions in my mouth. I thought about the last time I'd shared a meal at that table and wondered if Bentley could eat pizza with chopsticks. Knowing him, he probably could, or at least he'd say he could. My frustration over what had happened rattled me to my core. How did I let myself end up in this situation? Would I ever be able to forget him?

Gina swallowed a bite of pizza. "Did Bentley tell you what was going on? Why would he do that to you?"

"I don't know why he did what he did. I really didn't

want to hear his explanation." I knew how dumb that sounded, but it was the truth. I stood and placed the plate on my counter, but I grabbed my glass on my way to my comfy chair in the living room, leaving my friends at the table. I wrapped my legs with one arm as I continued to drink. Before I knew it, my glass was empty again. "Hey, Seth, is there more wine?"

Seth walked over to fill my glass. "Don't you think you should slow down since you're not eating?"

"No, I don't." He was right of course, but I didn't really care. With more wine, I'd finally begun to relax.

Gina and Seth joined me in the living room.

I looked at them and smiled. "You two should hook up. You're cute together." I giggled as my head spun.

"Andi, I think you need to lie down. This has been an eventful day." Gina looked at me with sympathy but not pity. That was why I loved her.

"Don't you think Seth's cute?" Either my words were coming out in a slur or my ears were hearing things wrong. I felt really dizzy as I stood.

Seth was at my side in an instant. "Why don't you go to bed? It's late, and we can talk about Gina and me hooking up tomorrow." His smile was bright but laced with concern for me.

"Fine, but I'm really not tired." I grabbed my phone off the coffee table and started to my room. I turned back to see my friends looking at me. "Guys, I'm fine. Thank you for the food. I'll clean up in the morning. You two should go and enjoy your night. I'll call you both tomorrow."

Gina paused before standing. "Love you, Andi."

I smiled. "Love you too, G."

After the door clicked closed behind them, I locked it and continued to my room. Once I'd crawled into bed in a T-shirt, I looked at my phone and stared at the green message icon. As I went to set it down, it dinged with a message from him.

Bentley: You're mad. I get it. It wasn't my intent.

The wine was still swirling around in my brain. I blinked to focus on the screen. As my eyes filled and my heart raced, I typed.

Andi: I am mad. No, you don't get it. What was your intention?

Send. The pain in my chest from my shattered heart was sobering me up. My phone dinged again.

Bentley: I do get it. My intentions were clear. I wanted the best for you.

Andi: And that would be you?

Bentley: I guess we'll never know.

Bentley: Bye, Andi.

I couldn't peel my eyes from the blurry words, nor could I reply, because he was right—we'd never know. My nose tingled, and my chin quivered. Just a week ago, I had been in rehearsals and dreaming of making it big. Now I was unemployed and alone.

How I'd let that happen was beyond me. I didn't want him. I didn't want to sit around, buzzed and depressed. I looked at the *Edge* on my dresser. My sadness returned to the anger I'd felt earlier. Screw him and his intentions. *Fuck!* I hadn't needed him before, and I didn't need him now. That was what my brain was saying. My heart was feeling the complete opposite.

THE CRITIC

Thoughts of our time together replayed in my head. His strong lips, rippled abs, perfectly messed-up hair, striking eyes . . . I shook my head and tried to rid my brain of the images that kept appearing. Then I realized I needed to rid my heart of it because I had begun to fall hard for Bentley Chambers.

Once morning came, my head felt as if it weighed fifty pounds when I attempted to lift it off the pillow. My hand went to my forehead as I dragged myself out of bed and glanced at the clock on my nightstand. Wow, it was already one in the afternoon. I'd never slept so late. One look in the mirror, and the previous night came back to me: wine, Seth, Gina, text messages . . . shit. I wiped the eyeliner off the bottom of my eyes and brushed my teeth, which felt covered in burlap. Then I grabbed my phone and reread the text messages from Bentley. Well, I really just read the last one. *I guess we'll never know.* Nope, I supposed we wouldn't.

With my phone in hand, I meandered to the kitchen for a glass of water. I decided to curl up on my couch, but I was interrupted by a knock on the door. I didn't get up to answer, hoping whoever it was would go away. Then I heard Gina's voice calling my name, so I got up and let Gina in.

"Girlfriend, I brought lunch!" Her voice was as bubbly as she was beautiful. She headed to the kitchen table and opened the brown bag she was holding.

Once it was open, my nostrils filled with the familiar scent of Chinese food. I stood rooted in place.

"What's the matter? Did you eat already?" Her eyes saddened.

I swallowed hard, past the sorrow lodged in my throat, and walked over to the table. I stared at the chopsticks next to the containers.

"I'll get you a fork. I know you hate these." She headed toward the kitchen.

My hand caught hers. "No! I'd like to use these." A tear escaped as I stared at the black-and-red wrapper.

"Okay, what gives? Spill it. Since when does my best friend cry at the drop of a dime, much less over chopsticks? Is it your job? Because if it is, then we need to talk." Gina continued to open containers.

"I really don't want to talk about it. What's there to talk about? We're done." I set down the sticks.

Gina's forehead creased as her eyebrows rose. She stuck a fork in one of the containers and grabbed a piece of broccoli. "Don't you mean it's done?"

Now it was my turn to be confused. "What?"

"You said, 'we're done.' Did you mean 'it'? The play? Or are you talking about something else?"

I hadn't even realized I'd slipped up. "Yes, of course I meant the show. It's over." I shifted the food in the container with my sticks.

"Well, what if I told you that I got a great job offer yesterday?" She smiled and popped a piece of chicken in her mouth.

Finally something to smile about! "That's great! I'm so happy for you! Where is it? Come on, give me deets!"

She swallowed and wiped her mouth with a napkin. "Well, it's on Broadway!"

"Oh my God! I'm so excited for you! That's amazing!"

We both jumped up and hugged, spinning around. Her happiness radiated off her, and I was so happy to be able to enjoy it with her.

She didn't let go of me when she said, "They're still building the cast, and I gave them your name."

I pulled back and looked at her. "What?"

"Okay, don't flip out on me. First of all, this all happened before you lost your job. I don't want you to think that I thought you were going to lose it, because I didn't. But this is already going to be on Broadway, and yes, the main characters are cast, but the supporting actress sprained her knee when she fell off the stage showing off for the male lead." Gina burst into fit of giggles. "I wish you could've been there. I'm sorry she got hurt, but honestly, Andi, I was laughing so hard I thought I would pee my pants." Gina grabbed two diet sodas from the fridge. "So what do you think?"

What did I think? "Thank you so much for doing this for me." It was a dream come true, but my tone was less enthusiastic than I'd intended. I was truly grateful, but I continued to stare at the chopsticks in my hand.

"Andi, please talk to me." Gina's voice sounded as if she were a minute away from pleading for answers.

I set the sticks down and rolled one with my index finger. "I fell for him, and he didn't feel the same. It's been years since I've felt this way. To be honest, I don't know if I've ever felt this way."

"What makes you think he doesn't feel the same?"

"See these chopsticks?"

Gina nodded.

"We had takeout the other night, and I didn't know how to use these."

She giggled. "Yeah, I know. That's why I was going to get you a fork."

Fork. "See, that's the thing. He taught me how to use these stupid things and told me he had confidence in me. He made me believe that I could be the absolute best and that I was special to him. So why didn't he tell me that he's in the habit of helping actresses? He knew how I felt about accepting help from him, but I swallowed my pride, and I did it. Bentley gave me confidence. He made me feel good about myself. Then he ruined everything. I just don't understand why. Out of all the things he could have done, this is just unacceptable."

Gina took a deep breath. "I don't know him well enough to answer that. All I know is I think you're wonderful, and I knew he would too. Maybe he just wanted to support you."

"Or maybe he just wanted to sleep with me." I dropped my head in my hands and sighed. "Damn him."

"Did he say he'd slept with Lucy?"

I shook my head.

"Then maybe he didn't," she said. "I love you, but you could have totally blown this out of proportion. I could tell he had confidence in you, or he wouldn't have wasted his time."

Gina made sense, but she still hadn't made me feel better. "Really? His time? It's amazing he had time to spend with me since he was apparently coaching Lucy too." My voice rose, and I felt immediate remorse for using this tone with her.

"But you don't know that for sure, do you? You only think you know what happened." Now her tone mirrored mine.

"No, I don't know anything anymore." I should have

let him explain. I had drawn my own conclusions, and that was different than having them confirmed.

"Okay, look. It's done, right? So how about I call the casting director and tell him you're interested? He said he saw you in a summer stock production in Boston, so he's familiar with you and is happy to hear you may be available. What do you think?" Gina's hands were clasped under her chin. "We can work together in the city! It's a short gig, only a short run." She batted her eyes.

"That'd be great. I was going to spend the day looking through the trades and calling some contacts, but I appreciate you opening this door for me." For the first time today, I smiled and meant it.

Bentley

I woke up feeling like shit for the way I'd left things with Andi, but I dragged my ass to the shower and got ready to go back to the city. My bag was packed. I took a minute to look at my last message to Andi. I shook my head and headed out the door.

The car service I'd hired was waiting for me. As we drove back to New York, I wondered why this had happened. Would I ever have a normal relationship? I'd thought she was different, and it hurt to realize I'd been wrong. My phone vibrated in my jacket pocket, and my heart skipped a beat until I saw Brett's name on the screen.

Brett: Bro, you coming home today?

Bentley: In the car now. Be there soon.

Brett: Cool. Lunch?

Bentley: Yeah, okay.

Brett: Come to the club.

Bentley: Okay, see you around noon.

My apartment was silent when I got in. I tossed my keys on the side table and sat in my favorite chair, thinking about the past few days. How she could flip on me so quickly baffled me. For her to think I'd told her those things just to get her into bed pissed me off. Maybe she'd been using me for a good review. *Fuck!*

I needed to get out of my apartment and my own head. I splashed some cold water on my face and went downstairs to grab a cab.

Once I was inside my brother's club, Carly, a beautiful blonde I'd had a one-night stand with, greeted me. I should've known better than to dip my pen in company ink, but since she worked for my brother and not me, I'd figured why not? But according to Brett, she'd asked about me once or twice, and I wasn't in the mood for any come-ons today.

"Hey there, handsome. How are you?" She undressed me with her soft brown eyes before licking her lips. "Your brother will be here in just a minute. He's on a call, but he told me to take care of you until he gets here."

"Thank you, Carly." I didn't want to give her the wrong impression, so I stayed impassive.

Her long blond waves bounced as I followed her through the club. The White Orchid was expanding their restaurant business, and from the look of it, they were doing well.

She led me to a private table, and rather than leaving, she sat down. "So how have you been? I haven't seen you in a while." Her chest rose, making my eyes gravitate toward the swell of her breasts.

"I've been good. Busy but good." Hopefully that sounded believable. I was anything but good.

"Why don't I get you a drink? Whiskey on the rocks?"

"Yeah, that'd be great."

She gracefully rose, giving me ample time to study her. Where the hell was Brett?

Before I could ask Carly, he appeared, looking exhausted. "Hey, man, sorry I'm late. I needed to take a call." He turned toward her. "Scotch, neat."

She nodded and left.

"It's fine. Is everything okay?"

"Yeah, same shit, different day," he said. "I swear, you're lucky you have a normal woman because what I'm dealing with is insane."

My heart clenched. I wondered if Andi was thinking about me. Brett leaned back in his chair as Carly set our drinks down.

"Would you two like a menu?" She addressed both of us but stared at me.

"I'll have my usual, and bring the same for Bentley," Brett said.

Carly nodded before she walked away.

He chuckled. "She still wants your ass."

"Yeah, well, I'll pass. Right now I just need to get my head on straight. I had a bit of a thing with Andi last night."

"By the look on your face, it wasn't a good thing. Care to elaborate?"

I sat back and fiddled with the small drink napkin on the table. "Andi lost her role in the show yesterday. The understudy, Lucy, read for the part alongside Andi, and she got it."

"Okay, and Andi's mad at you why?"

"Because after the audition, Lucy thanked me, with a hug, for helping her." I shook my head. "Andi thinks I slept with her when all I did was call an acting coach friend for her. I met Lucy when she played in a different show sponsored by the guild, and when she didn't get this role, she reached out and asked if I knew this coach she wanted to work with and if I could get her in. That's all I did. This is un-fucking-believable." I took a long sip of my drink, relishing the slow burn.

"So Andi totally misunderstood the situation, and you didn't try to correct her?" Brett's expression changed to disbelief.

"Yeah, that's half right. Except I did try to correct her, but she wouldn't listen. I don't know. Maybe we're better off apart." I stared at the ice in my glass.

"I'm not one to dole out advice, but if you care about this chick, then do something about it."

"Yeah, maybe. I haven't cared this much about anyone ever. From day one, I knew she was the one, and before we could find out where we were headed, we ended." I looked at Brett. "So what else is going on with you?"

Our food arrived, and Brett shifted our discussion to sports. I couldn't believe we'd both rather be talking about the Yankees' lineup than the women in our lives.

After lunch, I went to the office to talk to Scott. He'd sent me a message about an opportunity that was right up my alley. I wasn't sure what that meant, but nonetheless, I was intrigued. I'd welcome anything that would get my mind off Andi. The office was buzzing with reporters talking to editors, advertising sales people setting up boards at their desks, and layout designers doing their thing. I smiled at my coworkers and waved to Vanessa, who was on the phone, as I made my way to Scott's office. I knocked on the open door.

"Hey, there's my main man. Come on in." Scott rose from behind his desk and shook my hand. "I've missed you around here. Did you have a good week off?"

My mind quickly replayed my week. "Yeah, for the most part. You know, it's Jersey."

I chuckled, and Scott glared at me. He's a Jersey boy, so Jersey-bashing had been our joke for years. From the first review I'd written, Scott told me I had the potential to achieve big things. He'd taken me under his wing, and I just soared. I couldn't have done it if he hadn't believed in me. I thought of Andi. That was all I wanted for her to know—that I believed in her. I shook my head to clear my mind.

Scott motioned to the chair in front of his metal desk as he sat behind it. "Have a seat. I have a proposition for you."

"So what's up?" I asked. Scott looked excited, and I couldn't wait to hear what he had to say. I could use some good news.

"Well, our owners, Chatfield Unlimited, have been looking at starting a paper in the UK."

Chatfield Unlimited was a huge newspaper holding company, and they had various papers under their umbrella, the *Edge* being one of them. Since they'd taken over the *Edge* about two years earlier, the periodical had become one of the largest selling trade publications in the city. Our online presence had also grown.

"I remember hearing about that at the last all-hands meeting. What does that have to do with me?"

"Well, their expansion is going to include an arts section, and your name was brought up to run it."

I was stunned silent.

"Bentley? Buddy, you okay?" Scott chortled. "Isn't that great? Mr. Chatfield personally asked for you."

I leaned forward. "He wants me? Why not you? I mean, you're the editor. You understand the ins and outs of this business better than I do. I just review shows."

He shook his head. "They want you there and me here. You've made a name for yourself, my friend, and it's high time people outside the theater industry acknowledge that."

"I'd be leaving the city? What about my job here?" My heart raced as I thought about leaving my home behind. Not to mention my family. Brett needed me, and the thought of leaving him wasn't a pleasant one. Then Andi came to mind. Maybe this wasn't a bad idea.

"Let me clarify." Scott reached in his drawer and pulled out a manila folder. "It's a temporary position. You'd set up the arts section and stay until you found someone there worthy of handing the reins to. It could be three months or longer, that's up to you. They're only requiring a minimum of three months in England. Once you got back, you'd have to maintain an online presence as well as make periodic visits, which of course they'd take care of."

I opened the folder and saw the salary they were willing to pay me. Although I tried to remain impassive, I knew my eyes widened.

"Nice paycheck, right?" Scott smacked his hands on his desk and stood. "I know you love your job here, and it'll be yours when you come back. You aren't leaving the company, you're just—"

"Leaving here." I stood and looked at the folder.

"Think about it, but they need an answer soon. They want you there within the next six to eight weeks. They realize you'll need to tie things up here and make the necessary arrangements. They're setting you up with an apartment in London, so your housing is taken care of."

I nodded as my heart raced with excitement. Something in my gut told me to go for it, so I did. "Scott, I think this is perfect timing." I thought of Brett, but I could be back before anything happened with the baby. "Okay, I'll do it. I need to review the contract, but you can tell Mr. Chatfield he has a tentative yes."

"Fabulous." Scott shook my hand. "I'll miss your ugly mug around here, as I'm sure most of the women will, but this is a great opportunity."

I laughed. "Thanks, Scott."

As I left the office, I couldn't believe what had just happened. Oddly, I was excited about this change. London boasted big name shows, and the actors usually received rave reviews. *Yeah, this is perfect.*

CHAPTER 9

Andi

Waking up refreshed and nervous was better than the way I'd woken up yesterday. My audition for *Acceptance* was scheduled for four in the afternoon. The director had e-mailed me the script and told me I'd be auditioning for the role of Victoria, a small, but nevertheless important part.

Gina had decided that if I got the role, we'd go out and celebrate. Actually, she said no matter what happened, since we were going to the city, we were going to party. I could use a drink and some fun, so game on!

I met Gina at the train station, and I was surprised to see Seth waiting on the platform. "Hey there, handsome." I wrapped my arms around him.

He tightened his arms around me before releasing me. "I've been so worried about you. Then Gina called and said you had an audition in the city today and that we were all going out afterward. I'm so happy for you."

"Well, let's not get our hopes up quite yet, but I'm

glad you're here. I may need a shoulder to cry on." I nudged him, and he laughed.

"You won't need a shoulder, but mine is yours if you want it." He nudged me back, and we made a game of elbowing each other while chuckling.

"Okay, you two weirdoes, our train is here. Let's do this!" Gina laughed and handed me my bag.

In what seemed like no time at all, we were at our stop. As we walked through the streets, I took in everything. People either loved or hated New York, and I loved it, all of it. I didn't care that the man on the corner just ate something out of the garbage, street performers at every corner wanted money, or a man in nothing but his underwear and a cowboy hat was playing a guitar in Times Square. I turned the corner, and there it was—Broadway. Calm determination washed over me. That was where I needed and wanted to be.

I turned and realized Seth and Gina weren't behind me. I scanned the street and saw Gina standing next to half-naked guitar dude, getting her picture taken by Seth. I snickered at her antics. That was a total G move. She was in the Square all the time, and each time she got her picture taken with someone or something.

She ran up to me, holding her phone. "Look! I finally got my picture with him!" Gina giggled as Seth stood next to her, shaking his head.

"I'm very happy you got your Kodak moment, but I need to get to the theater," I said. "You can hang out here if you'd like."

"Nope, we're coming in. I have to check out the makeup area. Rehearsals start on Monday, and I need to check out all the actors' skin tones so I bring the right items with me."

Walking into the theater made my skin prickle with excitement. Small crystal chandeliers hung from the ceiling, and I ran my hand over the red velvet seats as I walked down the sloped aisle. My eyes lifted toward the stage, and I was engulfed by nerves and anticipation of what this audition could mean for me. I tried not to think about the future and just live in the present, but it was difficult. A single spotlight shown on center stage, and I stopped in my tracks to look at it. *Wow. Just wow.*

The auditorium was empty except for the three of us, and it almost felt like the calm before the storm.

"I'm going to check out the back and see who's there. Okay, Andi?" Gina said.

I nodded as I walked to the stage. Seth went with Gina to check things out behind the scenes. Six black steps led me to where I'd always wanted to be—on a Broadway stage. It didn't matter that it was small; it was Broadway. As usual, the worn stage floor had tape markings for the actors. I stood on the X directly under the spotlight. As I looked out to where the audience would be, I flung out my arms and spun. I wrapped my arms around my middle and spoke the lines the director had e-mailed me. My voice echoed as I imagined other actors saying their lines. *Acceptance* was heartfelt but not passion-filled. It was the story of a family that was brought together by adoption, and it spread the message that family was who you shared your heart with, not just your genetics. I was auditioning for the role of a social worker who brought families together.

Stepping forward, I practiced a few lines of the scene between Rose and the adoptive parents. My body relaxed as the words rolled off my tongue through the theater. I moved to stage right and imagined audience members before me. I briefly shut my eyes for a bit of dramatic pause before I spoke again, addressing the faux audience. The scene was gripping, and I made sure my gestures complemented and enhanced the story. I actually brought myself to tears, which wasn't difficult after what I'd just gone through with Bentley. My eyes closed, and I heard applause.

A man walked up to me from the side curtain. "Andrea Jordan? I'm Hank, the director. It's wonderful to meet you." He extended his hand as my nerves spiked.

That wasn't how I'd intended him to hear me. I was just practicing. "Hank, I was just rehearsing. I can do much better."

"Oh, no need. I knew you were perfect for the role before you got here. This was just a formality for the producer." His lips curled into a genuine smile.

I swallowed hard. "Who would that be?"

"Joselyn Burley. Do you know her?"

My breath of relief came out in a rush. "Nope. I was just curious." And thankful that Bentley and his mother's theater guild weren't involved. I didn't have anything against the guild, but I didn't want to be linked to Bentley.

⟵◦◦◦⟶

After we'd finished our celebratory dinner and cocktails, we headed to a club Gina insisted we just had to go to.

"I heard this place is the shit!" She was practically bouncing up and down in her seat.

Seth and I laughed at how animated she had become.

"So what's the name of this awesome place?" I asked.

"The White Orchid. From what I gather, the bartenders are hot!" She looked at Seth and shrugged. "Just as an attempt to get Andi's mind off you-know-who."

"I'm sitting right here and a man is the last thing I need. Let's just enjoy each other and have a good time." My voice came out harsher than I'd intended. The club sounded familiar, but I couldn't place it. I figured Gina had mentioned it before.

"Andi, I love you like a sister, but you've been moping, and I can't stand it. Now you have a job, and there's nothing wrong with taking in this moment and letting loose. So we see some eye candy in the process—there's nothing wrong with that. I'm not telling you to throw a guy down on a bar or dance on a table. Just have fun and relax."

Seth choked on the beer he was finishing. "If the two of you are going to be throwing dudes down on the bar, maybe this should be a ladies' night."

Gina flippantly waved at Seth. "Oh shut up, you'll have fun too. Save me a dance tonight, and you'll see." She winked.

I snickered at the look on Seth's face. He was clearly planning on doing just that. Those two played it way too cool with each other—they needed to sort things out.

After we'd paid our tab, Gina crowed, "Let's blow this popsicle stand and club it!"

As we hopped in a yellow checkered cab, my mind lingered on the man I missed. Yes, I was happy to be going out, but when Gina mentioned dancing with Seth, all I could picture was me dancing with Bentley. We'd never shared a dance, and we probably never would.

THE CRITIC

The White Orchid was sophisticated yet still young and fresh. The DJ spun tunes for the people gathered on the dance floor. A floral scent permeated the air, very different from any club I'd ever been in. Normally, we went to dive bars that smelled of beer and chicken wings, so flowers were never a thought. I watched couples talk, girlfriends laugh, and men look for their next conquest.

Seth led us through the small crowd to find stools at the bar. Only women occupied those seats, making Seth's smile grow.

I rolled up on the balls of my feet and whispered in his ear, "I thought you liked Gina?"

He smiled and kissed the top of my head. "Don't worry about me. Let's get you a drink."

We found three stools together and sat at the beautiful bar. It was magazine-cover worthy. Top shelf liquor lined the glass shelves, and Gina hadn't been lying when she'd said the bartenders were hot. The blond looked as if he'd stepped out of *Surfer GQ*. I looked at Gina, who was beaming with excitement.

A different bartender turned as he wiped down the bar and placed napkins in front of us. My heart sank. Brett. *Fuck me, this is his place. No wonder I recognized the name.*

"Well, if it isn't the woman who brought my big brother to his knees." His award-winning smile radiated, but his eyes were laden with mischief.

"You're Brett, right?" Gina tried to break the odd thickness that suddenly filled the floral-scented air.

His lips quirked. "Yeah." He chuckled. "And you're Gina." He tossed her a quick wink. "So, ladies, what'll it be? My signature Manhattan Martini?"

"That sounds great. Have you met Andi's friend, Seth?"

I wasn't sure what Gina was up to, but I didn't want Brett to think I'd moved on.

"Hey, Seth. Good to meet you. I'm Brett."

They shook hands, and Brett took our drink orders, completely unfazed by Gina's introduction.

When he returned with my wine, Seth's beer, and Gina's martini, he got the attention of Mr. GQ. "Hey, Ty, can you cover for me? I'll be back." The hot blond nodded. Then Brett signaled to me. "Andi, can I have a minute?"

My eyes shot to Gina's, which were as wide as pancakes, and then back to Brett. "Um . . . sure, I guess." I left my drink and slid off my stool.

Brett came out from behind the bar. He placed his hand on the small of my back as he led me upstairs to what had to be a VIP area. It didn't escape me that although Brett was hot as hell, his touch did nothing to me—no sparks, no tingling. Nothing like when his brother touched me. Bentley didn't even have to touch me for me to feel it. Brett motioned for me to sit in a plush booth that looked as if it had been built for lovers.

A beautiful waitress approached. "Can I get you anything?"

She'd addressed her question to Brett, so I tuned her out until she asked if Bentley would be coming in that night. My head snapped up and caught her name tag on her large breasts. "Carly, I think we're all set. Thank you."

She sized me up before smiling at Brett and leaving.

He watched her go. "I know this is none of my business, but what the hell did you do to my brother?"

I was floored. "Excuse me? You're right, it isn't your business."

Brett ran his tongue over his pearly white teeth. "Maybe not, but from the way he talked about you at lunch, I thought you two were serious. Then I talked to him yesterday, and he said it was over and he was done. So tell me Andi, how does my brother go from gushing to nothing overnight? How do you go from being with him to being here with someone else in a New York minute?"

Serious? He'd said we were serious? And over. "He lied to me." That was the only answer I had.

"What are you talking about? You didn't even let him explain, did you? Do you even know him?" He shook his head. "Fuck."

"Look, this isn't a good idea." His frustration was clear, and I didn't need to hear him bash me for pissing off his brother. My heart was damaged enough.

"Andi, let me tell you something about my brother." His voice was deep and bordered on chastising, which made me cringe. "He is the one of the kindest, most generous people I know. You rushed to judgment, and that was a mistake."

I recoiled in my seat. I was sure my cheeks looked like a basset hound's, and the look in Brett's eyes confirmed that. I felt all my muscles fall, making it hard for me to keep up a strong presence.

"I'm sorry, but he's the most important person in my life," Brett said, seeming to study me with each word. "I've fucked up so much, and if I didn't have him, I'd lose my mind. Bentley has always been there for me—he's that kind of guy. He likes to fix things and help people. He cares about his profession and all that encompasses."

"I don't know that he cares about me anymore, and I don't need his kind of help. I'm sure others out there can benefit from his expert tutelage, if they haven't already." My stomach twisted as I wondered how many actresses he had helped.

Brett smiled. "Us Chambers men, when we care, we truly care. It isn't a flippant emotion."

"He once told me that he had a deep reach in our industry. I didn't think that meant he reached up actresses' skirts."

That earned a lip curl and a shaking head from him. "And you know this how? Did he tell you that's what happened? Because the story I got is completely the opposite." He took a sip of his drink and studied me.

"Wait, he told you about this, and you're sitting here questioning me? What do you mean opposite?" Bad decision to leave my drink on the bar. I could've really used it. Actually, I could have gone for a shot. *Where did that waitress go?*

"When he told me what you thought about him and that Lucy chick, I figured he was assuming the worst, but he wasn't, was he? You think my brother has a habit of sleeping with actresses. Maybe you should get the facts before you jump to conclusions." Brett smirked. "My brother doesn't mix business with pleasure—he leaves that to me. You know what's funny? We've both done it once, and we both lost the women we cared about. Except the one he did it with was the one he did care about. Ironic." He drained his drink and placed the tumbler on the table.

"I don't need this." What had I done? I began to slide out of the booth, but he put his hand on my arm to stop me. My body stilled. I looked him dead in the eye as I tried not to lose it.

"Andi, wait."

His voice wasn't harsh, but it still pierced through me. I felt like an errant child. "No, I won't wait. I met your brother because of his hatred of my acting. Do you realize how hard it was for me to ask for his help? And then have it become more?" My voice cracked. "Just when I thought I was special to him and fell for him, I found out I wasn't the only one." The hug Lucy had given him was very familiar, and I'd hated it. Imagining them in each other's arms made me see red. "He knew my reservations from the beginning, and he discounted them. So if I seem a little on edge, I have a reason. I don't have flippant emotions either."

Brett raked his hand through his hair. "Look, all I know is he cares about you. I know for a fact he didn't sleep with Lucy—he set her up with some famous acting coach. I also know you didn't let him explain that. This is on you as much as it is him."

My face heated as his words spun in my head. *A coach? He didn't run lines with her? Oh my God.* "Oh."

He let out a deep breath. "If he had told you about helping Lucy and still wanted to work with you, what would you have said to him?"

All I could do was stare at him because I didn't have the answer. The air felt heavy, and my heart hurt with the thought that I'd let go of a man whom I had quickly fallen for. "I don't know."

"Maybe you should think about that." Brett slid out of the booth and stood. "He's a great guy, and I think you realize that or you wouldn't have cared about any of this. He's not the type to take a week off from work for just anyone. I've never known him to do that." He rubbed his chin before leaning toward me. "You hurt my brother, and if you two work this out, which I hope you do, don't do it again."

My eyes glassed over, and his handsome image blurred.

"I need to get back to work," he said. "It was good seeing you. Feel free to stay and have a good time with your friends. Your night is on me." With that, he turned and walked away.

Before I knew it, Seth and Gina were squeezing into the booth. Thankfully, Gina had my drink in her hand.

"What was that about?" Gina said.

"Bentley."

Gina placed her hand on mine. "Are you okay?"

"I don't know." That was the truth. I had no idea if I'd ever be okay.

Seth chimed in, "Well, we're here to celebrate, so let's get this party started."

I smiled at them. They were right—we did need to celebrate. But I needed to figure out what to do next, and staying at that club and having a great time wasn't what I wanted.

Traveling to New York City for rehearsals for the week made me crave the big city life. Once the show ended, I'd miss the sounds of the train, the horns and sirens blaring, the yellow cabs weaving through the city streets. Hopefully, I could land something else then, but what really weighed on my mind was Bentley.

After my heart-to-heart with Brett, my head had swum with questions. I'd been trying not to think about Bentley, but when I passed the newsstands, I couldn't help picking up a copy of the *Edge*. His picture next to his latest review haunted me. I missed those deep blue eyes. The image of his tousled hair and chiseled jawline felt like a vise on my heart, and since when did he have his picture in the paper?

I'd read all of his latest reviews. Some were praise, and some weren't, but the one I hated the most was when he appeared in a photograph with the star of a show that had received a lot of acclaim in the trades. Her name was Jaclyn Love Hart, which sounded phony. I wondered if she was as fake as her name, which was wrong of me. She was stunning, and by his smile, he seemed happy. Who was I to be jealous when I was the one who'd pushed him away?

When I finally got home from the grueling yet enjoyable week, I peeled off my Converse sneaks, which felt as if they'd been molded to my feet. The air was getting warmer as summer drew near. My feet were beginning to swell. I kept forgetting that New Yorkers walked . . . a lot. Cabs were too expensive to keep taking, and the subway lines still confused me a bit, so I walked too. The chardonnay in my fridge was calling my name, and after I answered by pouring myself a glass, I planted my tired ass on the soft sofa. I couldn't stop myself from looking at yet another picture of "Mr. Chambers and Ms. Hart" in the society section. They were arm-in-arm at the benefit gala for the Shooting Stars Theater Guild. The vise on my heart turned into a blade that sliced right through me. Would we have been at that gala if we were still together? Would I have been the one in the gorgeous black gown?

My eyes betrayed me, refusing to look away from the stunning couple. The tips of his fingers peeked out from around her small silk-covered waist. I could actually feel his palm pressed against the small of her back as she smiled brightly; I'd have been smiling too. I set the paper down and decided I'd had enough of the happy couple.

Questions lingered in my mind. Did he miss me? Did he think of me? Did he wonder what I was doing? Did he still want me? I glanced back at the picture and came to one conclusion . . . the only conclusion: no.

I refilled my glass and polished it off before grabbing my phone. No calls, messages, or texts. He didn't miss me. My mind enjoyed the wine coursing through it, but my heart hurt. I made a call to the local cab company.

Sixty minutes later, I was back in the city, sitting in a packed theater and waiting for Ms. Hart's show to begin. The show's program sported pictures of the cast, and her headshot was prettier than the pictures in the paper. I perused the auditorium, looking for him, but the house lights dimmed. I didn't even know if he was there or not.

Ninety minutes and two standing ovations later, the theater emptied. Ms. Hart had been as wonderful as Bentley had said in his review. Her stage presence was as large as she was beautiful. If she weren't an actress, she could have easily been a beauty queen. For a fleeting moment, I felt as if they were meant to be together, two gorgeous people who exuded confidence and strength.

I didn't know what had possessed me, but I took the aisle to the back of the playhouse and waited to see the woman up-close and personal. I ducked behind a crew member and followed him backstage, trying to go unnoticed. Then my world halted when he came into view: Bentley in her embrace. Ms. Hart's long hair was draped over his arm, and her cheek rested on his shoulder. Bentley's back looked broad and strong as he held her close. My skin prickled. What had I done? I'd pushed him away and into the arms of another woman.

Her eyes opened and met mine. As she pulled out of the embrace and stared at me, Bentley turned. His smile faltered as his brows drew together and creases formed on his forehead.

"Andi?"

Going backstage had been a mistake of epic proportions. I had nothing to say. My chest heaved, and my lungs burned for air. For a brief moment, I was rooted in place, but once he stepped closer, my feet moved. I turned to hurry away. As I pushed through the stagehands, praying my legs wouldn't betray me, he kept calling my name, each call louder than the last. I needed to keep moving and get as far away from them as I could. I heard his voice through the crowd, but I kept going. I should have been happy for him, for them, but at that moment, I couldn't be. Maybe someday, but not now.

"Andi, wait!" His voice echoed down the back hallway, sounding closer than it had.

I came to a door that sported a "No Exit" sign. *Shit!* I stopped and pivoted, praying my body could absorb the emotions that were ready to burst from me. Being upset with him wasn't fair—this was all on me. As I tried to muster some version of a smile, I stared at him. He had a look on his face that I couldn't decipher. Guilt? Happiness? Dread maybe?

He appraised me from my hair to the tips of my

stilettos. "You're here." A smile grew across his gorgeous face.

I nodded as he took a tentative step forward then another. With one deep breath, my chest would be against his, so I stepped back.

"Don't run from me." He took my hand and attempted to pull me toward him.

My feet stayed rooted as he tugged on my arm, and my head shook. "I can't. I don't want to see you with her. She's a wonderful actress, but . . ." Feeling as though I would lose all my composure, I whispered, "Did you help her find her passion too? How many of us are there?" It was an unfair question, and I really didn't want to know the answer, but I wanted him to know where my mind was. Was I being petty? Yeah, probably, but my sarcasm was keeping my tears at bay.

He swallowed hard, his Adam's apple bobbing. "I helped her, yes."

"I see." My head lowered, and my eyes stung. That wasn't the answer I'd expected or wanted.

"Why did you come? Did you know I'd be here?" He studied me with his head cocked. His brows rose, waiting for my reply as a glimmer of hope passed over his face.

I felt his deep blue eyes penetrate my soul as my heart broke. How could he not see what he was doing to me? "I talked to Brett." I shrugged.

"He told me. So, that was a bit ago. Why did you come here?"

Normally, his soft voice would have comforted me, but right then, it did the opposite. "Never mind, it doesn't matter now." I tried pulling my hand from his, but he just gripped it tighter.

"It does matter. What did he say to you that made you want to see me?"

My face heated with embarrassment. "He said you cared about me, but he was clearly mistaken. It's fine, really. Can you please just let me go?" His charcoal-gray dress slacks and black loafers were the only things in my line of vision. I kept trying in vain to pull my hand from his grasp.

"No, it's not fine, and no, I'm not letting you go until you meet Lyn." His voice was calm, which unnerved me.

"What? Why do I need to meet her? Meeting your girlfriend will only make me feel worse. If you've found someone who makes you happy, then I'm happy for you, but I can't handle meeting her."

His eyes were soft. "Andi, you don't understand."

I nodded. "That's where you're wrong. I do understand, and I take full responsibility. You tried to explain. I didn't let you, and now I've lost you." My voice hitched, making me pause. "This hurts too much, Bentley. You've moved on. Please just let me go so I can try to do the same."

With his index finger, he raised my chin. I kept my eyes away from his.

"Look at me," he asked. "You're doing it again. You're jumping to conclusions. Let me explain."

I shook my head. "I'm sorry. I need to go. Your girlfriend will be looking for you soon, and I just . . ." I raised my eyes to his, allowing a tear to fall. "I can't meet the woman who has you now. I'm very sorry . . . for everything." I swallowed the lump in my throat. I should've trusted him and at the very least let him explain about his relationship, or non-relationship, with Lucy. "Thank you for everything you did for me, but you should be celebrating with her." Just saying that made me want to be ill. All I wanted to do was go outside and wail until I had nothing left in me. I was crushed and surprised I was still breathing.

I heard a giggle and looked behind Bentley to see Ms. Hart gliding toward us like a runway model. My heart jackhammered. He dropped his hands from my face, and I whisked away my tears. I was sure my face was a mess, but at that point, I really didn't care.

She walked up. "I'm sorry for laughing, but I couldn't help overhearing you. I'm Jaclyn Love Hart—well, that's my stage name. My real name is Lyn Chambers." She extended her hand.

Chambers?

"I'm Bentley's cousin. You're Andrea, right? I've seen your picture."

I accepted her hand, feeling utterly foolish.

"It's nice to meet the woman who stole my favorite cousin's heart," she said.

I managed to squeak, "It's nice to meet you too." I looked at Bentley, who had his arms crossed in front of him as his eyebrows rose to say, "I told you so." *Wait, I stole his heart?*

"I need to go to our post-show cast meeting and scrape off this make-up. Thanks for coming to the show. It was good to meet you." Lyn's smile was genuine and bright, which made me feel horrible for the mean things I'd thought about her.

I'd been wrong . . . again. I really needed to stop making assumptions. "Very nice meeting you as well.

You're a very good actress. Congratulations on your success. The show was wonderful." I was rambling, trying to cover my earlier faux pas with a smile.

"Thank you." She turned to Bentley. "Thanks again, cuz. I'll talk to you tomorrow." She kissed his cheek, hugged him, and scurried away.

I realized I wanted to be back in those arms and feel his body against mine. We were alone again, and it was time for me to eat crow. "I'm sorry. When I saw her, I just thought—"

"You thought I'd moved on and that I'm in the habit of screwing actresses." His cheeks rose as he smirked.

"Yes. No. I don't know what I thought, but I didn't like what I saw." My lips pressed together as I struggled to keep my emotions in check. "Can we go somewhere and talk?" I was wringing my hands, and if I didn't calm down, I was going to twist off a finger.

"My place isn't far. Do you want to come over? Or we can go somewhere less private." The look on his face told me where he'd prefer to go.

"Your place will be fine." I felt a bit of relief and thanked God she was his cousin. I didn't think I would have survived her being his lover.

Bentley

I had her with me. Her obvious jealousy confirmed what Brett had told me—she did care. I needed to make her realize that we belonged together and she needed to trust that my feelings for her were genuine. Then I'd tell her about London.

A short cab ride later, and we were entering my second-floor walk-up. The building was a vintage brownstone with an old brick façade, which was what I loved about that part of the city. It wasn't pretentious or glamorous—it was real.

I opened the door to my apartment and let Andi in. I followed close behind her.

"Wow, this place is spacious." Her voice was filled with surprise. "It's just gorgeous."

My apartment was large by NYC standards, but to me, this was just home. I owned the building and hoped to renovate it someday when I had a family. She dragged her hand along the back of the sofa as she walked around, taking in the soft earth tones and the décor. The pictures of skylines and different architecture scattered throughout seemed to capture her attention. She stopped at one picture, and my heart clenched.

"Is this . . . ?" She pointed at the picture and looked back at me.

I rested my hands on her waist and my chin on her shoulder. I took in her warmth as I pointed at the older boy on the left. "That's me, and that little guy is Brett." I felt my smile growing as I recalled when we'd taken that picture.

She turned in my arms, and I studied her. Her eyes were rimmed in pink, a faint black smudge underneath her lashes, and my chest constricted. I'd never wanted to upset her. All I'd wanted was to make her happy.

Her bloodshot eyes looked around the room. "Is this where you grew up?"

"Yeah. When my parents moved out to the

Hamptons, I stayed here. My grandfather owned this building, and he handed it down to Brett and me. Brett wanted a more upscale apartment in the city, but this was home to me, so I bought him out." My voice was full of pride.

"I see." Her soft hand ran down my chest. "Can we sit and talk?" She licked her lower lip, making me want to do the same.

A wave of relief, followed by nerves, washed over me. "Yeah, I'd like that."

CHAPTER 10

Andi

He sat next to me on his supple leather loveseat, which felt like warm butter. "Would you like a glass of wine?"

"No, thank you." I needed to keep my mind clear. The wine I'd had earlier had landed me here.

We spoke in unison.

"Andi . . ."

"Bentley . . ."

He chuckled. "Ladies first."

"Okay. I wanted to say that I'm sorry for jumping to conclusions tonight with Lyn. It's just . . . when I saw her, all I could remember was being in your arms like that after you helped me." I shrugged. "Just like when Lucy hugged you, I felt replaced and jealous. I'm so sorry."

"Andi—"

"No, wait, I have more to say, and if I don't get it out, it may stay trapped forever." He smiled, and I continued. "I realized, when your arms were wrapped around Lucy, that I don't know you very well, and it made me wonder, how I can feel the way I do about someone I don't really know?" I lowered my head. "I may have overreacted when Lucy thanked you for helping her. After talking to Brett, I realized that I was very wrong about you and her." I exhaled, needing to say more. "Apparently, I jump to conclusions when it comes to you, and that isn't very fair. I hope you accept my apology."

"I believed in you, Andi, and yes, you're forgiven." His palm went to my cheek, raising my head. "All I ever wanted for you was success. I've always thought you had talent, and when we worked together, I finally felt it. This is my fault too. I should've told you, but I really didn't think it mattered. I don't have a relationship with Lucy. I met her at a workshop the theater guild sponsored, and she mentioned a coach she wanted to work with but couldn't get a hold of. He's a friend of mine, so I put in a good word for her, that's all. I'm sorry for hurting you; it's the last thing I wanted to do." His eyes remained fixed on me, waiting for me to understand his intentions.

He pulled me into his arms and held my head against his broad chest. His heartbeat was steady, and I could feel it in my own body.

"I fell for you. Hard," he said. "I feel as if I've known you for years. I'm not going to lie, I got hurt when you judged me, and more than that, I've missed you over the past couple weeks." His embrace became tighter as the sting from his words coursed through me.

"I need you, Bentley. I haven't really needed anyone in a long time, and it scares me. I pride myself on being on my own and working my ass off, and when I let you in, I wasn't alone anymore. I loved that. But then I felt as if you weren't only with me. Can you understand that?" I pulled back to look at him.

"I can and do understand. All I wanted was the best for you. Maybe that's why my reviews were hypercritical. Watching you flourish is all I've ever wanted. Well, until I gave you my heart. Then all I wanted was all of you." His arms relaxed as his hands cupped my face. "We haven't known each other a long time, but how about we change that? You've told me about your parents and your dreams. Maybe I should tell you about mine."

Bentley's voice was so sincere I wanted to crawl back into his arms, but I didn't. I curled my legs under me as I agreed to get to know each other.

He wove his fingers in mine and stroked the back of my hand with his thumb. "My family is the most important thing to me. I'd do anything for them. When I was growing up, my mom took me to shows all over, and that started my love for the theater. I'd envy the actors standing on a stage, bringing characters to life. There's nothing better than feeling what they are at the exact moment you're supposed to. It transported me in a way that made me want to tell the world, or at least other New Yorkers, about it, so when I was old enough, I started sending reviews to different publications in hopes they'd print one. Then it happened. I saw my name on a byline, and my dream came true. So when you told me about your dream about having your name in lights, I got it."

"What about your dad?"

He chuckled. "My dad's a doctor. He wasn't home much, but his job was why my mom had time to take me and Brett to the theater. My brother didn't catch on to it like I did though. I think he just liked going to ballets to see the women in tights." Bentley shook his head and shrugged.

I laughed, picturing Brett going backstage to get the dancers' names and numbers.

"But my dad always told me that if I worked hard, then nothing was impossible." His voice was full of the same pride it had been before.

I smiled because hearing the way he'd turned his love for something into reality made me happy and feel encouraged. Hearing about how his parents supported him made me envious. "The support you grew up with is so wonderful. My parents weren't all bad. I didn't want for anything growing up. I didn't want anything but Julliard, and that's the one thing they didn't give me. I suppose it wasn't theirs to give, but their support would've been nice." I shrugged. "Maybe it's all for the best, and it happened for a reason."

"What reason?"

His eyes met mine, and I was drowned in them. "You. I wouldn't have met you. If I'd gone to Julliard, who knows what shows I would've been in? Who even knows if I'd be here right now? So maybe by my parents forcing me to go it alone, they made me fight harder and go after a critic who pissed me off." My lips quirked, trying to contain a smile.

The roar that Bentley let out made me laugh too. "I pissed you off, huh?"

I grinned. "Yes, you know you did. But think about it, if you'd written wonderful things about me, I wouldn't have tracked you down to tell you off."

"About that . . . you lied to my assistant." His eyes narrowed, and his lips twisted.

"I did."

"My doctor's office? Really?" He shook his head with a soft chuckle.

"Well, I needed to come up with something, and that seemed plausible."

"And she told you where I was?"

My eyes went wide, and I shook my head. "Oh, please don't be mad at her. It slipped out. She wouldn't give me your phone number or anything. I tried my hardest to get it out of her, and she didn't budge." The last thing I needed was to be responsible for him firing her.

"Don't you worry about Vanessa. I may have to send her flowers for the slip-up." He beamed, making me care for him more than I already had.

I brought my hand to my chest and exhaled in relief. "Maybe I should send her a gift too."

He leaned in and kissed me. "It's getting late."

It was. I had been hoping he wouldn't notice because I loved this side of him, but he was right. My legs uncurled from beneath me. As I moved to get up, his hand touched my knee.

"Stay the night with me. I'll go back with you in the morning." His voice was sexy and warm at the same time, making me want to stay longer than one night.

"I need to be back in the city early tomorrow, and I don't have clothes with me." It dawned on me that he didn't know about my new job—or did he? "I'm in a new production in the supporting role."

His smile told me he knew. "I heard."

"You did?"

"Yeah, Gina told me."

"Gina? When did you talk to her?" I felt lines form on my forehead from my confusion.

Bentley's lips curled up. "I ran into her at a coffee shop. She was pretty animated when she saw me. Then she told me to fuck off because you didn't need my help anymore."

I laughed and nodded. I found it odd that she hadn't told me about it, but I was sure she had her reasons. "Sorry about that. She's my best friend and was probably just protecting me."

"I get it, and I'm glad you have her." He laced his fingers with mine.

The feeling of being connected with him sated me, but I needed to leave. "I should really get going." I stood and slung my purse over my shoulder.

He quickly blocked my path with his body. "Please stay. We don't have to have sex or even sleep in the same bed. I just want you here with me."

My heart did a flip then a flop. Thoughts scurried through my head. Could I just stay and not totally jump him? Would my body forgive me for missing out on a fabulous orgasm? "Okay." I'd make it up to my body another time. "I'll stay, but I need to leave early tomorrow morning."

The biggest smile spread across his flawless face. "Follow me, and I'll get you something comfortable to sleep in."

I followed him through his apartment and up the stairs to his very large bedroom. The rich wooden four-poster bed covered in a gorgeous deep plum comforter looked beyond inviting. His room was understated, opulent, and masculine. I saw writing awards on his dresser, pictures of famous news articles, and a stack of theater programs piled in a wicker basket.

"Wow, great room!" My words came out louder than I'd intended.

"Thanks. Let me grab you a T-shirt and sweats. Then I'll get out of here." He pointed toward a closed door. "That's the bathroom. You should find everything you need in there, including a new toothbrush in the top right hand drawer. Towels are under the vanity, and if you need anything else, just let me know."

I took in everything he said, but it didn't feel right. "Where are you going to sleep?"

"I'll grab the couch."

"No." That came out before I'd thought about it, but right then, thinking wasn't on my mind. His arms wrapped around me and my head on his chest while I slept was. "I want to be with you."

"Andi . . ." His voice was laced with concern. "I don't want to push you."

"You said yourself that we didn't have to have sex." I placed my hand on his bicep, which twitched under my touch and did all sorts of things to my insides. "Please? I want you to hold me."

"Well, if you put it that way, how can I say no?" He placed a soft kiss on my forehead.

"You can't, so get changed, and I'll be back." I grabbed the clothes he'd pulled out for me and went into the bathroom.

I took off my clothes and folded them before I slid on his white T-shirt. I decided against the sweats and grabbed the new toothbrush, brushed my teeth, checked myself in the mirror, and headed back into the bedroom. He was already in bed with his arms behind his head, showcasing his strong shoulders and fabulous chest.

Wow. I pulled back the covers and slid in next to him. As soon as my leg hit his, I wondered what he was wearing. I lowered my brows, studying the comforter as if I had x-ray vision.

"Boxers." The smirk on his handsome face drove me all kinds of crazy. "And you aren't wearing my sweat pants."

All I could do was smile. I lay on my right side with my hands in the praying position under my cheek. Bentley slid his arm under the pillow as he rolled onto his side to face me.

"You really are beautiful." He tucked my hair behind my ear, and his knuckles lingered on my jawline. His hand rested on my neck as his thumb teased my earlobe. "This is going to be harder than I thought." His deep blue eyes penetrated mine. "All the times I saw you perform, I hoped we'd be here like this one day."

"You did?" I whispered.

"Yeah. I'd watch you, and my chest felt as if it would burst as I waited for you to look in my direction and catch my eye, but you never did. Then, when I saw you in the diner, I panicked."

"Well I didn't know it was you when you walked in that diner, but I found it difficult to breathe too. Then you were gone." I remembered that night. He'd been stunning.

"Even though I was desperate to talk to you, I knew what was coming the next day, and well, I punked out," he said. "When you walked into Brookstone, my heart stopped, but when you started chastising me, I was so happy."

"Happy? Why were you happy?"

"That fire that I knew was buried deep inside you surfaced. You're special." He inched closer and kissed my forehead. "I noticed something in you that day in the corner store."

All I could do was smile. My lips itched to kiss him back, but if I did, I'd never stop. There wasn't a square inch of him that was undesirable. "I still can't believe that was you. How bizarre. Really, what are the chances?"

"I don't know, but I'll never forget it."

"So, your brother." My voice fell a bit. Something was up with Brett. I could tell he was hurting.

"Yeah?" Bentley's fingers caressed my arm.

"He told me he was in a messed up situation."

He brought my hand to his lips. "He is." He squeezed my fingers

"What's that all about?"

Bentley let out a deep sigh, and his face grew sad. "It really isn't my story to tell. Let's just say he should have thought with the head above his shoulders."

"Oh." I respected him for not telling me Brett's story, but I wanted to know more about him. He truly admired Bentley, and I could see that it went both ways.

Bentley smiled as he kissed my knuckles before lacing our fingers together. "So have you talked to your parents? Did you tell them you'd made it to Broadway?"

"No. I thought about it, but then I got an e-mail

from my mother saying that I should come home for a party at their club." I shrugged. "That really isn't my scene. I had one close friend there, and she hated it as much as I did. I can't imagine she'd be there either, and I don't want to see the rest of those people. I just don't want to go and be asked a million questions about what I've been doing with my life."

His deep eyes looked into mine. "I'll go with you if you'd like. Just let me know when."

My lips curled into the biggest smile they could. "You would? Really?"

He pulled me closer, until we were chest to chest. "Yeah. I'd love to be there for you."

The word *for* didn't escape me. "Okay, it's a date."

His arms grew tighter as my hands gripped his muscular back. I knew how much he wanted me when his erection grew against my pelvis. I arched my back to look at him. His eyes were hooded and exuded desire. For me. This beautiful man desired me, and at that moment, all I needed was him.

"Bentley? I know you said we didn't need to have sex and you wanted to get to know each other, but I'm done talking for now." I placed my lips against his. I didn't move them, just rested them there. Our eyes opened at the same time. I felt his warm breath on me, and his hand inched up my shirt.

"Are you saying you want to have sex with me?" His voice was playful and sexy as hell.

"No. I want you to make love to me."

Before I knew it, his lips were on mine, and ours tongues danced as our hips grinded in a steady rhythm. My panties grew damper with each swirl of his hips. A moan escaped me, and my breath hitched. He lifted my shirt as I slid my thumbs under the band of his boxers. I actually had to move them forward then down to lower them as far as I could. My shirt was tugged over my head as my hands went back to work on his shorts. He rolled onto his back, and I made my move. I straddled one of his legs as I stripped him. His cock bobbed as if it was saying, "Take me." So I did.

I lowered my mouth to the tip and licked it as if it were the best piece of candy I'd ever tasted, and at that moment, it was. Feeling his smooth skin against my tongue was bliss. I took him deep into my mouth as my tongue continued its ministrations, making Bentley groan in pleasure. His enjoyment was more of a turn-on than anything else. I cupped him as I gingerly stroked between his legs, making his hips thrust forward. I took him as deeply as I could, licking, sucking, and enjoying him.

"Andi. Please. God. I need to be buried in you." His voice sounded animalistic, almost a growl.

I kept going while I let out a hum. He grabbed the tops of my arms, and I released him with a quiet pop before he effortlessly pulled me toward him. He flipped me over and planted his mouth on my breast. My hands flew into his hair. He worked between both left and right breasts before he trailed kisses down my stomach. My muscles quivered in anticipation. My need for him was growing at an accelerated pace.

Either I was holding my breath, or it had evaporated. "Bentley, I need you too, please."

He moved so he could reach the drawer of his nightstand to grab a condom. My heart sank a little at the thought of the other women who had been in his bed. I knew I wasn't the only woman he'd been with, but going forward, I needed to be. I watched his deft fingers roll the rubber down his long, hard shaft before he brought them between my legs and touched me in the most intimate, sensual way.

"You're so wet and ready for me." My hips rose as one of his fingers entered me then another, making me throb around them. "I've missed you."

He moved up my body and rested on his forearms. The weight of his body warmed me as I wrapped my legs around his waist. As he slid into me, my chest rose, and my heart filled with love. I couldn't love this man already, especially after everything we'd been through, but my feelings were definitely headed in that direction.

We moved in unison. My body trembled as I began to contract around him. He was deep inside me, and the feelings that radiated from him penetrated my heart. He rounded his hips, just about sending me over the edge. He pulled out, and I immediately needed him back. I pulled him back with the heels of my feet on his toned ass.

"I want this to last." His voice reverberated through me. His scruff-covered cheek brushed against mine. "You smell so sweet. I'm going to take my time and ravish you until you splinter into a million pieces around me."

I rolled my head to the side, giving him access to the curve of my neck.

His tongue grazed my earlobe, and he whispered, "I'm going to make you come now."

All I could do was nod. Before I knew it, he was inside me, filling me in the most delicious way. His movements were steady and deliberate. He definitely knew how to please me. As his pace increased, I shook. He grumbled something completely inaudible as his eyes rolled back under his hooded lids.

In the most tender way I'd ever been touched, Bentley placed his hands on the sides of my face and leaned down to kiss me, beginning at my forehead, to the tip of my nose, to my chin, and back to my lips. No words. Just us and whispered kisses.

Bentley

I couldn't take my eyes off her. She drifted off to sleep, and I prayed she felt what I did. When she'd asked me to make love to her, I'd never felt so relieved. I pulled her closer, and she shimmied toward me in her sleep. I buried my nose in her hair and absorbed everything about her as sleep claimed me.

When I woke, she was facing me in the morning sun. Looking into her ocean blue eyes was the best view I'd ever had.

"Good morning, gorgeous," I said.

Her arms stretched above her head, making her breasts jut toward me. She squeaked and relaxed back into my arms. I stared at her while I kept my hand on her back.

"You look great in the morning." She smiled and played with my hair. "I think you're sexy." She giggled. Apparently, she was a morning person.

I laughed. "Oh yeah? Well, you aren't so bad yourself."

THE CRITIC

"I'm sure I'm a mess." She trailed her finger down my jawline. "But not you, Mr. Chambers." She gave me a cute, crooked smile. "You wake up all pretty and flawless . . . very fuckable."

"Did you say fuckable? Is that even a word?"

She laughed and raised her right shoulder. "I don't know, but if it isn't, it should be. Just like lickable." Her soft pink tongue grazed my chin.

"Lickable, huh?"

"Yeah. Lickable."

"I'll show you what's lickable."

Before she could say a word, my mouth was on her breasts. My tongue claimed her nipples one by one. I continued down her taut stomach until I reached her hip bone. My name came out of her mouth as a benediction.

I positioned her body until we were face to face. "I'm going to make you mine. I need to make you mine."

As I claimed her she sighed, "Yeah. . . . yours."

This was definitely the way to wake up, but we still needed to discuss London. "Let's have breakfast." I figured talking would be better on a full stomach. I rolled out of bed and grabbed her hand. "Come on. Let me cook for you."

She tossed on a T-shirt and the sweats she'd ignored last night while I put on basketball shorts. We walked to the kitchen, and I opened the fridge to see what I could make us.

I called to her. "Do you like eggs?" When she didn't answer, I looked toward Andi.

She was standing in the family room with the manila folder open in her hands. "What's this?" Her face was pale and her forehead creased.

I closed the fridge and walked over to her. "Come sit with me."

She scanned the papers. "You're leaving? When were you going to tell me?"

I raked my hand through my hair. "Well, in all fairness, I didn't know you'd be here, but I was going to tell you before I left."

She yelled, "In all fairness? That's fair? What do you find fair about this, Bentley? We talked last night. You had ample time to tell me about this before you took me to bed. What did you want? A couple more romps before you dropped this bomb on me?" She closed the folder and tossed it on the couch. "Well, I hope it's fair that I'm going now."

She hurried into my room, and I chased her. I stood in the doorway and watched her strip off my clothes and put hers back on.

"Andi, let's just sit down, have some breakfast, and talk about this."

"I've lost my appetite." She pushed past me and hustled through the living room toward the front door.

I was right behind her. I couldn't let her leave like that. I put my hand on the door before she could pull it open.

"Move." She glared daggers at me.

"Let's talk about this. You haven't even called for a cab. Just stay. Don't go."

"So now you want to talk about this? What if I hadn't found the folder? When would we have talked about this? Oh wait, you already said—before you left. Well, I'm leaving now." She tugged on the door, which hardly budged. "Let me out." Her chest rose higher with every intake of breath.

I reluctantly moved my hand, but I positioned myself in front of her. She dropped her shoulders and looked at me. The spark that had been in her eyes just a few moments ago was gone, just like our happiness.

"Come with me," I said.

Her brows scrunched together. "What?"

"To London. You can come too. We can be together there."

She shook her head. "You're crazy."

"Yes, about you I am." My eyes pleaded with her.

"So you want me to drop everything I've been working for and move across the Atlantic with a man who didn't think twice about withholding important information until he saw fit? I don't think so." She shifted to the left to try to get around me.

I decided to let her go. Once she was out the door, I called after her, "You were always the one for me. I just want you to know that."

She stopped and looked back at me. "I thought you were the one for me too."

"Then don't leave just yet. Please, Andi. I'm sorry."

"I'm not sure what you think that will change. I can't move away. My life is here. Everything I've ever wanted is here." She sucked on her lips, obviously realizing what she had just said.

I walked toward her. "I see. Well, I'm not going to live there permanently, just for a few months." I watched her breathing slow to a normal pace. "The longest I'll be there is a year. I'll still be connected to the theater business, so if you decide to forgive me and come along, you could work there."

She lowered her eyes. "I don't think I can."

"You can't forgive me or come to London?" *Please let it be London.*

"London."

"Can you at least come back inside? I just got you back, Andi. Please let me make this right." I placed my hand on her elbow. She didn't pull it away, which was a good sign. "I'll make coffee." I gave her the best smile I could. I knew she loved her coffee.

CHAPTER 11

Andi

I was exhausted, and I'd just woken up. Granted, we hadn't slept much, but my brain was on information overload. Our relationship had been so strained, and most of it was because of me overreacting and jumping to conclusions, which Bentley had forgiven me for. I guessed it was my turn, so I agreed to hear him out.

He handed me a cup of coffee and sat next to me. "Thank you for staying."

"You didn't give me much choice." I blew on my coffee before gingerly taking a sip.

"Andi, you always have a choice."

I raised my brows, and he scrubbed his hand across his face.

"Look, I didn't handle this correctly, but to be honest, having you here with me last night was more important than anything else. I'd been dreaming of having you in my arms again. Please forgive me for not broaching the subject of London. When Scott told me about this position, I thought it was great timing. We weren't seeing each other, and if I was thousands of miles away, I could try to keep my mind off you." He placed his hand on my knee, which made chills race up my spine.

"The thing is I'm happy for you. I mean, this is quite the opportunity. From what I saw, you'll be in charge of the arts division. That's pretty major. You should be proud and willing to go, but I don't know that I can. You've always said writing is your art while acting is mine, and I'm just getting to where I need to be."

"I understand, and I don't think you should make a decision right away. You have an open invitation to join me."

I took another sip of my coffee and set it down. "Thank you." I gave his hand a quick squeeze and stood. "But I do need to get going."

"I can drive you. Let me just change."

I grabbed my cell from my bag. "I'll call a cab, but thank you." He watched me make the call, the muscles in his chest contracting. I didn't want to hurt him or us, but I needed to breathe. When I hung up, I said, "They have a car around the corner. So I'll see you later."

"I'll call you later." He placed a chaste kiss on my lips and opened the door for me.

"Bye, Bentley."

The cab was already waiting outside. Once we were on our way, everything started to hit me. Just thinking about Bentley leaving made me sad. I needed advice, and the only person I fully trusted was Gina. I could only imagine her reaction—she was going to flip. I called her and told her I needed to talk to her and that I'd be home in about an hour.

Before I knew it, we were sitting on my sofa, drinking wine at ten in the morning.

Gina took a sip of her wine before placing the glass on the table. "So what's up? You look totally stressed. Oh my God! Did you see Bentley?"

"Yes, I did. To make a long story short, once again, I misinterpreted the situation, but that's all cleared up." A smile grew across my face.

"Ahhh . . . I know that look." Gina snickered. "So you guys are good then?"

Now it was my turn to take a sip of my wine. "Well, that's what I wanted to talk to you about."

Gina sat back and made herself comfortable. "Okay, shoot. What's up?"

In one quick breath, I said, "Bentley is moving to London and wants me to go with him."

"I'm sorry. I thought you said you might be moving to London." Sarcasm laced her words. "Is that what I heard?"

I shook my head. "No, I'm not going. He asked, but I said no." I let out a frustrated groan. "I just don't know, G. Part of me wants to go. I'd be with him, and the theaters on the West End are amazing. It could be a great experience, but what about everything here?"

"It would be totally cool, but I would miss you terribly. But hey, we both have passports. I can come visit." Her voice filled with enthusiasm.

I'd forgotten all about that show we'd done in Canada a couple years earlier. At least I knew my passport was valid. I shook my head. "Bentley's job there is only temporary. That's why I don't think I need to be there. I mean, we can chat online and, I don't know, email each other, I guess."

She shook her head. "Look, this needs to be your decision. You may not think you need to be there, but is that what you really want? Do you need to decide today?"

"No. He won't be leaving for at least a month." I drained my glass of wine.

"Then play it by ear. You two are just starting to really know each other. Make your decision later, and for now, have fun with each other." Gina winked. "If you're good, I'm going to take off. I'm meeting Seth for dinner, and I need time to primp."

"I think I'm good." I walked her to the door. "I'm happy to hear you and Seth are getting along."

"He's pretty great, but you come first. If you need me, I'm here. Got it?"

I saluted her. "Yes, ma'am."

The door closed behind her, and I took the wine glasses to the kitchen. She was right—I had time, and I was going to make the most of it. If I didn't go with him, I would do my best to make him want to hurry back to me. I decided to draw a bath, and as the water filled the tub, I thought back on my life since I'd met Bentley. Granted, we hadn't started off in a very conventional way, but we still cared for each other. All bullshit aside, I knew that for sure. I climbed into the hot water and did my best to relax.

⊰◦◦◦⊱

My next few weeks were filled with rehearsals and meeting Bentley for late dinners then dessert at his place, which included hot sex . . . my favorite. We rarely spoke about his upcoming move. We had a few weeks left before I needed to make my decision, then he'd be gone.

Gina and I were tired of traveling to and from Jersey every day, but finding an apartment to sublet in New York was difficult, not to mention pricey. Plus, who knew where I'd be living in a few weeks, so we continued commuting. Seth and Gina had been hanging out while I visited Bentley, and Seth came to the theater when he wasn't working to make sure we got home okay.

My play was opening on Thursday, and I was a nervous wreck. I knew Bentley would be in the audience, but he'd told me his colleague was writing the review.

On opening night, I paced the halls, waiting for my cue. My senses alerted me to Bentley's presence before he spoke, but his voice still startled and relaxed me.

"Hey, nervous Nellie. I think you need to relax." Bentley turned me toward him and smiled. He had a press pass around his neck.

"Yeah. Okay." I half smiled. "I'm so worried. What if my parents show up?" When I'd replied to their country club invitation, I invited them to the show and left two tickets for them at Will Call. My stress level escalated when I thought of them sitting in the audience.

"Babe, you'll be great. Don't worry." He cupped my cheek. "Whether they're here or not, just go do your thing. You got this. Okay?"

"Yeah."

No sooner had I said that than the stage manager waved at me, indicating I had five minutes.

"Now go be great." Bentley kissed the top of my head. "I need to get out of here before we get scolded." He laughed.

THE CRITIC

After a deep breath and my biggest smile for Bentley, he went to his seat, and I walked toward the stage I'd been dreaming of for years.

What a show! The audience was on their feet as the cast and I linked hands to bow. The curtain lowered, and I ran offstage into Bentley's waiting arms.

He picked me up and swung me around. "Awesome. Just awesome. I knew you had it in you!" He reached to the side and grabbed a bouquet of long-stemmed red roses mixed with white baby's breath and wrapped in silver tissue paper. "Congratulations, sweetheart!"

I inhaled the pretty scent of the blooms as my eyes scanned the area. I'd left backstage passes with the tickets for my parents.

"They aren't here." Bentley's eyes looked sad.

I shrugged and nodded. "I'm going to go get changed and find Gina." As I began to walk away, I was hoisted into the air.

"Oh my God, Andi! That was amazing. What a great show!" Seth twirled me around and set me down. "You were fantastic!" He looked at Bentley. "We haven't officially met. You must be . . ."

"Bentley. It's good to meet you. Seth, right?"

They shook hands.

"Yeah. Right," Seth said.

"Okay, guys, I need to change, peel off my face, and go find Gina. Then we can head out for a drink or something. I have way too much energy to go home!" I felt as though I were bouncing off the walls.

Bentley's blue eyes caught mine, and they were full of

lust. I was sure he had a way for me to spend my energy, but I really wanted to be with my friends and for them to get to know my guy.

I placed my hand on the back of his neck and lowered his ear to my mouth. "Later."

He let out a soft moan, and I left with a wink. In my small dressing area, which I shared with other cast members, I noticed a large bouquet of pink roses in a crystal vase. I grabbed the card nestled among them.

We're sorry we didn't make it.
Congratulations. We are very proud of you.
Love,
Mom & Dad

My heart swelled. I was twenty-six, and parental approval or pride wasn't necessary, but it still felt good.

I brushed my hair, ruining the gallon of hairspray in it, and pulled it into a ponytail before I scraped off the theater makeup. I replaced it with light blush and a touch of gloss and set out to hang with my friends. We headed to a small restaurant—nothing fancy but perfect. I noticed Gina and Seth getting very flirty with each other as we were seated.

"So your parents sent you flowers?" Gina took a sip

of her wine, waiting for my response.

I nodded. "They said they couldn't make it, but they were sorry, and they were proud of me."

Bentley kissed my cheek. "That's good, right?"

"Yeah, that's more than I expected. I'll see what happens when I see them." My lips formed a tight grin.

"You mean the country club bash?" Gina half-smiled. She knew how much I disliked going there.

"That's the one." I turned to Bentley. "You'll be with me, right?"

His smile was panty-melting. "I wouldn't want to be anywhere else." He lightly brushed my lips with his.

I took in his masculine scent. "Good. Thank you." Our eyes locked. We needed to get out of there.

"Are you reviewing the show?" Seth's voice was laced with concern.

"No, I'm not," Bentley said. "A colleague of mine, George, is. I didn't think it would be appropriate if I reviewed it. But if I was going to, it would be a wonderful article and one that I've wanted to write for years. Something to the tune of, 'Ms. Jordan is a show stopper.'"

Seth sneered at him. "That's a lot different from your last review."

I shot Seth a look to cut it out. I knew he was just trying to protect me, but I'd moved past it. He needed to do the same.

Bentley's eyes narrowed. "I was doing my job. Are we going to have a problem?"

"Not if you're not going to review her anymore."

I knew Seth's heart was in the right place, but I

needed to step in. I put my hand on his. "It's fine. Bentley made me a better actress. His critique helped me."

Seth ran his tongue over his top lip in frustration. "Fine. But . . ." He looked at Bentley. "Your words cut her and left scars. Maybe you don't see it that way, but when you trash someone's art in print, you run the risk of hurting them. I get that it's your job, but you don't have to be so harsh. Have some feelings, man."

Bentley's hand tightened on my thigh as Seth spoke. "Point taken."

His reaction to Seth was calm. I half-expected Bentley to defend his work as always, but he didn't. I wasn't sure why he'd reacted that way, but I was thankful they didn't have an argument. Gina had asked me if she could tell Seth about London a few days ago. I'd felt bad that I hadn't mentioned it, so I gave her the go ahead. Maybe that was why Seth was even more upset with Bentley.

"Let's get you home. You've had a big night." Bentley's grip loosened on my leg, and he took my hand. He dropped cash on the table. "Gina, always a pleasure. Seth."

I quirked a smile at my friends and headed out with Bentley. His pace quickened as he hailed a cab. Once inside the yellow checkered sedan, he gave the driver his address.

"Bentley, I need to get home."

"I'm just going to pack a bag, and I'll drive us to your place." The tension radiating off him was palpable. I supposed Seth's words had something to do with that.

"You're coming with me?" I was surprised and

delighted.

"Yeah, I am."

"Don't worry about Seth. He was just being protective. G told him about London. I haven't talked to him about it yet, so that could have impacted his attitude" I kissed Bentley's bicep.

He nodded. "I know. I'm glad you have him, but you have me too. I want your friend to understand that. We're part of each other's lives now."

My heart filled with joy at those words. I rested my head on his shoulder.

<hr />

The next morning, I called my parents to thank them for the flowers. My mother asked me about the show and apologized again for not attending, which pleased me. The production was slated for a one-week promotional run on Broadway. Then it would be going on the road with the original actress in the part of Victoria. The director had asked me to be the understudy, but still not knowing if I was moving or not, I'd sadly declined. Thankfully, he understood. The last thing I'd want to do was burn a bridge. In this industry, you needed all the support you could get. Sadly, because of this, my parents wouldn't be able to attend any of the performances I'd be in.

"Mom, did you get my e-mail? I'll be attending the summer kick-off event at the club."

"Yes! Your father is so thrilled he'll have his baby girl there. I am too. It's been too long since you've attended anything with us."

Guilt washed over me, and I knew that was what she wanted. I knew Mom was genuinely happy for my recent success, but she still carried a bit of animosity about the way I'd rejected the country club life.

"Well, I don't exactly live there." I rolled my eyes.

Bentley walked out of my bedroom, looking completely edible in his faded jeans and dark gray T-shirt. I smirked and continued listening to my mom.

Once she stopped gushing about how wonderful the event at the club would be, I said, "I'll be bringing a date with me." I braced myself for shouting.

"Who is this man?" she asked.

I tried to stifle a laugh and looked at Bentley. I wasn't sure how to describe him. I scanned him from head to toe, and my skin prickled at how extremely attractive he was.

"He's a friend of mine." I shrugged as his brows furrowed.

"Well, if you must bring someone, I suppose he can stay in one of our spare rooms. You need to realize the importance of this event. Your father's colleagues will be there, and he's vying for a seat on the Club Board of Directors."

My mom still treated me as if I were a teenage girl who needed her virtue protected. I gripped my phone tighter. "We'll stay at a hotel nearby, but thank you for offering him a spare room." I squeezed my eyes closed.

"Andrea Jordan! Are you telling me he's *that* type of friend? Young ladies shouldn't parade about town with a man they're bedding. Men don't buy the cow if they get the milk for free."

I let out a hearty chuckle. *Cow? Milk?* "Bedding? Really, Mom? Just let us take care of our arrangements, and I'll see you soon." After I hung up, I looked at

THE CRITIC

Bentley.

His hands were in the back pockets of his jeans, making his muscular chest broad and very tempting.

I tilted my head to appraise him. Something wasn't right. "Is something wrong?"

"Friend?" His voice had a twinge of sadness.

"How would you like me to describe you to my mother? 'Hey, Mom, I'm bringing my hot lover with me'?"

He strutted toward me. When he was about six inches away from me, I looked up into his serious eyes. "How about boyfriend?" My mouth fell slightly open, and he pulled me to him. "That's what I'd like to be called."

I bit my lower lip. "Bentley Chambers, are you asking me to be your girlfriend?" I couldn't help the sing-song tone in my voice.

"Yeah, looks that way. So?" He brought his lips to the pulse point on my neck and gently sucked my most tender spot. "What do you say?"

A slow groan escaped me as my head rolled back. "Hmmm . . ."

He chuckled. "Hmmm? Does that mean you don't know?" He kissed my neck.

"I think I may need more convincing."

I smiled when he scooped me up and carried me to the bedroom. He set me on the bed and hovered over me as if he were going to do a push-up. His eyes met mine, and my body felt as if it were melting into the mattress. My heart grew warm with feelings for him. Once our lips met and his tongue engaged in a seductive dance with mine, I knew that I wanted him as more than a boyfriend. I wanted him forever.

<hr />

Bentley and I spent as much time together as our schedules allowed. I had just finished the final performance of *Acceptance,* and my time on Broadway had concluded for now. We were going to The White Orchid to celebrate with Seth and Gina, who were close to becoming an item.

My handsome boyfriend hired a car service for us so we didn't have to drive. We all slid into the sleek black Cadillac and headed to the posh club. I wondered if Brett would be there and how he would act toward me. I twined my fingers with my man's, and he brought my hand to his lips and kissed it.

"Will Brett be there tonight?" I knew he worked a lot, but Bentley hadn't mentioned him.

"Yes. He's looking forward to seeing you again." I looked at Gina, who was smiling at Seth as if she'd just won the lottery. With him, I guessed she had. They were great together.

"Great, I can't wait to see him again too. You did tell him that we're better now, right?" I bit my lip.

"Yeah, babe. Don't worry." Bentley smiled, making me relax.

"Have you told him about London yet?" I knew telling his brother would be tough for him. He'd told me that his parents had thought his news was wonderful, but I knew Brett would be a different story.

"I did. He said he was happy for me, but I could tell he was holding back. He seemed better when I told him I'd be back in a few months." Bentley shrugged. "Leaving you and my brother is tearing me apart."

"I'm sorry. I really am. But think of the fun video chats we can have." I wiggled my eyebrows. I couldn't tell him I'd go with him, because I didn't know yet if that would be true.

He chuckled. "I'm going to hold you to that."

We arrived at The White Orchid and walked toward the bar, where we were greeted by the same hot blond bartender, Ty. His *GQ* smile was surely dampening the panties of the women sitting at the bar.

He shook Bentley's hand. "Hey, man. Your brother set you up in the VIP section."

Bentley nodded. "Thanks, Tyler. Is he around?"

Tyler quirked his head to the side. I looked over and saw Brett was talking to a pretty brunette who was rubbing her stomach. Was she pregnant? Was he the father? I looked at Bentley. His face paled and was etched with concern.

I placed my hand on his shoulder. "You okay?"

"Yeah, let's head up. Ty, tell my brother we'll be upstairs."

We walked away, and I looked at Gina and Seth, who had their eyes on Brett.

Gina scurried up to me. "Is that his girlfriend?"

"I don't know." I wanted to look back at Brett and the brunette, but I didn't.

She nodded, and we followed Bentley, who was walking with Seth. It didn't escape me the number of times Bentley turned back to look at Brett. My heart went out to him. We slid into a booth upstairs, and a waitress came by for our drink orders.

"Everything okay?" I rubbed Bentley's bicep.

He shrugged. "I honestly don't know. I told you my brother got himself in a situation, and it looks like he's dealing with it."

The waitress brought our drinks, and Seth raised his glass. "To you, Andi. Congratulations on your dream coming true. You deserve it."

We clinked glasses. Music pulsed through the club, and Seth took Gina's hand and led her to the dance floor. I was so happy for them, for all of us.

Brett came to our table and slid into the empty spot across from us. He forced a smile. "Hey, you two. Glad you could make it. Congrats, Andi. Bentley told me about the show."

"Thank you. It's good to see you again." I smiled, but I could tell that Brett needed to talk to his brother. "I think I'll give you two a minute. I'll be back."

"Please stay," Brett said. "I could use a woman's opinion."

His tone made me want to cry, and Bentley held my hand under the table. Something was going on, and I was nervous about what I might hear and what advice he may want. But he was my boyfriend's brother, so I'd do what I could. "Okay. I'll stay."

The waitress came back with a tumbler of amber liquor for Brett. He gave her a model-worthy smile and wink before he took a sip.

He set down his glass. "Did you see that woman I was speaking to downstairs?"

"The pregnant one?" My free hand went to my mouth. "I'm sorry, I shouldn't have assumed she was pregnant." I really hoped she was, or I'd just sounded like an idiot.

"Don't apologize, she is pregnant." He looked at Bentley as if they shared a big secret. Once his eyes were back to me, he blurted, "Claims it's mine."

"Claims?" Again with my mouth.

"Yup." He took a generous swallow before he set his glass down again. "I slept with her when my girlfriend and I had a fight. All I wanted was to get back at her for . . ." He shrugged. "I don't know what I was getting back at her for, but karma reared its ugly head, and now there's a chance I may have knocked up a chick I don't care about and permanently lost the one I do." He exhaled.

My thoughts went to my last conversation with Brett. This must have been his "mix business with pleasure" woman. My heart raced. "What are you asking me about?"

"I just don't know what to do. Nikki, the girl downstairs, is a bit promiscuous. So I've asked her to take a paternity test, but she won't do it until the baby is born—says it could harm the fetus." Brett took a longer sip.

"I can understand her concern. Do you really think she'd lie about you being the father?" I lowered my brows and studied him.

Brett shrugged. "It's possible. She's not the most trustworthy person." He sighed, and his shoulders went slack as he leaned back. "I just want my girlfriend back."

Bentley chimed in, "Have you talked to Julie?"

"Julie?" I asked.

"She's my ex." Brett's voice cracked.

"You love her." I knew by the desperate look in his eyes that I was right.

"Yeah. I've never loved anyone so much." He looked to Bentley. "And to answer your question, no, I haven't talked to her. Not for lack of trying, mind you. I've been using Aubrey . . ." Brett looked at me. "My best friend's wife is Julie's best friend, so I've been getting her to send messages to her."

I still was unsure what Brett wanted from me, but I'd take a shot at guessing. "If I were Julie"—I looked at Bentley then back at Brett—"I don't know that I could forgive you, and if I could, I don't know that it'd be without reservation." Tears gathered in my eyes, and my heart clenched. I knew that wasn't what Brett wanted to hear, and I felt like shit for saying it. "I understand you were broken up, but this other woman may have a part of you that's special. It'll bind you two forever, leaving Julie with a constant reminder of what could've been hers."

"Andi." Bentley's voice was stern, making me feel worse and a bit timid.

"No, it's fine." Brett forced a smile. "That's what she thinks, and I asked her opinion. From what I know of Andi, I figured she wouldn't hold back. I kind of had a feeling she'd say what she did. Thanks, Andi." He slid out of the booth. "Come and say bye before you leave. I need to get back to work." He drained his glass before he walked away.

I lowered my head to my hands, and tears fell from my eyes. My fingers whisked them away. "I'm really sorry I said that to your brother."

Bentley cupped my face. "You were being honest. I'd be a mess if I were dealing with what he is. Not having Julie is tearing him apart. Brett's a funny guy, and I haven't heard him laugh in a long time."

"I'm so sorry. This has to be hard on you too. I can see how much you love your brother." I wiped another tear away.

"I do. I hope he isn't the father, but at the same time, that woman could be carrying my niece or nephew. They'd be lucky to have Brett as a dad. I just think she's after him for his money." He let out a breath. "It sucks to be rich sometimes."

I nodded. My family had money too, and I knew what that was like. Granted, I didn't have any of it, but someday I might. "I didn't know you had money. You understand that isn't important to me, right? I'd never do—"

He put his index finger on my lips, silencing me. "I know you're not that type of woman, and I'm not that type of man. I love my brother, but he wasn't smart—he was drunk and doesn't think he wore protection. Let's not get caught up in his troubles, okay? This has nothing to do with our relationship, so let's not let it affect us, okay?"

My body heated when the word "relationship" rolled off his tongue. "We won't, but I can tell this is really bothering you."

"I just miss him. We don't see each other often. A lunch or a drink here and there just isn't enough."

Bentley's voice broke my heart. "Is that why you want to come back sooner than later? Because of Brett's situation? Maybe he should go visit you there."

Bentley looked toward the bar and nodded. "Yeah. If this baby is his, he won't have time for God knows how long, and he needs a break."

I gave him a chaste kiss and licked my lips. "You

know what?" I trailed my finger from his earlobe, over his delectable scruff, to his chiseled chin.

"What's that?" The right corner of his mouth rose as he looked at my lips.

I whispered in the sultriest voice I could muster, "My boyfriend is extremely sexy." My tongue grazed his earlobe as I blew a soft breath on him.

"Is that so?" His voice was so deep my thighs clenched together. Before I could answer, his mouth was on mine, and his hand under my shirt, teasing my back. "Let's get out of here."

He grabbed my hand and practically dragged me from the booth. We walked to the dance floor to tell Gina and Seth we were leaving. Bentley squeezed my hand, pulled me into an embrace, and swayed to the music. His hands were on the small of my back, and my fingers played with his hair.

"One dance, we say our good-byes, then we're out of here."

I smiled. "Sounds great."

Bentley

We practically fell into my apartment as we ripped off each other's clothes. I couldn't seem to get enough of her. I lifted her, and her denim-clad legs wrapped around my waist. I pulled her shirt over her head, tossed it away, and then lowered the cups of her bra with my teeth. Her back was pressed against the front door as we grinded our hips together. She tightened her legs, applying just enough pressure to my already-hard cock.

"I need to be inside you." I continued tasting her skin from her neck to her breasts.

She rested her head on my shoulder as I carried her into my bedroom. Once I set her on the bed, her bra was the next thing to hit the carpet. She unbuttoned her jeans and lifted her ass so I could slide them down, taking her panties with them. She sat up, unbuttoned my jeans, and slid them off, her hands caressing my ass.

"Naked, Bentley. I want to see my boyfriend." She licked her lips in what appeared to be anticipation.

I smiled. "I love the sound of that. I never thought I'd have you as my girlfriend. Shit, just having a real girlfriend is surreal to me."

Her brows furrowed. "You haven't had a girlfriend?"

My lips found the pulse on her neck as I grumbled, "Not one that lasted very long."

She grabbed my boxers and lowered them. With my hand between her legs, I teased her in the most tantalizing ways until she bucked her hips against my palm.

"Bentley . . . I. . . ."

She was ready to come apart, but I pulled my fingers out of her then licked them one at a time. Her mouth formed an O as I left her wanting, staring at my glistening fingers. Andi rose to her knees and placed her hands on my torso.

"You look like a statue." She studied me as her words made my heart skip.

"A statue?" My brows rose slightly as the left corner of my mouth lifted.

"Yeah. If I were going to carve a flawless body, it'd

look like yours." She bit her top lip. "I can't wait to lick every inch of you. I'll start here . . ."

She brushed my pecs with her lips. The warmth of her breath on my cool skin made me harder—maybe teasing her hadn't been my best plan.

Her eyes became darker as she continued. "Then I'll continue down . . ."

Her tongue slid down the center of my abs as I tried to contain myself and not spread her wide and give her what I wanted to—what I needed to.

"Until I have all of you in my mouth. I can't wait to taste you"—she peered up at me—"again."

I picked her up and laid her on her back. My arms held her legs apart while I pushed into her, relishing her wetness against me. My pace increased with want.

"Oh my God, Bentley." Her voice was heady with need.

The desire in her eyes captivated me as I pushed in and out of her. Not wanting this to end, I shifted us so that she was straddling me. I could think of nothing hotter than seeing her slide up and down my slickened shaft. We moved in unison as I grabbed her ass, controlling her speed.

"You feel incredible. Ride me, sweetheart." My hands moved to her hips.

She picked up her pace, and just when I thought she would fall into orgasmic bliss, I flipped us around, regained control, and stopped moving.

"Please don't stop." Her chest heaved as her back arched.

Resting on my elbows, I slid her hair behind her ears and took in her beauty. "I'm glad you're mine."

THE CRITIC

She sounded sexy as fuck when she said, "Me too."

We moved together, savoring each other until we came apart. I rolled off her and turned to my side.

I smiled at her. "You're pretty spectacular."

She smiled. "I'd say we're spectacular together."

I couldn't help but agree, but panic set in as I realized we hadn't used protection. "Andi, I didn't wear a condom." All I could think of was Brett. Unlike him, I was with my girlfriend, but we weren't ready to be parents.

"I'm on the pill." Her brows lowered.

The relief I felt came out in a sigh. "Are you okay?"

"Yeah, I'm fantastic." Her eyes met mine. "I've never had unprotected sex. Have you?"

"Once, but I'm clean, I swear." I cringed at the thought of that night.

"Oh." Her eyes fell, along with my heart. "Then I guess we're in the clear."

My arms opened in invitation. Andi scooted closer and laid her head on my chest.

"So, Mr. Chambers, tell me more about you."

"What would you like to know, Ms. Jordan?" Andi's sweet giggle made me smile as I played with her hair. I held her hand on my chest so she could feel my heartbeat. She seemed to want to cram all she could into the time we had left together, so I obliged, resigned to the fact that she most likely wasn't coming with me.

"Let's see . . . where do you like to go on vacation? Are you a cold weather guy, or do you like sunshine and heat?"

"My family has a place on the beach in the Outer

Banks. I'm not one for the cold, so Aspen is out." I laughed. "Do you ski?"

"Me? Hell no! I hate the snow, and the last thing I want to do is go Mach 20 down a mountain on a pair of narrow boards."

She was completely serious, and my laughter turned into a roar.

She propped herself up. "What? Mach 20 is fast, isn't it?"

"Um, yeah, babe, if you're a fighter jet."

"Oh, well . . . you know what I mean." We both laughed.

"Got it. No skiing or winter-weather activities." The tips of my fingers grazed her spine. "Andi?"

She looked at me. "Yeah?"

My eyes closed then opened slowly, drinking her in. "Thank you for being here."

A smile graced her face. "My pleasure. Let's get some sleep."

"Okay. Sweet dreams."

She leaned up and placed a faithful kiss on my lips. "How could they not be? You're in my arms."

CHAPTER 12

Andi

Waking wrapped in Bentley's arms was definitely something I could get used to, but sadly, it would be ending soon. I took a deep breath and smiled. I also enjoyed feeling his morning happiness on my lower back. I'd never been this close to a man before. The idea of finding someone to truly love me hadn't even been a blip on my radar before him.

He kissed the top of my head. "Good morning, gorgeous."

I sighed and turned in his arms, relishing in his warmth. "Hi."

"This is nice." He pulled me closer. "I don't want to leave this bed."

Our bare chests pressed together, making me not want to let him go either. I knew we'd eventually need to get up though. A sigh escaped me. "I don't either."

"My calendar is a little lighter than usual." His soft lips peppered my skin with tender kisses. "Scott hired a new guy to take over for me, and he's taking him to

THE CRITIC

some shows I would normally review, so I'm covered. Plus, Scott knows I need time to wrap things up here."

My heart skipped a beat when I thought of him getting ready to go. I was doing my best to support him with a smile rather than with tears, but letting him go was so hard. We'd moved quickly over the past weeks, but he was in my heart. I needed to trust him with it. I didn't want us to be that couple who avoided talking about things that scared them or that they might disagree on. We'd both been learning to be more open with each other. I supposed after being alone for so long, it was easy to dismiss the obvious.

"Bentley?" His eyes found mine, and I continued. "What about *Together Again*? Don't you need to be here for that?" Losing my part in that show no longer upset me, but I couldn't ignore the sting I felt when I thought about it.

"I went to opening night."

"Oh. I haven't read your reviews lately. I've been busy." I shrugged. "How was it?"

"Babe, what does it matter?" His index finger grazed my cheek.

I stared into his eyes. "Just tell me. She was good, right?"

"Yes, she's doing very well. My mom and the ladies in the guild were quite impressed with the entire production." His tone was steady and impassive.

"That's good. I'm glad their investment is paying off. It's a really great story."

He rolled us so his body hovered over mine, and he rested on his forearms. His hand moved my hair behind my ears. "I'm thankful for that show. It brought us together, which is funny. I never really thought about that before." He tilted his head.

"Thought about what?"

"*Together Again,* the title. That's what it did for us." He continued twirling my hair while smiling at me.

"Well, it did bring us together, but not again."

He smiled. "It was always you, Andi. It has been for years. So, yeah. Again."

He leaned down and kissed me. My fingers threaded into his hair, holding him to me. His kisses made me feel alive. Bentley had become my reason for happiness and made me feel alive. It wasn't acting, the thrill of the curtain rising, or my name on a marquee. It was him. I'd fallen hard for him. I couldn't tell him that yet, so I said the next best thing. "Make love to me."

No more words were needed. His hands skimmed my naked body as mine glided over his taut back and firm ass. I spread my legs and bent my knees, giving him access to my most delicate place. His tip grazed me in a controlled, sweeping motion, gently teasing me. I arched my back to encourage him to enter me. He shifted lower, took my nipple in his mouth, and nibbled it.

"Bentley, please."

His lips curled into a smile on mine as the tip of his cock teased me. "Do you want this?" I nodded, and he chuckled. "I'll take that as a yes."

He slid inside me with a groan, and my body reacted. I felt my pulse in my ears, and the heady feeling of making love to the man I loved was surreal. We moved in slow, fluid motions, as if music were playing. Our bodies danced to our own rhythm.

"You're so fucking wet for me." His voice was deep

and dripped in the sexiness that was all Bentley.

His hand went between us, and he gently pressed on my tender spot, sending me into oblivion. His mouth covered mine as I let out a sound I didn't know I could make. Our pace quickened, and my legs trembled.

"You . . . feel . . . so . . . good." His voice was ragged and deep, making my orgasm more intense.

Knowing I was the one who made him feel this way was more than enough for me. He held my knees, which were almost touching the mattress, and I watched the muscles in his face contract and his eyes close. He pushed deeper and deeper inside me as he rode out his climax.

"God, that was just . . . I don't know. Perfect?" He licked his lips then licked the thumb that had been rubbing my clit. "Yeah, perfect."

I smiled because I couldn't have agreed more—we were.

We finally got out of bed, and while I showered, Bentley made coffee. I relished the scent of his body wash as the liquid turned into bubbles on my skin. I thought of all that had transpired over the course of the past few weeks. How had it all happened? I guessed that everything did happen for a reason, even if we didn't know what that reason was at first. Now I knew. Bentley was my purpose. His move came to mind, as it often did. I just didn't know if I could walk away from New York. Yes, he was the most important thing to me, but I needed to make a living too.

Once I'd finished my shower, I grabbed a towel off the heated towel rack, which I could definitely have gotten used to. When I was dried and dressed, I headed to the kitchen. Bentley was on the phone. I hoped he was making plans with his brother, but when he set the phone on the counter, he just stared at it.

"Brett?" I guessed.

"Yeah." He grabbed two mugs off the shelf and filled them with freshly brewed coffee. "Black?"

"Yes, please."

He nodded and poured creamer in his.

"How is he?" I padded across the room and placed my hands on his hips. The rise and fall of his chest told me he was worried about him.

"He was ready to take the night off tonight and hang with us, but he said he needs to deal with some things first."

"I'm sorry."

"Me too." He handed me my cup. "I'm going to go shower. Then we can figure out the rest of our day."

I took a sip of my coffee and moaned. It was one of my favorite parts of the day.

"Want to wash my back?" He wiggled his eyebrows.

My lips curled. "As enticing as that is, no. I really need to get home."

"I'll go with you. Give me ten minutes." He set down his mug and hurried into the bathroom.

I sat on the couch, sipping my coffee and taking in his apartment. I was happy, and that was because of him. I was reading a magazine that had been lying on his table when his sexy voice broke my concentration and made my stomach flutter.

"You ready to go beautiful?"

I smiled at him. "Yeah."

We got in the car and drove toward my place. He

grabbed my hand and squeezed it while weaving through the crazy Manhattan traffic. He looked tense as he squeezed my hand tighter with each turn.

"What's the matter?" I asked.

"Nothing. I'm just thinking about Brett. How could he have done this to himself?" Bentley slid his hand through his hair.

"Well, technically, he did it to her too." I closed my eyes. "I'm sorry. That was out of line."

"No, you're right. I just wish I could do something." He glanced at me and quirked his lips.

"You're a fixer, and I get that, but you can't repair this one. Whatever happens, just support him."

"A fixer?" The muscles in his neck tensed. "What does that mean?"

"You enjoy making sure that everything works out the way you think it should. Maybe this time, you should just let the pieces fall where they will." I tried to sound sympathetic, but Brett had made his bed. Not everything was fixable.

He glared daggers at the road, and my heart raced. Had I said something wrong? His lips were set in a fine line. He looked too mad to talk about Brett anymore, so I decided to drop it and talk about something else.

I smiled at him. "So I was thinking—"

"You didn't seem to mind me 'fixing things' when I helped you run lines. Shit, without me, you may not have landed the role you just had," he snapped.

His voice shot through me like a bullet. I flinched, and I saw him grip the steering wheel until his knuckles turned white. I clenched my jaw as I swallowed down the boulder of pride in my throat.

"You could be right. The difference is I asked for your help, and unless I'm mistaken, there isn't a way to fix this. So just be supportive of him and the choices he makes." My fists clenched in my lap, and I counted to ten. I felt as though the rug had just been pulled from under me . . . again. The hammering in my chest made it difficult for me to breathe. "When you say I wouldn't have gotten the part of Victoria without you, what does that mean? Did you tell the director to hire me? I didn't get this because of my talent?" My voice hitched as I felt myself begin to fall apart, and I hated myself for that.

He pulled the car over. All I could do was stare out my window. *What the fuck just happened?*

"Andi." His voice was softer, but that didn't help.

I kept staring out the window and concentrated on a sprinkler in the adjacent yard. It moved effortlessly back and forth, nurturing the green lawn it sat on. I envied that sprinkler's uncomplicated existence. What I wouldn't have given to be like that.

"Andi, please look at me." He placed his hand on my thigh. "Just for a minute."

"Why?" I turned my head and looked at him. "Why would you say that to me?"

He brought my palm to his lips and kissed it. "I'm sorry. I really am. I had nothing to do with you getting your job. That was all you. I shouldn't have said what I did. I'm just stressed over the fact that my brother may be a father soon. You didn't deserve what I said, and I'm very sorry." He raked his hand over his stubble. "Please forgive me. I need you, and I really didn't mean a word of that."

The calm of the scene I'd just been staring at washed over me like the water on the grass. "I'm on your side, so I don't need to forgive you. You have me to lean on, but if you keep trying to push me away with your harsh words, one day you'll lean, and you won't be supported, because I'll be gone." I looked into his deep blue eyes, which were glassing over as he let out a breath. My words surprised me, but they were true nonetheless.

"I don't deserve you, Andi, and I'll remember what you just said." He placed another kiss on my hand before laying it on his lap.

We rode in silence to my apartment. I had forgiven him, but it still bothered me that he'd spoken to me that way. He parked in front of my building. Would he want to come in? I shook my head and leaned on my hand as I continued staring though the window. I glanced at him, but he remained calm, stoic, and silent. The thought of leaving him like this didn't sit well with me, but by the look on his face, I may not have a choice.

Bentley

I was an asshole. Looking into her eyes solidified that for me. Actually, asshole was a bit too kind. My mind raced as she went to open the car door.

"Are you coming in?" She sounded so unsure.

Did she think I was just giving her a ride home? Shit, I'd really fucked things up. I needed to get back in her good graces, and she had asked me in, so yeah. Time to get this runaway train back on track.

I forced a smile. "That was my plan."

Her lips curled into a sexy grin that put my racing

thoughts at ease. "Okay, good."

I opened my door and hurried to hers so I could help her out. I may have acted like an ass sometimes, but I knew right from wrong. When she put her hand in mine, I felt complete. We'd had amazing sex earlier, but for some reason, it didn't hold a candle to the feel of her hand in mine. She swung her leg out of my SUV and paused when I didn't move.

"Um . . . Bentley? I need room to get out." She looked at me as if I were rooted to the ground.

"I love you, Andi."

She looked as startled as I felt. I hadn't planned to declare my love for her in the street. I hadn't even realized I loved her until the words flew out of my mouth. *No, that's not true.* It was high time I stopped lying to myself and to her. I'd been pushing her away for a reason unbeknownst to me, but I was done with that. She needed to know how I felt.

Panic set in as her face paled at my declaration.

"You don't have to—"

She placed her fingers on my lips. "But I do." The color came back to her cheeks as she remained still. Her beautiful eyes looked directly into mine. "I do . . . love you, Bentley."

I was so relieved. I grabbed her face and kissed her as if I'd never kiss her again. When we broke our kiss, I scooped her out of the car and carried her into her home.

Once inside, I needed to make sure she hadn't felt pressured to respond. "Andi . . . what you said . . ."

She tossed her purse on the sofa and wrapped her arms around my neck. Her hair dangled as she leaned back to look at me. "I realize we haven't known each other very long, nor did we get off on the right foot. Shit, we didn't get off at all." I chuckled, and she blushed as she swatted my shoulder. "You know what I mean. But sometimes the length of time two people know each other is insignificant when it comes to their feelings. I guess the saying is true—when you know, you know." She shrugged.

I nodded.

"I've been falling for you since the first day I met you." Her eyes filled with the words she'd just said, filling my soul with adoration. Her body pressed against mine, and I held her, never wanting to let her go

"You mean the day you yelled at me at the restaurant?" I bit my lip, remembering the day this feisty woman attempted to put me in my place.

"Yeah, that day." She smirked.

"Andi, I fell for you five years ago when I wrote my first review. My heart started truly beating that night, and since I've had you in my arms, the beat keeps getting stronger."

"Yeah?" Her voice hitched.

My chest clenched. My thumb caught the tear that escaped her eye and wiped it away. "Yeah."

Our lips met in a gentle kiss. Then we walked hand-in-hand to her bedroom, where I planned on loving all of her.

CHAPTER 13

Andi

In love with me? He'd said it and said it first. I knew that I'd fallen for him, but for this gorgeous man to fall for me? Well, that was just a dream come true. We stared at each other as if we were each memorizing the other's face.

Bentley's expression was serene and content, relaxed. His phone buzzed and broke our trance. He picked it up from the side table and sighed.

"Is everything okay?"

"I don't know. Brett can't meet us tonight." He set down the phone and sat up.

"Oh, I'm sorry." I rubbed his bicep.

He grabbed my hand and kissed it. "It's okay. He has to go see Nikki about something." Lines formed on his forehead.

"I see. Well, why don't we just hang here? I'm sure we can find something to do."

He smiled. "Yeah, I'm sure we can. What about Gina and Seth?"

"Don't worry. I'll let them know we can hang out after we get back from my parents' next weekend."

"Andi, I'll be gone." He pulled me close.

"Oh. Well, then when you get back." I held him tighter.

"It's a date."

Spending the day with him was the right choice. "Bentley?"

"Yeah, babe?"

I pushed myself up and looked at him. My index finger trailed his strong jawline. "I really do love you."

He smiled. "I'm so glad."

"Me too, but we need to eat . . . Chinese?" I smiled.

"Mmm, that sounds great. Make sure to get chopsticks." He winked.

The way his eyes pierced mine, I knew he was thinking about the first time we'd had Chinese. That night hadn't gone as planned—I didn't know if we'd even had a plan—but the way he'd pushed me to do things and break out of the shell I'd unknowingly put myself in was something I'd never forget.

"What's that smile about, sweetheart?" he asked.

"Just thinking about you. I hope I get a better fortune cookie this time."

"I don't need a cookie. We make our own good fortune, and I have mine right here." He cupped my cheeks, and the warmth of his hands spread through me like the afternoon sun.

My lips curled into a smile. I supposed he was right, but I knew that without him, I'd still be a little lost. His lips pressed to mine, and my stomach fluttered. I swore that every time he kissed me, it was like the Rockettes were dancing their famous kick line inside me.

After he placed our order, he pulled me to the couch, and we talked about seeing my parents soon. I knew my mother would love his looks and that he came from money. My parents had always thought I'd end up married to a doctor or become a successful business woman, but I hoped they'd realize that I was happy and just be happy for me.

"Are you excited about going home?" His voice was like velvet.

My back was to his front, so his warm breath caressed my neck. I played with his hand splayed on my thigh. "I'm excited for them to meet you." I tilted my head back to look at him. "I mean, how could they not love you?"

"Did they like your other boyfriends?"

"I really haven't had anyone to introduce them to, so . . ." I shrugged.

He sat up straight, making my body fall back against the couch cushions. I looked into his eyes as he hovered over me. His brows lowered as he studied me. "How is that even possible?"

"Because other than my prom date, I haven't had anyone to speak of or that I would've gone through the trouble of introducing to my parents." I smiled. "Until you."

He lowered his head and pressed his lips to mine. "Until me, huh?"

"Yeah."

"I'm flattered, Ms. Jordan." He chuckled.

"You should be, Mr. Chambers." I smiled and

watched his eyes light up.

⋘—◈◈◈—⋙

Gina came over while I packed a weekend bag for the trip to my parents' place. Bentley had made us reservations at a posh hotel not too far from the country club.

"What dress should I wear? This one?" I pulled out a black lace sheath gown. "Or this one?" I held up a black silky gown.

"Mmm . . . the first one."

"I think so too." I set the gown in the garment bag hanging on the hook on the back of my door.

"So, tell me. What are you going to tell your parents about Bentley?" Gina snapped her gum.

I shrugged. "Well, my mom knows he's coming. I told her I was bringing a friend."

"A friend, huh? What'd she say to that?"

"The usual mom stuff." I stood and put clothes into a small suitcase. I walked to my dresser and pulled out a black lace panty-and-bra ensemble to match my dress. With my back to her and a smile on my face, I said, "Bentley said he loved me."

Silence.

I turned around, and my best friend looked like a deer in headlights.

"Are you okay?" I couldn't help but laugh as I placed my undies in my small case.

"Andi, this is big. Love? He loves you?" Her voice hit all different octaves.

"Is that so hard to believe?"

"No, I mean . . ." She pushed off my bed and took

my hand. "You're an amazing woman. I'm just so relieved. I've been worried about you"

"Why?"

"Because, my friend, I don't even need to ask if you love him. It's written all over your face, and it has been since that day you told him off at the Brookstone."

I grinned. "I do, G, so much. I disliked him—no, I hated him—for so long that I almost didn't want to love him or give him the satisfaction or something? So I'd start shit then regret it. But when I saw him in the arms of another woman, my heart seized. I was so jealous, and that's when I knew, or when I admitted to myself, that I not only need him, but I love him."

"What other woman? When was this?" Gina's arms crossed, and I expected her foot to start tapping on my carpet.

"It was his cousin. She starred in a play I went to, and when I went backstage, I saw them hugging." I closed my eyes and rubbed my arms. "I felt lost for a moment. It was as if I was having an out-of-body experience. It was horrible."

"Well, I imagine it was." She gave me a hug. "I'm so happy you're happy. So does that mean you're going with him?"

Gina grabbed my suitcase and rolled it into the living room while I carried the garment bag. I laid it over the back of the chair and sat on the sofa with my friend.

"I don't think so. Maybe I'll visit, but my home is here, even if London is temporary. So tell me . . ." I needed the scoop on her love life and to get my mind off England.

She flipped her hand and studied her manicured nails.

THE CRITIC

"What is it that you'd like to know?"

I shoved her shoulder.

Gina laughed. "Okay, Seth is amazing. He's kind and totally hot. Have you ever seen his abs? Holy shit! I could do laundry on them."

"I have seen his abs. They're quite nice."

"Quite, yes." She giggled. "He's just a great guy."

I nodded. Seth was one of the best, and I was happy for her. She and I made plans to double date when I got back. We acted like two giddy schoolgirls, gushing about our boyfriends.

My phone chimed with a text from Bentley telling me he was coming up. I opened the door a crack so he could walk in.

"I'm going to miss you," Gina gushed.

"I'll only be gone a few days."

"I know, but what will I do with my time?" She giggled, and I rolled my eyes

"Am I interrupting girl time?" Bentley's sexy voice gave me chills.

"Nah, Andi was just telling me how amazing you are in bed." Gina smirked and winked at me while Bentley's brows rose. "Call me and let me know how it goes with your parents."

I walked her to the door. "Yeah, I will. Now leave and stop causing trouble."

"Have a great weekend, you two." Gina walked out.

I laughed. "She's the best." I turned to Bentley and studied him. He was wearing black golf shorts and a light blue golf shirt. His eyes looked like the depths of the Caribbean Sea, while his body was broad, firm, and perfect.

"You like what you see?" Bentley rested his hands on my hips.

"Yeah, I do. Is that okay?" I batted my eyes a bit, hoping to delay our departure.

"It's more than okay, but we'd better head out, or we'll never make it on time. I'll be too busy having the pleasure of my girlfriend." He winked. "I'm sure you'd have a hard time resisting me since I'm so amazing and all."

"That sounds so much better." I kissed his cheek, ignoring the amazing comment.

"It does, but let's get out of here. I'll show you how amazing I can be later."

I sighed and nodded. Bentley grabbed my bags and we went outside. Once inside his black Infinity SUV, I inhaled deeply and closed my eyes; it was all Bentley. I was encased in his cologne. It was clean, spicy, and very masculine, and it did weird things to my insides.

As we drove down, I couldn't help noticing the flowers. After spending so much time in New York, I'd missed New Jersey. I'd never thought I'd say that, but the only flowers I saw in the city were being sold on street corners. My mind wandered to my parents and what they would think of my boyfriend. I glanced at him. His strong chin rested on his left hand, elbow on the door as his right guided us through traffic.

His eyes shifted toward me. "What's that look for?" He smirked and looked back at the road.

"I just hope my mom keeps things in check this weekend. Like I told you, my parents had a plan for me, and that included marrying a rich, successful country club guy." I regretted my words as soon as they left my lips. The creases on his forehead made me sad. "I didn't mean that you aren't successful, because you are. It's just . . ." I really needed to shut up. I was just digging myself further into a hole.

"Should I tell them I'm worth over five million? Would that make them happy?"

"Yeah, right." I laughed.

He nodded, his expression a mixture of sadness and humor.

I gaped at him. "You have over five million dollars?"

He looked at me. "Does it matter?"

"Obviously it doesn't matter to me, considering I fell for you before you told me that."

Bentley's eyes softened. He reached across the center console and grabbed my hand. "Let's just be us and have fun." His lips curled into a smile that reached his eyes.

I nodded. I wasn't going to open my mouth again. Lord only knew what I'd say. Instead, I turned the radio on. We listened to 90s music and sang along to most of the songs. Bentley's voice was even sexier when he sang. He made me melt more and more every day.

After we checked into the hotel, we changed and got ready to head over to the club. I slid on my black lace gown, which was extremely fitted. Thankfully, it had a bit of give and a small slit in the back, so I had some mobility. My breasts looked perfectly lifted, and the neckline exposed just the right amount of cleavage. The dress also made my ass look as if I did squats on a regular basis.

I glided out of the bathroom to find Bentley adjusting his bow tie. My man in a tux was a sight to see. "Wow, you'd better hold my hand tonight, or the women in there will be all over you."

He turned to look at me, and if I hadn't known better, I'd have said he stopped breathing.

"Andi, wow. You look beautiful." He strutted toward me and grasped my hand. "You better believe I'll be holding on to you."

I really wished we didn't have to leave, but it was time. "Let's do this."

Getting into his SUV in a form-fitting gown proved to be a bit of a challenge. Bentley held my door while I tried lifting my leg, which didn't really work. Then I tried to hoist myself up by using the seat for support, which also failed. I was ready to hike my gown over my knees to regain some mobility.

Bentley chuckled. "Let me help you, Ariel." He scooped me up and set me in the car.

"Ariel?"

"Yes, you know, the mermaid?"

"Yes, I know the mermaid, but really?" I giggled.

He leaned in and kissed me. "In that gown, you look like a princess, but definitely not one created for children."

"Mmmm . . . okay." I smiled as his eyes perused my body in a way that made my insides clench. "I'm glad you're here with me."

"I wouldn't want to be anywhere else."

Bentley pulled up to the country club, and a bead of sweat ran down my back. The young valet in a red jacket opened my door and offered his hand. I had visions of myself tumbling out onto the pavement.

THE CRITIC

Before the valet could help me out, Bentley handed him the key and some bills. "Thank you, I'll take it from here." Bentley bowed slightly at the waist as he offered me his hand. "My princess."

I glared at him as I welcomed his help. "Let's leave the princess comments to ourselves, shall we?"

Bentley chuckled as he closed the door. "Whatever you wish, Your Highness."

I swatted his arm. We were laughing when we walked into the Royale Club's ballroom.

"Wow, nice place." Bentley took in the surroundings. "Do you see your parents?"

"Nope, but I see a bar. Let's go."

Bentley laced his fingers with mine as we walked across the marble floor. I saw many familiar faces, so I smiled and nodded. Then I saw the girls from high school who'd thought they were bitchin' but that was all they were—bitches. They didn't act as though they'd seen me, but they definitely saw Bentley. Was I invisible? I rolled my eyes and continued toward the bar.

"They friends of yours?"

I looked at Bentley, and he raised his chin toward the clique of women staring at him. I shook my head. "Nope. I never got along with them, but they look like they'd like to get along with you."

Before I knew it, his lips crashed down on mine as if we were all alone. His firm, tender tongue caressed my mouth. When he broke the kiss, I was breathless.

Our eyes met as he cupped my face. "You're gorgeous, and I'm yours."

I smiled and felt blood rise in my cheeks. "So are you."

He kissed my forehead.

"Ahem. Andrea."

"Mom, hi! I didn't see you there." I leaned in to kiss her cheek but received an air kiss instead.

"I'm not surprised. You were occupied." She addressed Bentley. "So you're the friend."

"Hello, Mrs. Jordan. I'm actually—"

"My boyfriend." I glanced at Bentley. He was smiling, which made me do the same.

"Oh. I didn't realize. It's good to meet you." My mom extended her hand. She grinned as she inspected his features for a bit too long.

Bentley shook her hand. "This is a wonderful club. I noticed the greens when we pulled in. They look like they're in great shape."

"Oh, you play?" Apparently my mom appreciated not only his looks but the fact that he played golf.

"I've been known to, yes."

Just then, my dad walked up. "There's my princess." He leaned down and kissed me.

Bentley chuckled, but he reeled it in quickly as I playfully glared at him.

"Charles, darling, this is Andrea's boyfriend, Bentley. He plays golf." My mother wore an expression that said she'd just solved life's great mystery.

"It's good to meet you, Mr. Jordan." Bentley outstretched his hand to my dad.

"You as well. We'll have to get you out on the course. Do you have a handicap?"

Here we go. Golf talk. I rolled my eyes, which would be a common occurrence that night.

Bentley squeezed my hand. "Yes, sir, I do. I ended with a five last season."

I was shocked. "That's really good, babe!"

Bentley shrugged as if it were no big deal.

He'd definitely impressed my dad though. "Well, then. We won't just get you on the course—we'll get you in a few member-guest tournaments." My dad winked and put his hand on my mother's back. "Darling, we should go say hello to Joseph and Marguette." He kissed me on my cheek. "We'll see you in a bit. Have fun, kids."

My parents walked away, and I turned toward Bentley. "Wow! Ass-kiss much?" I laughed.

"Hey, he asked. I told him."

"I didn't even know you played."

He whispered in my ear, "I like putting it in the hole. When it rims the top and then slowly hits the sweet spot. Then I do it all over again. Sometimes my stroke is firm, and other times it's all finesse."

The warmth of his breath and the images he put in my head that had nothing to do with golf, instantly dampened my thong. I took a sip of my drink.

Bentley finished his. "Want another?"

"No, I think I'm going to go outside for a minute. It's a bit warm in here."

Bentley gave me a knowing smirk. "Okay."

Bentley stayed inside while I went out to the patio near the ninth green. Another woman was standing there alone. Her gorgeous dress hugged her curves, but I smiled at the red stilettos peeking out from the bottom of her gown. She defied the club's boring dress code—I liked her already!

When I got closer, I was a bit shocked. "Bev?"

She turned. "Andi?"

We laughed as I scurried toward her for a hug.

"You look amazing! I always thought you were beautiful, but this . . ." I stepped back and looked at her with our arms stretched to the side. "God! You look so different!" My hand went to her raven hair, which had once been fair. "This color is amazing on you. Your mom must have flipped!"

Bev laughed and smiled. "Thank you. I got tired of being called 'heavy Bevvy.' It's been so long! But you're pretty as ever! I didn't know you were back in town. Last I heard, you were lighting up the stages on Broadway."

"Really? You heard that?" I was so sorry we had lost touch when she went to college.

"Of course I did. Do you think your mother didn't tell mine? I mean, you're a successful actress. I'm just a teacher in the poor part of town."

"I think your career is wonderful. You have a gift, but you always have."

She smiled and glanced to her right as a gorgeous man walked by. He was tall, dark, and broad. By the look on Bev's face, she'd noticed that too.

"Holy shit! Who's that?" I asked, turning to watch him walk away. He walked inside as Bentley walked out.

Bev shrugged. "I don't know. I've never seen him before, but I'd totally rock that!" Her eyes followed Bentley. "Are they having an all-male revue tonight, or did they add hot guys to the silent auction?" I smiled and was about to say something, but she cut me off. "Oh my god, he's walking over here."

Bentley sidled up to me and rested his hand on the

small of my back. Bev's face turned beet red, and she sucked in her lips to suppress a grin.

"Bev, this is my boyfriend, Bentley. Babe, this is Bev. We went to high school together."

"Ahh, someone who knew Andi in her glory days. We'll have to chat later," he said with a smile. They shook hands. "It's a pleasure, Bev."

She nodded. "Likewise."

"Baby, they're about to get the event started. We should get back in," he said calmly.

I nodded. "Bev, may we escort you inside? Unless you're here with someone. I wouldn't want to get my ass kicked."

Bev forced a smile. "No, I'm alone."

Those three words tore at my heart. She was too amazing to be alone. Maybe the hot mystery dude would sweep her off her feet.

"Well then, shall we?" Bentley bent his arms as he stood between us.

We placed our hands on the crook of his arms, and we walked into the room. Waiters and waitresses were passing out glasses of champagne to the people starting to fill the tables.

I looked at Bev. "We're at table fifteen. You?"

"I'm at table twenty-three. The bitch table." Her eyes pointed at the clique from hell.

"I'm sorry."

Bev nodded. "Yeah, me too. I can't stand them. At least you were bold enough to tell them to fuck off when they acted like stuck-up bitches. I just stood behind you." Her face reddened when Bentley chuckled.

"Please, excuse my language."

"No, really, it's okay. I was picturing my princess here telling people off." Bentley kissed my forehead.

My lips twisted. "Yeah, well, you know me. Not the type to really hold back."

"No, you're not. That's one of the things I love about you." Our eyes met, and I wanted to get lost in the depths of his.

"Okay, you lovebirds, I'm off to hell. Thank you for the escort, and it was great meeting you, Bentley. Andi, let me get your number." She reached into her clutch and pulled out her cell phone. We exchanged information, then we went to our tables.

My parents were sitting at our table with some of their friends. Bentley and I were definitely the only ones who didn't have an AARP card. My mom introduced us as the wait staff set salads in front of us.

"So what do you do Bentley?" my dad asked. He had the, "I hope you're good enough for my daughter" tone, which I completely hated.

"I'm a journalist."

"Oh, impressive. For which paper? The *Times?*"

Everyone's eyes were focused on Bentley.

"No, sir, I write for the *Edge*."

"I'm not familiar with that publication," my father said.

Here we go. Dad's voice of disapproval was just waiting to come out. At that point, it wouldn't have mattered if Bentley was good enough to be on the PGA Tour. If Dad thought Bentley's job wasn't good enough, then that was all it would take.

THE CRITIC

"It's a trade journal. That's how I met your daughter."

A woman named Gloria piped up, practically choking on her merlot. "Oh my! Are you *the* Bentley Chambers?"

"Well, I'm the only one I know." Bentley winked and speared a piece of his salad and popped it in his mouth.

"Wow, your reviews are critically acclaimed." She looked at my parents and leaned in as if sharing a huge secret. "He's won several literary awards. Harold and I were just at a show where he praised the actress . . . oh . . . what was her name?" She snapped her fingers. "Harold, dear, what was her name?"

The man to her right, whom I assumed was her husband, shook his head and shrugged.

She squinted, and her eyes rolled up as if she were looking into her brain for the answer. She pointed at Bentley. "Hart! That's it."

Bentley smiled.

I was so happy this woman knew his work. "I saw that show as well. Ms. Hart is a very good actress."

"So then you reviewed Andrea's new show?" My mother's question silenced everyone at the table.

He shook his head. "No, not this last one. I reviewed one she did in Jersey and haven't reviewed any since we started dating. It would be a conflict of interest."

"That's actually how we met. He came to my show, reviewed it, and the rest is history." I took a long sip of champagne. They didn't need any details about how he'd hated my performance or our confrontation afterward.

"That's wonderful, honey." My mom smiled.

I whispered in his ear, "Thanks for saying I sucked." I smiled and bit my lower lip.

"My pleasure." The band started playing as we waited for our main course to be served. "Dance with me." Bentley stood and took my hand. He looked at the others at the table then at my parents. "Excuse us."

We were the only couple swaying to the music, but I didn't care. I was in the arms of my man, and that made me happy.

Our bodies moved in sync as he pressed his hips against mine. His hand glided up and down my bare back. "You look amazing in this gown, but I can't wait to get you out of it." His right hand slid down the curve of my ass before resting on the small of my back.

"Sounds good to me. Can we get out of here?"

"You're what I want to eat, but I think we should at least finish our dinners." He nibbled my ear, which made my knees weak.

I placed my lips to his ear. "Bentley, I love you."

He smiled. "I love you too."

After the song was over, we made our way back to our table. I glanced at Bev, who looked as if she were in hell. It reminded me of the lunchroom we'd suffered through, with all the cool kids at one table. I prayed they were being nice to her. She looked amazing, and her personality was even lovelier, but those women were brutal. Bentley kissed my hand before he pulled out my chair for me.

"So tell me, Andrea, how is life in the big city?" Mrs. Hodges asked. She was dripping in diamonds and looked as though she was infused with Botox, which wasn't surprising—her daughter was sitting next to Bev.

"I actually live in Jersey and work in the city."

I began to eat my dinner, hoping to be able to leave

sooner than later.

"Oh." Her one word was extremely condescending, but I wasn't in the mood call her out on it. She turned her attention to Bentley. "And you, Mr. Chambers? Is your apartment in the city?"

Bentley wiped his mouth with the black linen napkin. "Actually, I own a brownstone, but yes, it's in the city. However, I've been offered a job in England."

My mother cleared her throat. "You're moving?" She looked at me. "Andrea?"

Bentley spoke before I could address my mother. "Yes, Mrs. Jordan, I will be moving, but it isn't permanent. The longest I'll be gone is a year." Bentley grabbed my hand under the table.

I turned to him and smiled.

"Andrea, dear . . ." My father's voice was sympathetic as his eyebrows lowered.

"Dad, it'll be fine. This is a wonderful opportunity for him, and as he said, it isn't permanent." There, that sounded convincing. But I needed to get off this topic before I turned into an emotional wreck. "So, Mother, this event, it's for charity?"

"Yes, all the proceeds go to several different charities. There's a silent auction as well. We have some lovely prizes—you should take a moment to look at them." My mother was on the planning committee, and I was sure she was happy each table was full of people with deep wallets.

"Sounds wonderful. We'll take a look on our way out."

Bentley and I continued the small talk while we finished our meals. We glanced at each other knowing we wanted each other for dessert, which brought a smirk to his face. I placed my napkin down.

Bentley stood to move my chair. He placed his hand on the small of my back as my father stood.

He walked over to us and shook Bentley's hand. "It was wonderful meeting you. We'll have to get you on the course this summer."

Bentley smiled. "Thank you. I'll look forward to it sir."

I was so thankful he hadn't brought up London. I didn't tell him not to before we'd arrived at the club. If he had, I didn't know what my parents would have said.

"Please, call me Andrew." My dad acted as if I were with the next Master's champion. "Be sure to take care of my little girl."

I glanced between my father and Bentley and realized they stood eye to eye.

Bentley's fingers flexed on my waist. "You can be sure of that, sir."

My mom walked over and gave us both a hug good-bye. "Sweetheart, don't be a stranger. And please call us know when your next show is or if you just need to talk."

The relief in my heart was immense. "Thank you, I will."

We said our good-byes. I looked toward Bev's table and saw her sitting next to the hot guy we'd seen outside. I caught her eye and waved. She smiled as she waved back. I needed to make sure to keep in touch with her. She was real people, and I loved real people. The other women at the table looked at me, and I couldn't pass up strolling over there hand-in-hand with the hottest guy in the room.

"Hi, everyone." I looked around the table then at Bev, who was hiding a smile in her napkin. "Well, isn't this a high school flashback."

Their eyes appreciated my boyfriend as if he were as rich as the dessert. I couldn't help but snicker. They must have been boggled over how the "nerdy drama club girl" got this super-hot guy. Well, they could kiss my perfectly toned ass.

"Andrea, who do you have there? Did you call Rent-a-Date?" Angelica Hodges asked.

Angelica had been the nastiest of them all in high school. I'd never forget how awful she had been to Beverly, calling her all sorts of names and making snide remarks about her weight. Putting her in her place would be fun.

"Angelica, you're looking . . ."

She adjusted in her chair and arched her back, pushing her no-doubt-fake D's out farther.

"Older," I said.

Bev laughed.

"Bentley Chambers." His voice was deep and sounded extra sexy. I wondered how he did that. He extended his hand to her. "Andi's boyfriend."

Angelica took his hand in a way that insinuated that she wanted him to kiss it. He just released it and took mine to his mouth instead.

"Bev, I just wanted to tell you we were leaving," I said.

She stood to give me a hug. While we were linked, she whispered, "I'm in Satan's lair."

I laughed as we pulled apart, but I gave her a sympathetic look. I leaned in again. "Who's that guy?"

Bev smiled and told me his name was Dane. *Hmm, great name for a hot guy.*

"Well, Dane hasn't taken his eyes off you," I said.

She glanced back. "I don't know about that, but he's the only normal one here. Want to meet him?"

I glanced at Bentley. He must have overheard us, because he nodded and took my hand as we walked over to Dane. He stood, and if I hadn't been holding on to Bentley, I may have wavered in my stilettos.

"Dane, this is my friend Andi and her boyfriend, Bentley," Bev said.

He smiled at me and shook Bentley's hand. "It's a pleasure."

"Very nice to meet you. Make sure you take care of my friend Bev here, okay?"

He gave me a nod, making me grin. Something about his presence made me feel as though he were ready to toss Bev over his shoulder caveman-style and have his way with her. I couldn't help but smile at that image. His eyes raked over her, making my insides quiver. How Bev could just stand there and appear unfazed was beyond me. I looked at Bentley, who raised a single brow at me. I shrugged—he'd clearly busted me scoping out Dane.

I gave Bev another quick hug good-bye. "Don't let these bitches bring your night down. Dane wants your ass!"

She snickered. "Trust me, I'm not a timid high school girl anymore. These tramps can suck it." Her eyes flickered to Dane and back to me. "And I'll suck that."

We laughed as Bentley took my hand.

"Excuse us, but Andi made me miss dessert," he said. "I need to take her home and have her instead. I'm famished."

Bentley and I walked across the room, leaving Bev giggling. Dane had a look of understanding, and the bitches' mouths hung open. I was overcome by his words. The man was like hot caramel, and I was the ice cream melting in his presence. My heels clicked on the marble as we rushed across the room. I prayed I didn't skid across the shiny floor.

His hand tightened around mine as if he knew my steps were uncertain. "She's cool. I liked her."

Bev *was* cool, and I hadn't realized how much I'd missed her. In the past, I would've worried about leaving her with those skanks, but not tonight. She was ready to kick ass and take names later. With Dane next to her, oozing alpha male, she was primed for a great night.

I welcomed the brisk evening air as we approached the valet. Bentley handed him our ticket.

Bentley

To say I hadn't been nervous walking into the club to meet her parents would have been a lie, but having her hand in mine as I did it calmed me. I looked at my beautiful girlfriend as we sat at a red light, and I said a silent thank you to anyone who was listening.

Andi's eyes shifted toward me. "What are you staring at?" She shyly smiled, and my heart melted.

"You. The way you handled those uppity women and

the things you said about the shows and me just blew me away. You blow me away."

"Well, they were horrible to Bev in high school. She was overweight, and they called her names like 'heavy Bevvy.' It was awful. Back then, she was shy, so I stood up for her." Andi sighed.

"And to you?"

"Hmm?" She laid her head on the seatback. "Were they mean to me?"

"Yeah, did they call you names too?"

"Sometimes, but I didn't let it bother me too much. It bothered me more when they picked on Beverly. People don't understand how words can be weapons. It's sad really. We have this wonderful language with over a million words in it, and the cruel ones flow so easily while the others stay unspoken or maybe just on the pages of the dictionary."

The thought of anyone being mean to Andi made my heart ache. Then I realized I'd done that. I had been mean to her with my words. My mind raced, trying to think of all the bad reviews I'd written and how people had counted on them, not only those who read the reviews but the actors and directors involved. "Shit."

"What's the matter, babe?" She placed her hand on mine.

I stared out the window as we pulled into the hotel parking lot.

"Bentley? Are you okay?"

Her thumb rubbed the back of my hand, and with each pass, I felt more guilt.

"I'm sorry I hurt you with my words." I looked into her eyes as the valet opened her door.

She held up her index finger and pulled her door closed. Her body swiveled so she was facing me. "Apology accepted." She placed a soft kiss on my lips. "Yes, your words hurt me, but you weren't being malicious. If it weren't for your reviews, I wouldn't have been able to grace the stage of Broadway with confidence." Her eyes glassed over. "As much as I hate to admit it, you were right. I wasn't performing as I should've been. I was going through the motions, and you made me feel the emotions that I lacked."

All I could do was nod. This was the first time I'd ever questioned my work. I had always vowed to stand behind my words, and I prided myself on the honesty I brought to each review.

"Don't change who you are or, as you told me not so long ago, your reviews won't be worth the paper they're written on. Now let's go to our room, and I'll take your mind off all this."

"I love you, Andi." Those were words that I hoped to say more times than I'd be able to count.

"I love you too."

And those were the words I hoped to hear just as often.

CHAPTER 14

Andi

My one-week run on Broadway opened doors for me. The director, Marcus, was directing another show that started rehearsals in the fall, and he asked me if I'd be interested in reading for the lead role. Naturally, I couldn't turn down that opportunity, but sometimes the hardest part was timing. Since it was only the beginning of summer, I needed to either find another short-running play or a short-term job.

Gina and I decided we needed to look for a place in the city. She was working there every day since she had back to back jobs, and she was getting tired of the commute. Seth wanted to move as well, and we liked the idea of having him as a roommate. Even though they were officially dating, I wasn't sure how Bentley would feel about that.

My buzzer sounded, and I half expected to see Gina with the classifieds in her hand, but my hot boyfriend came in instead.

"Hey, you! What are you doing here?"

Bentley gave me a kiss. "Do I need a reason to visit my girl?"

"No, but what if I wasn't here? It isn't like I live around the corner." I walked into my kitchen. "Would you like something to drink?"

Bentley relaxed onto my sofa. "No, thanks. I just had lunch."

"Oh, so you've been in Jersey?" I opened a Diet Coke and sat next to him.

"I had to go see Mack about the show." He fidgeted with his shirt, and creases developed in his forehead.

"You don't have to feel badly about mentioning Mack or the show. Really, it's fine. I'm in such a better place now." I put my hand on his thigh and felt his muscles tighten. "What's wrong?"

He picked up my hand and placed my palm on his cheek while he took deep breaths. "A very large producer picked up *Together Again*. They're going to Broadway then touring major cities when that run is over. It's going to be pretty big and . . ."

I nodded. I knew what that meant for the cast and what it could have meant for me, but I was happier now. "That's fantastic! This must be why Seth wants to move to the city. You didn't think I'd be happy?"

Bentley walked across the room to my window, which overlooked a park. His chin rested in his hand as he just stared outside. "I thought you'd be might be upset."

"Babe, look at me." He turned as I padded across my carpet to him. I placed my hands in his and held them against my chest. "Everything happens for a reason. You're my reason. I'm really content with the way things are right now, so it's all good." His arms snaked around me, lifting me off the carpet.

I wrapped my legs around his hips as he carried me to the couch and sat. My hands went into his hair, and I studied his face. He looked more gorgeous today than he had yesterday. "So, Mr. Chambers, what do you have planned for today?"

"Well, that's another reason why I'm here. My parents are having a birthday get-together for Brett, and I wanted to know if you'd go with me." His lips turned up slightly, forcing a smile. "I think they want to take his mind off everything that's going on, and I'd love for them to meet you before I leave."

I nodded and tried to contain my sadness "Okay, when?" My heart hammered at the thought of meeting his parents, but from what I could tell, they were nice people who supported their children.

"Sunday afternoon at their place in the Hamptons." His thumb grazed my breasts as he raised his hands up my ribcage. He lowered his forehead to mine, and I watched his chest rise and fall with each breath.

"I hope your parents like me."

He played with my nipples, making me not really care who liked me. "They will love you. I promise."

"Hey, Bentley?"

"Mmm hmm." He was sprinkling kisses on my neck.

"I want you." My head fell back as his tongue glided from my collarbone to my earlobe.

His teeth nibbled my soft flesh. "Babe, I'm yours."

He carried me into the bedroom, and we spent the majority of the day in bed, loving and holding each other.

THE CRITIC

As we drove up the Chambers' long driveway in South Hampton, I felt my hands getting sweaty. I'd chosen to wear a cotton floral dress and a pair of wedge-heeled sandals. My man looked hot in his beige golf shorts and navy polo shirt, which brought out the depth of his gorgeous eyes. We'd stopped and picked up a bouquet of flowers for his mother. Even though the party was for Brett, I wanted to bring his mom something. My nerves surfaced as Bentley pulled up behind a beautiful Maserati.

"Wow! That car is gorgeous," I said.

"That's Alex's car."

I glanced at him.

"Brett's best friend and co-owner of The White Orchid," Bentley said.

"Yes, I remember you telling me about him." We got out of the car, and I smoothed my skirt.

Bentley took my hand. "You look beautiful. I'm glad most of Brett's friends are taken, or I'd have to break some arms today."

"Yeah, okay." I smiled and shook my head. "It wouldn't matter if they weren't. I'm yours."

"Mine. You better believe it." He kissed me hard and deep, and I let out a slight groan.

"Hey, bro, want to keep it PG in Mom's driveway?"

We broke our kiss, and Bentley chuckled as we turned to see Brett on the porch. We walked up to the front door, hand-in-hand. He hugged Brett with his free arm, never letting go of me.

"Hey, man, happy birthday." Bentley pulled a card

from his back pocket and handed it to Brett. "Don't spend it all in one place."

Brett kissed my cheek. "Hey, Andi, it's great to see you again. I hope my bro is treating you well."

"Yes, very well. Thank you." I felt my cheeks rise with my smile.

"Great, well, everyone is just about here. Let's go inside before Mom misses her favorite child." Brett's smirk was adorable.

Bentley countered with, "Does she even know I'm here?"

I enjoyed listening to their banter. Those guys really loved each other, and I was glad to be there. We followed Brett inside, and I took a moment to look around. Although the home was large, it looked comfortable and not pretentious in the least.

"Sweetheart! You're here." A pretty woman walked up to Bentley and hugged him. Her hair was deep brown and in a perfectly-styled bob.

Bentley looked over her shoulder at Brett and mouthed, "Told you," and held up his index finger.

Brett shook his head and rolled his eyes, making me smile.

"Mom, this is my girlfriend, Andrea Jordan. Sweetheart, this is my mom, Madeline Chambers." Bentley pulled me to him, and I felt my cheeks redden.

"Andrea, it's so nice to finally meet you. Bentley has told me so much about you." She gave me a gentle hug.

"It's a pleasure to meet you too. Please call me Andi."

"Well, Andi, I'm very glad you're here. All the kids are on the back patio. Come, let's go."

THE CRITIC

She took my hand, and I heard Brett and Bentley snickering behind us. We walked outside to a gorgeous patio. Sun bounced off the water of the in-ground pool, making it sparkle. I looked at the others, who were laughing and having a good time. A pregnant, pretty woman sat on a chaise lounge between the legs of a man who was rubbing her belly. Bentley's cousin Lyn was eyeing Tyler, who was playing cards with an older gentleman. When his eyes met mine, I instantly knew he was Bentley's father.

He walked over to us. "Son, it's great to see you." He clapped Bentley's back. "And who is this beauty?"

"Dad, this is my girlfriend, Andi."

"Well, it's a pleasure to finally meet one of Bentley's girlfriends."

"Pleasure to meet you too." My voice was a little tense, and I could tell Bentley heard it.

"Excuse us, please." Bentley pulled me toward the pool. "I've never brought a girl home before."

"Never?"

"No, never. They've briefly met my dates before, but I've never brought a girl over for a family function or dinner." He kissed the top of my head. "Just you."

I felt my body relax. "Good. Unbelievable, but good." I couldn't help being happy about that. At least I knew they wouldn't compare me to anyone else. I took his hand, and we walked toward the others.

The pregnant woman looked at me and stood to greet me. She swatted her husband's hand when he grabbed her ass. "Hi, I'm Aubrey. I'm so glad to see you. There's way too much testosterone out here." She laughed.

Her husband came up behind her and placed his hand back on her belly. He outstretched his other to me. "Hi, I'm Alex." He looked at his wife. "Baby, you know you love my testosterone."

Aubrey rolled her eyes and giggled. I noticed Brett look at them with a hint of sadness. I didn't know if it was because the one he loved wasn't there or because Aubrey's protruding belly made him think of his situation.

Lyn came up and gave Bentley a hug. Then she turned to me and did the same. She was absolutely stunning. Her skin was perfect, and I knew what theatrical makeup could do to someone's complexion.

She sighed. "Andi, it's so great to see you two together."

"Are you okay?" I couldn't help noticing she looked sad.

"Yes, thank you." She kept stealing glances at Tyler.

I leaned in and whispered, "He's very good looking."

She smiled, blushed, and countered with, "And doesn't know I'm alive."

I looked up and saw Tyler staring at her. "You're wrong. Don't look now, but he's coming over here."

"Hey, ladies, can I get you a drink?" His movements were effortless, and his voice oozed sex. He really was something, and I could tell he affected Lyn.

"I'm all set," I said. "I think I'm going to head over to the others."

Lyn's eyes opened wide, but she could handle him. I shot her a wink and walked away.

We spent the afternoon laughing and getting to know each other. They were a great group of people, and I was happy to be a part of them. The guys talked about baseball and if the Mets were going to show up that year. Alex laughed and said there was only one New York team—and it wasn't the Mets. Their witty banter and team bashing was all done with obvious love and respect. I loved being there.

Tyler broke up the MLB talk by mentioning the upcoming events at the club. He said his cousin Jake's band, Raging Urge, would be making an appearance at the club. Alex hadn't been keen on the idea at first— something about a rock band playing at his club was abnormal. Tyler had told him that they needed to broaden their scope. Lyn smiled and nodded, but I thought she would have agreed with just about anything Tyler said.

"I saw them in upstate New York a few months ago, and they were fantastic!" I said with excitement.

Everyone just looked at me.

"Didn't you have their concert shirt on at Brookstone?" Bentley's brows lowered as he tried to remember.

I beamed at his recollection of my attire that day. "Yeah, I did." My smile grew as I watched his do the same.

"Well, you can't go wrong with rock 'n' roll, and if Andi likes them, then I'm sure I will too." Bentley kissed my temple and whispered, "Do you realize how sexy you are?"

My cheeks heated, and I crossed my legs. I shifted my eyes toward him. "Ditto."

Aubrey became very excited as she said, "Well, Walker-Stone is handling the marketing announcements, and according to Julie, Raging Urge has quite a following. She went to see them play in a bar upstate too when she came back from Europe, and she said they were very good and easy on the eyes. Maybe you were there at the same time, Andi. Julie is the best, not to mention so much fun. I'm sure you'd love her." She let out a schoolgirl giggle, which surprised me. Alex shot Aubrey a pained look as she looked toward Brett, and her cheeks paled. "I'm so sorry. I didn't mean to . . ."

Brett forced a smile. "It's fine. You can't avoid your best friend, and neither can I, since she heads the marketing for the club."

The air became thick and heavy, and it had nothing to do with the humidity. Alex and Tyler grimaced at Brett sympathetically. I suddenly felt very uncomfortable and out of place. I knew some of the history, but apparently there was a lot more.

Alex turned toward Bentley. "So Brett tells me you're moving to the UK? That's awesome. We love Europe."

I placed my hand on Bentley's shoulder. "I think I'm going to see if your mom needs anything."

"Want me to come with you?" Bentley asked.

I smiled. "No, thank you. Stay out here and hang with your friends." I kissed his cheek before I made my exit. We'd been skirting around the "moving" issue for a while. Whenever it came up, my chest felt heavy and sadness enveloped me. I needed to get away while they talked about his new job.

The home was so lovely, and I smelled coffee brewing. In the kitchen, I found Madeline putting candles in a beautiful two-tiered cake. She looked at me, and her eyes actually looked as if they were smiling.

THE CRITIC

"Hi there, Andi. Were they getting crazy out there?" She stuck the last candle in the top tier and clapped. "Another year gone. I can't believe it." Her hand went to her heart.

"Time does fly. Can I help you with anything?"

"Have a seat, sweetie. How about you and I have a glass of wine before we take out the cake and coffee?" She pulled out two crystal glasses and set them on the granite countertop. "Is white okay, or do you prefer red?"

"White is perfect, thank you."

She poured us each a glass. "Come let's sit for a minute."

I should've been nervous, but I was quite calm. Madeline seemed genuine and kind. We sat at the kitchen table, facing each other.

She sipped her wine before smiling at me. "So, Andi, tell me a little bit about yourself."

"Well, I'm an actress, but you know that already. I'm between shows right now, but I have some temporary things lined up." I brought my glass to my lips and savored the tart liquid.

"Yes, Bentley told me you were originally cast in the show our theater guild sponsored." Her brows rose, and that small gesture spoke volumes.

Had he told her why I wasn't in it anymore? My pulse quickened, and I was sure she could tell I was nervous now. I swallowed hard. "Yes, I was, but it didn't work out. It was the best thing really. I wasn't right for that part." I tried to keep my voice even. "You see, Bentley reviewed the show, and let's just say it wasn't a glowing review."

"I'm sorry it didn't work out for you, but one has to do what's best for them. You landed on your feet though. That's very commendable." She rotated the stem of her glass with her thumb and forefinger. "I heard his review was rather . . . strong."

"Yes, it was. After I read the review, I tracked down your son and gave him a piece of my mind."

Madeline laughed. "I heard. Good for you! You should stand up for yourself. My son definitely has a way with words. I've taught him to always be truthful but also as kind as possible." She shrugged. "In his defense, his words have made him who he is—professionally, anyways."

"Yes, well, after that, Bentley really helped me dig deep and find the actress I needed to be. For that, I'll always be thankful."

"How are you handling his upcoming move? He told me he asked you to go with him." She took a sip of wine, her eyes peering at me over the rim of the glass.

"He did." I fiddled with the small napkin on the table.

"Can I assume by your lack of enthusiasm that you aren't going?" Her tone was kind and laced with some sort of womanly understanding.

"I love your son, I truly do, but this is a big decision. I just don't know." I shrugged.

"What are you two talking about?" Bentley's voice echoed through the room. "You're not giving up my childhood secrets, are you, Mom?" He chuckled.

Madeline walked back to where the cake was sitting, carrying her wine glass in one hand and waving him off in the other. "Andi and I were just having a little girl time." She winked. "Now make yourself useful and carry this cake outside. Andi and I will get the coffee."

Bentley chortled. "Yes, ma'am." He kissed his mom's cheek before he lifted the cake off the counter. When he walked past me, he whispered, "I love you."

⸺⧓⧓⧓⸺

We decided to stay at Bentley's place since it was closer to the Hamptons and we were both tired. In the car, he grabbed my hand. "My parents really liked you."

I rolled my head on the headrest to look at him. "I liked them too. Your mom is wonderful. When she speaks of you, she just oozes love. She's very proud of her boys. I can tell."

"Yes, she is. When Brett and I were younger, my mom never missed an opportunity to tell us she loved us and that she was proud of us. I remember when I was a teenager, I once told her I wanted to be a stripper just to get a rise out of her." Bentley laughed with me. "And you know what she said?"

"What?"

"'That sounds lovely, dear, as long as you're happy and you do your best.'"

"Really? Wow, my parents would've freaked."

Bentley chuckled. "Wait, she wasn't done. Then she hit me with, 'Let me know when you're performing so I make sure that isn't the same night I go with my girlfriends.'" He shuddered as I burst out laughing.

"That's priceless! I assume you never took to the stage?"

"That would be a negative. It was bad enough trying to get rid of the mental image of my mother stuffing a dollar bill in someone's G-string."

"Well, I'm sure she was kidding, right?" That didn't sound like something Madeline would do.

"I have no idea, and I honestly don't want to know. The point is my mom never said we couldn't be what we wanted to or that she wouldn't be proud. She just had a way of guiding us without actually giving blatant directions." His face softened as he spoke of his mom.

"I wish my parents would've been like that. Can you imagine if I said that to my mom? Instead of Ivy League colleges, she would've had a convent on the phone."

"Not that you wouldn't rock a nun's habit, but you'd kick ass as a stripper. Maybe I should have a pole installed in my home to test that theory." He winked and turned the corner.

I gaped at him. "Ha-ha. You're very funny, Mr. Chambers, but I don't think that'll happen." We laughed as we pulled up to his apartment.

Bentley

We held hands walking into my place, and rather than releasing her, I held on tighter. I looked at our fingers, and I realized with her there, I was truly home. I would miss her terribly if I couldn't convince her to come with me.

She flexed her fingers and looked at me. "Everything okay?" Her eyes softened, and her cheeks flushed.

"Perfect. Everything is almost as it should be." I walked to my sofa and pulled her along with me. As I sat, I made sure to position her on my lap.

"Almost?" Her voice had become shaky.

"Andi, I don't want you to go back to Jersey." I held on tighter to her.

"I don't have anything with me, but I can stay the night if you'd like me to." She smiled, but she didn't seem to have understood what I wanted.

"No. I don't want you to stay the night."

Her face fell. "Oh. You're confusing me."

I picked up her hand and placed it on my heart. "Not just tonight. I want you here all the time. Would you consider staying here with me? Gina can move in too, after I leave. Then I won't have to worry about either of you commuting back and forth to Jersey. It makes sense. You both need a place to live in the city, and mine will be available."

The pulse in her wrist quickened under my fingertips. I watched her chest rise and fall with each quick breath. My nerves spiked, which I was sure she could feel with her hand on my chest.

"You can think about it if you need to," I said. "But know that I love you, and even if you say no, it won't change how I feel. I just want you here with me when I wake up and before I go to sleep. If you'd rather wait until I was gone, that's fine too."

She pivoted so she was straddling me. The skirt of her dress rose, and my hands found the smooth skin of her thighs as she placed her hands on my cheeks. "I don't need time to think about it." She placed a chaste, sweet kiss on my lips. "Living with you isn't something that requires a lot thought. I'd love to live with you, and I'm sure Gina will be grateful as well."

"Then it's settled. Every night when I go to sleep in

London, I'll be able to picture you in my bed here. Just knowing that makes me happy."

She licked her lips, and I felt my excitement growing beneath her. I claimed her lips as my hands pulled her ass closer. She tilted her hips and ground against me, rubbing me with her hot panties. I needed to be inside her. I pushed off the couch with shaky legs and carried her down the hall . . . to our room. I planned on loving her until we fell asleep in each other's arms.

CHAPTER 15

Andi

Bentley and I sat at the table, me with my coffee and him with his orange juice. I couldn't help staring at him. He looked so great in the morning that it really wasn't fair. I'd pulled my hair into a ponytail just to look halfway presentable, and he was naturally beautiful.

He looked at me. "You're staring."

I laughed. "Am I? Hmm . . . I hadn't noticed."

He leaned forward, took my hands, and brought them to his lips. "I'm going to miss you."

I swallowed hard. "Today's the day, isn't it?" I knew he had an early meeting. Time was about up.

"Yeah, I actually need to pack. I've procrastinated long enough." He grabbed his cell off the table and handed it to me. "Scott texted me last night. I saw this when you were in the bedroom."

I took the phone and stared at the screen.

Scott: Hey, buddy. Get packing. Chatfield wants you on a plane day after tomorrow. Meet in my office at 10 am tomorrow to get ticket and info.

I stared at the message until my vision blurred with unshed tears. I set the phone down and dabbed my eyes with a napkin.

"Andi, I didn't know. I mean, I knew it would be soon but not tomorrow. I wanted to help get you settled here before I left."

I slowly nodded. "It's okay. Gina and I can handle it." *Be strong, Andi.* "I can help you though. Do you even know how much to bring?"

"I don't. I'll just wing it, and what I don't have, I'll buy there."

"Okay." I walked into the kitchen and set my cup in the sink, trying not to lose it.

Bentley came up behind me and spun me in his arms. "Shower with me. We can worry about packing when I get back. We can go get some of your stuff too."

"I'll call Gina and tell her our plan. If she's okay with it, which I'm sure she will be, then I'll pack some things." I tried to sound chipper, but it was definitely forced.

He could tell, but he didn't call me on it. "Sounds good, but after we shower." He pulled me along as he walked backward toward his room.

<hr />

Bentley drove us to his office and then gave me his car to take to Jersey. "Pack what you need, and you can get the rest later. I'll call you when I'm done with my meeting."

I slid into the driver's seat. "Thanks for the car, and I'll talk to you later." He leaned in and kissed me. "Bye."

He tapped the car door and walked away. The word "bye" felt heavier today. I needed to change that to "see ya later" or something less final. I weaved through traffic and crossed into Jersey before I used my speakerphone and dialed Gina.

"Hey, Andi."

"Hi. Are you around? Can you meet me at my place?"

"Yeah, are you in the car?"

"Bentley's car, yes." I glided my hands over the steering wheel as if I were touching him.

"Oh, hey, Bentley!" Gina giggled.

I laughed. "He's not here, but I'm sure he says hi."

"Oh. Ha-ha. When will you be at your place?"

"About thirty minutes or so."

"Okay, I'll bring food. Love you."

"Love you too."

"Bye, Bentley." She giggled and hung up.

I shook my head and smiled at my friend's goofiness. Yeah, I'd be okay as long as I had Gina to keep me entertained. I turned on the radio and listened to a talk show until I pulled into my complex.

<hr>

Gina came over with subs and chips from a nearby deli. "I'm starving."

My stomach growled. "I guess I could eat."

We sat at the table and unwrapped the hoagies.

"So, I have news." I took a bite of my sandwich.

"Yeah?"

"I've decided I can't go with Bentley, so he's offered us his apartment. Isn't that great?"

She tilted her head and studied me. "Yeah, it is, but are you sure you don't want to go with him? You don't have anything lined up right now. Even if you only went for a week or so, take a vacation."

I shook my head. "That's just putting off the inevitable. I'd leave, and he'd stay there. It's better this way."

"Nope, not buying it. But it's your life. You need to be comfortable with your decision." Gina continued to eat her lunch.

"I don't know if I'm comfortable, but hey, we have a place in the city now. So that's good." The more I tried to convince Gina the more I started to believe my own words.

She grinned. "It is. Okay, so when is all this moving taking place?"

"Tomorrow."

Gina started coughing. "I almost choked. I thought you said tomorrow."

"I did. He's leaving tomorrow. I'm actually here to pack up some things and head back to his place. I thought maybe you'd help me. Then we can go grab some of your stuff and go to the city together." I pushed my lunch aside. "What do you think?"

"Yeah, I can do that. I suppose I need to tell Seth and my landlord."

"Shit, I forgot to call Seth! I can talk to Bentley if you want Seth to move in with us."

She shook her head. "I talked to him yesterday, and he said his landlord agreed to a month-to-month lease, so he's okay for now." Gina stood. "Let's get moving! We have a lot to do. I'm going to head out and grab boxes."

"Sounds great. Thanks, G."

I emailed my landlord my notice and headed into my room to pack. As I looked around my room, I thanked God I had to give my landlord thirty days' notice. It would take me that long to go through everything and pack what I wanted to take. I took the pictures and news clippings out from around my mirror and smiled at how far I'd come.

I grabbed my duffle out of my closet and packed a couple days' worth of clothes and my toiletries. My shoes were a different story—I gabbed about a week's worth of those. I loved my shoes, and just taking one or two pairs wasn't an option.

Bentley: Hey, babe. You at your place?

Andrea: Yes, but I'm getting ready to leave soon. Waiting on Gina. How's the meeting?

Bentley: Over. I'm taking care of some things in the office and then I'm done. Can you pick me up or should I take a cab?

Andrea: I'll come and get you. I'll call when I'm on my way.

Bentley: Drive safe. Love you.

Andrea: Love you too.

Gina came back with boxes and tape. "Hey, I talked to my landlord, and she's letting me out of my lease early, so I only have five days to pack up. So if you're okay here, I'm going to go home."

"Sounds great. Thanks for everything." I pulled her in for a hug.

THE CRITIC

I pulled up to Bentley's office building, and he was standing outside. He waved when he saw me and gave me his brightest smile. He was happy, so I was happy for him. He walked over to the driver's door and opened it for me.

I hopped out. "Thanks. I wanted you to drive."

"That's what I figured." He winked and pulled me into a searing kiss.

It didn't matter that we were on a city street and horns were blaring—we needed every stolen moment possible. Once I was buckled up, he pulled away from the curb.

"So what happened in your meeting?" I asked.

"Well, Mr. Chatfield gave me the contract, which I signed after consulting with my attorney. I'll be there for a minimum of three months. Then I'll need to return at least four to six times over the course of the year, unless something happens. Then it could be more. He gave me a key to my apartment, or flat as they say there, and my airline ticket. I guess it was all standard stuff really."

"Sounds like everything is taken care of then." I smiled and looked out the window until we stopped in front of his brownstone.

He opened the front door and handed me the key. "Here, you're going to need this."

"Thanks. I guess I will."

I had my duffle slung over my shoulder, and Bentley carried my small box of shoes. We set everything down, and he pulled me onto his lap.

"I have something for you," he said.

"You do?"

He reached into his backpack and handed me an airline ticket. It had my information, and my flight date was tomorrow from JFK to Heathrow.

"Bentley?" The thin piece of paper trembled between my fingers.

"Look, I know you said you weren't going with me, but when they told me my flight information, I decided to buy you one too. It's refundable or the date can be changed, and I'll cover whatever fee they charge you." He placed his hands on my arms and looked into my eyes.

I inhaled his cologne and tried to memorize the scent. "Thank you." Yeah, that was all I had. Just thank you. I leaned into him and held him around his waist.

"So Brett invited us to the club tonight. I'd like to go. Is that okay?" He kissed the top of my head.

"That sounds like fun. I'll tell Gina to meet us." I knew he wanted to see his brother, and a night out would be fun, but it was our last night together. I would have preferred us to be alone, but it wasn't about me.

He picked up the small box and looked at my duffle. "Is this all you brought over?"

"I'll get more stuff tomorrow. I just wanted to get back to you."

"How about we find a place for these?" He winked, and I followed him into the bedroom.

I couldn't take my eyes off him. The way he moved with such confidence, I envied that. I envied him.

"I want you to make yourself at home and feel free to take whatever space you need," he said as he set my box beside the closet.

THE CRITIC

I took off my clothes while his back was to me. "Right now, all I need is you."

He pivoted, and his eyes went wide when he took in my black lace bra and panties. The way he looked at me from head to toe made me melt. "Wow, am I going to miss you."

"No talking. Just make love to me." I lay on the bed and held my hand out to him.

The mattress dipped as he lay down. "I can't not talk to you. I won't talk about tomorrow, but I need to tell you that you're the most gorgeous woman I've ever known and I'm going to love you forever." In no time at all, he was naked and on top of me. His hands caressed the sides of my face as we stared at each other. He pushed my hair off my face. "I've always loved your eyes." He gently kissed each lid.

I opened my eyes and watched the man I loved make his way down my body, one kiss at a time. His head was between my legs, and I felt his tongue graze my inner thigh. My legs fell open as he moved to my most sensitive spot. His breath was warm on me, making my hips buck. He looked up at me and smiled as he tasted me. He moved up my body the same way he'd gone down, kissing every inch of me.

"You taste great." His tongue plunged in my mouth as he entered me. His movements were slow. "I need to savor you, Andi."

All I could do was nod. The feeling of fullness overwhelmed me, and it wasn't from connecting physically but because we were connected emotionally. My hands trailed down his muscular back as he picked up his pace.

"I love you, Andi." He grunted, and we came in

unison.

I looked into his deep blue eyes. "I love you too."

⋙◈◈◈⋘

The club was hopping, and Brett was busy pouring drinks. He motioned to Bentley to head up to the VIP room. Gina and Seth walked in as we were heading up the stairs, and I waved at them to follow. We turned the corner and saw a "good luck" banner hanging on the wall. Bentley stopped in his tracks and put his hand on his chest.

I snaked my hand around his arm. "This is amazing."

Everyone was there, including his parents, Alex, Aubrey, and Lyn. We walked in hand-in-hand and said hello to everyone. The only time he released me was when he hugged someone. Otherwise, our fingers were interwoven.

Brett came charging up the stairs and slung his arm around Bentley's neck.

"Brett, no trips to the ER tonight," Madeline scolded.

"Yeah, Brett. You don't want to hurt Mom's favorite son." Bentley winked at his mom.

"You mean the one that's leaving her? That number one son?" Brett sauntered over to his mom and wrapped his arm around her shoulder. "Don't worry, Mom, I won't leave you." He kissed her cheek, earning an eye roll from Bentley.

His father laughed. "Those boys will never change." But his smile told me he was happy about that.

We spent the rest of the evening sharing great wine and food while the DJ played retro dance tunes. Brett had really outdone himself.

THE CRITIC

He tapped the side of his glass with his fork. "Excuse me." Everyone turned their attention to Brett. "I'd like to thank you all for coming tonight to give my brother a send-off as he leaves for London tomorrow." He turned his attention to Bentley. "I love you, bro, and I'm proud of you." He raised his glass. "To Bentley."

Everyone said in unison, "To Bentley."

Brett walked up to us. "Andi, if you need anything while he's gone, I want you to call me. You got it?"

I nodded as words evaded me.

Brett hugged Bentley. "I'm gonna miss you man."

"I'll miss you too, little brother."

I really didn't want the night to end, but Bentley had a morning flight, so we headed out, went home, and laid in each other's arms until the sun rose.

When I woke, the air in the apartment felt different—almost heavy. Bentley was already in the shower, and I rubbed my hand over his side of the bed. This was what it would be like waking up alone in his bed. What hurts was that it was my choice. I heard the water turn off in the bathroom, so I decided to get up and make some coffee. I promised myself that I wouldn't be a basket case. That would just make him feel bad, and I didn't want to do that to him.

"Hey, babe, having your morning caffeine?" He kissed the top of my head.

I noticed his suitcases by the door. "Are you leaving already?" My voice hitched.

"In a few minutes." He poured a glass of orange juice.

"But you have a while until your flight." I felt as though I would suffocate. How could I say good-bye to him? I wasn't prepared. I'd avoided this moment for so long that I didn't know what to do. I stood and took a breath. "I'll be right back."

I walked into the bathroom and brushed my teeth. The mirror didn't lie—my hair was a disaster. I smoothed it with a brush and washed my face. I needed to get something for Bentley before he left, so I opened the small box I'd brought over and took out a candid picture Gina had taken of us. She'd texted it to me, and I'd printed it out for him. Back in the family room, Bentley was looking out the window.

I slyly put the picture in his backpack. "Bentley?"

He turned and came to me. "Babe, are you okay?" His thumb grazed my cheek.

I leaned into his hand and shrugged. "I'll be okay. Do you have everything? Your passport? Ticket? ID?"

"Yeah, I have everything. Andi, I don't want a drawn-out good-bye. I can't—" He held me close and rested his forehead on my shoulder.

My hands were on his back, which had begun to tremble. I gently rubbed his back as my tears fell.

He looked at me with tear-soaked cheeks, grabbed my face, and pulled me into a searing kiss. Our tongues moved, and I savored his taste, knowing I wouldn't feel his lips for a long time.

He broke the kiss and put his forehead against mine. "I'm going to miss you so much." His warm breath caressed my face. "I love you." He grabbed his suitcases and backpack and gave me a smile. "I'll call you when I land."

I tried to smile and hide my sadness, but it was a lost cause. I gingerly nodded, and when the door closed behind him, I sobbed. I went to the window and watched him get in his car. My hand went to the glass, and I said, "I love you too."

I walked around Bentley's place, trying to absorb the fact it would be mine and Gina's home while he was away. The pictures were sparse, and aside from a few books and literary awards, his built-in bookshelf was bare. I knew I could fill them with some of my favorite books, which I kept in a box at my place. I didn't have beautiful bookcases to showcase them, but I would here. I picked up one of his framed reviews. A gold-and-black ribbon hung from the bottom: "2012 Award Winner." I smiled and felt a sense of pride. He really was the best critic in the city, and he deserved awards. Three others had the same adornment, as well as a few other awards from different agencies. My heart swelled at his accomplishments. It was no wonder the owners of the *Edge* wanted his help.

I opened the drawers in the credenza below the shelving, and my heart stopped. He had programs from the shows I'd been in over the past five years. He had some from other shows too, but mine were banded together. I pulled them out, crossed my legs, and sat on the floor to look through them. I honestly couldn't believe he'd kept these, even some I didn't have. I flipped through the pages and noticed yellow sticky notes on some of them. He'd written what stood out and what didn't. Most of the notes about me weren't wonderful, but I wasn't shocked. I knew he didn't like how I'd performed in those shows.

The last program was for *Together Again,* and there were multiple notes stuck in it. My hands trembled as I opened it, remembering his review. I didn't know why I needed to read his notes, but skipping them wasn't an option.

"Andrea Jordan makes me feel things I've never felt. I can't stop staring at her, and like the very first time I saw her, I knew she was someone special. Just like the first time I critiqued her, many years ago, I knew she could do better. What I wouldn't give to have the chance to meet her. Her eyes are captivating and staring into them wouldn't be a chore but a delight. Maybe someday I'll have that chance."

My eyes filled. This wasn't the review for the paper—this was for him. He'd thought about me for years, just like he'd always told me, and there was the proof in his handwriting. I replaced the programs in the drawer and pushed it closed. Memories flooded me. We'd moved past the bad ones, and I was a better person for it.

My phone chimed, and I instantly grabbed it. I prayed it was Bentley so I could tell him I loved him, but it was Gina.

Gina: Hey, I'm on my way over. I want to thank Bentley for letting me stay there and give him a farewell hug.

Me: He left.

About five minutes later, there was a knock on the door. Gina walked in the unlocked door and stared at me sitting on the floor, holding the note Bentley had written.

She came and sat next to me. "Oh, Andi, are you okay?"

I shook my head. "No, I don't think I am." I handed her the note and watched her brows go from low to high.

"Wow," she said.

"Yeah, wow." I stood, and Gina followed.

273

THE CRITIC

"What are you doing, Andi?"

"I was just looking around. That's all."

"No, that's not what I mean." Gina's hands went to her hips. "I mean, what are you doing? What are you waiting for?"

Bentley's words flooded my mind. *"I'll ask again, what are you waiting for? You want this, right? To be on Broadway under the bright lights with your name on the marquee? You say you need me, but what for? A good review? Because a critic doesn't slingshot you into stardom. You need to control the pull and release. The slingshot can only go as far back as you decide to draw it."*

I looked at Gina with wide eyes. "It's the slingshot."

She tilted her head. "What?"

"And the chopsticks. He told me I was conventional and that I always went for the fork. I need to eat soup with chopsticks."

"Andi, sweetheart, please sit down. You're scaring me. Would you like a glass of water or something?" Gina took my hand to lead me to the couch, but I stopped and shook my head.

My voice became frantic. "No, I need to pull the sling back and not be a fork. I need to go to London. I have to be with Bentley." I ran to my room with Gina on my heels.

"What can I do?" Gina was picking up my clothes as I took them off and tossed them on the floor.

I grabbed my toothbrush and tossed it in my duffle. "Take me to JFK." I opened my dresser drawer and grabbed my passport and ticket.

"You're going?" Gina beamed and grabbed my purse off my dresser.

"Yes. I don't have a job right now, and there's no reason I can think of to be without him. He supported me and helped me achieve my dreams. It's time I repaid the favor." I slung my duffle over my shoulder and handed Gina my key to the apartment.

"Then let's get you on an airplane."

We rushed outside and got in her car. I looked at my watch. I had a little over two hours before the flight took off. We could totally do this. I logged on to the airline's website from my phone and checked in online, sending the boarding pass to my cell. I wasn't checking bags, so I should be fine.

"I'm proud of you," Gina said as she drove.

"You are?"

"Yeah, this is very un-Andi-like, and it's about time you did something spontaneous. You're following your heart. You've followed your dream and achieved it, and while I know being on Broadway made you happy, I think Bentley is the one who makes you feel whole."

We came to a screeching halt in front of the terminal. I leaned over the center console and hugged my best friend. "I'll miss you."

"I'll miss you too. Come home with a cool accent. Now go."

I opened the door and hurried inside.

I had to go to the kiosk to print my boarding pass because my cell had only one bar of battery life left, and if it died, I wouldn't have my information. I felt as though I'd answered twenty questions before the machine spat out the glossy paper.

When I finally made it to security check-in, my heart fell at the sight of what appeared to be one hundred people in line. My pulse raced at the possibility that I'd miss the flight. Security seemed to be moving in slow motion. I looked at my watch. Shit! Only fifteen minutes until the boarding *process* began. There were still about twenty people ahead of me. They really needed more agents. *Don't my taxes pay for this?* I was beyond frustrated and nervous that I was going to miss the flight.

The thought of calling Bentley crossed my mind, but my cell had died, so that wasn't an option. I took my shoes, belt and light jacket off and tossed them into the bin along with my cell. Once my belongings were on the conveyor belt to be checked, I walked through the people scanner. The man nodded giving me the all clear, which I was thankful for after seeing the person in front of me get patted down.

I grabbed my things, threw my shoes, belt and jacket back on, and rushed to the gate, zig-zagging and dodging people and their luggage. All I could do was pray I'd make it.

Bentley

I'd been sitting on a hard plastic seat in the terminal, watching planes land and depart. I wondered how many people in those little oval windows had left behind someone they loved or if they were going to see them. How did the pilots and flight crews cope with being away from their families? I looked at my watch and realized we'd be departing soon. I reached into my backpack to put my headphones away and saw a picture of Andi and me. I took it out and touched her face before I turned it over and read what she'd written.

You're my purpose.
I'll miss you more than
words can describe.
I'll be waiting for you.
All my love, Andi

My heart constricted as I heard them call my flight. I held the picture in the same hand as my boarding pass, grabbed my bag, and got in line. Thankfully, I was in first class, so I'd be boarding first. The seat next to me would be empty. Andi had that ticket—how I wished she could be with me.

I looked around at the other passengers. There were businessmen and women and maybe a family or two. I smiled at the little brown-haired girl having a bit of a tantrum because she didn't want to go to London—she wanted to go to Disney World. She reminded me of another brown-haired spitfire.

"Bentley!"

I turned my head. I could have sworn I'd heard Andi's voice, but I didn't see her in the group of people.

THE CRITIC

I must have been over-tired. I looked at the picture and murmured, "Are you trying to drive me crazy?"

"No, I'm trying to get on a plane." A hand touched my elbow as chestnut waves draped over my arm. "Nice picture. They're a cute couple."

I looked at her. "Andi, what are you doing here?"

She was breathing heavily as though she'd been running through the terminal. "I couldn't let you go without me or this." She held out a shiny penny and smiled. "For good luck."

A smile grew across my face as my heart filled with more love than I'd thought could be possible. I held her and looked into the eyes that had captivated me since I'd first seen them in a small corner store. "Keep it. I'm the luckiest guy in the world. I have you."

EPILOGUE

Later and Back in the States

Andi

After months of rehearsals, *Romance My Heart* was ready to be performed for critics. Normally that would have made me nervous, but Bentley had watched the preview and said he couldn't wait to write a review. His new colleague would be reviewing it as well since we were a couple, but Bentley had been promoted to managing editor since his return from London. He planned to write a supplement no matter what.

My cab pulled up to the theater, and my eyes went to the illuminated marquee. I'd seen my name there during the day, but seeing it at night made my heart fill with pride. I paid my fare and stood on the sidewalk for a beat, just staring in awe. "*Romance My Heart* Starring Andrea Jordan" My skin prickled.

Then he appeared like something out of a fairytale or chick flick. My gorgeous boyfriend wore a black tux and held a single red rose. I slowly approached him, but I wanted run and wrap my legs around his waist.

"Hey, handsome." I rolled up onto the balls of my feet and gave him a chaste kiss.

"Hi, beautiful." He handed me the rose. "This is for you. Congratulations."

I twirled the stem between my thumb and forefinger as I brought it to my nose. "Thank you for the flower and for being here. You look amazing." My eyes trailed the length of him. He was just perfect.

He kissed my hand before taking it and leading me into the auditorium. He guided me though the ornate lobby toward the doors that led to the stage. I needed to get to my dressing room—I was already running behind schedule.

"I'll see you after the show, babe. I need to go get ready." I smiled.

He nodded. "We'll be here waiting for you."

I kissed Bentley hard before walking away. I wondered who "we" was.

The show went off without a hitch. The audience gave us a standing ovation, and I heard my man yelling, "Brava," through the crowd. I glanced toward his voice, but I couldn't see his face. Just hearing him made me smile.

After the cast hugged in excitement, we headed off to our dressing rooms. When I opened the door to mine, my smile could have wrapped around my head. I couldn't believe "we" meant Bentley and my parents. He stood next to them, looking as happy as I felt. They'd finally made it to a show, and by the looks on their faces, they'd enjoyed it.

My mom rushed to me and gave me a hug. "Sweetheart, you were fantastic." She released me then hugged me again.

My dad stepped in and took me out of her arms. "Baby girl, you were just wonderful. You're very talented." He pulled back and looked into my eyes, which had begun to fill with happy tears. "I'm so happy you followed your dreams."

My mom came back to his side and put her hand on his arm.

"Thank you both for coming. This is really a pleasant surprise."

Just then, Bev opened the door. I was stunned.

"Wow, Andi, you were brilliant! You had me in tears and then laughing in the next scene. You know I don't have those emotions." She chuckled. "I'm so happy Bentley thought to invite me."

I hugged Bev. "I'm so happy you're here! Thank you for coming. I know theater isn't your scene. Are you here alone, or did that hot guy from the club come with you?"

Her face turned as red as the rose Bentley had given me. "No, Dane's not here, but wow, do we need to catch up!"

"Yes, we do!" I squeezed her arm.

The squealing that could have shattered crystal informed me that Gina had entered the room. "Holy shit, Andi! That was amazing!" She grabbed me, almost knocking me down.

"Thank you!" I looked behind her for Seth, but he wasn't there.

"He's talking to the stage director. He'll be here in a few."

I nodded.

THE CRITIC

"Well, since most of us are here, I'd like to propose a toast." Bentley handed everyone a glass of champagne, which he must have been pouring while I hugged my girls. He brought me a glass and took my free hand. His chest rose, and his eyes were full of love. Love for me. "Andi, when I first saw you perform, I hoped for this moment, when you'd finally find all the passion and talent I knew you possessed and for your dreams to come true. To be here with you"—he waved his glass toward the others in the room—"and everyone who loves you makes my dreams come true."

My heart raced at his words. I glanced at the others in the room. My mom's eyes had glassed over, and my father was looking at Bentley as if he'd just gained a son. Gina and Bev looked at him as if he were the finest thing on earth, which to me he was, and Seth, who must have entered the room while I was focused on Bentley, was looking me. When he winked, my attention went back to Bentley.

Bentley continued. "You're the love of my life. I know we haven't known each other for very long, but I wanted you to know how much you mean to me."

A single tear trickled down my cheek. "I love you too."

"So I've set up a small party for you at our place. The caterers are there now, and I have a car waiting to take us there. Let's get out of here and go celebrate."

Everyone cheered Bentley's toast. After we'd all gotten a few sips of champagne, I told them I needed time to change. They walked out of my dressing room, talking about the show and the party, but I grabbed Bentley's arm, bringing him to a halt.

"Can you wait? I need help with my zipper." I bit my

lip and looked at him with imploring eyes.

Bentley raised an eyebrow, looking at me with a gleam in his eye. My zipper was on the side of my dress and not the back, so he knew damn well I could get out of it myself. Once the door was closed and locked, he sauntered to me, making my insides clench.

His hands rested on my waist. "Zipper, huh?"

"Yeah, do you think maybe you could help?" I sucked on my bottom lip and gently grazed it with my teeth, followed by my tongue.

His eyes smoldered as he raised my arm and reached for the top of the zipper. He slowly drew it down, and slid the straps over my shoulders making it fall and pool at my feet. My black bra and panties were all I had on.

"My girlfriend is stunning." His eyes raked over my body from head to toe. "We don't have enough time now to do what I want, but believe me, when we're alone at home, this"—his hand went between my legs and cupped me—"is all mine." Our eyes locked, and he smiled. "You're mine, Andi."

"And you're mine."

I placed my hands on his shoulders and melted into him, just as I'd wanted to when I first saw him. Our lips locked in a searing kiss. His tongue massaged the inside of my mouth, and mine reciprocated in pure passion. Once we'd had a taste of each other, it was hard to stop, but knowing that my dad was waiting for me was enough to put out my fire for a little bit.

After Bentley stepped out the dressing room, I washed up and changed into my casual clothes. Then I walked out of the theater hand-in-hand with the man of my dreams. We were greeted by fans asking for my autograph. I beamed at Bentley, who looked almost as happy as I felt. With him by my side, I signed programs and took selfies with fans.

We strolled around to the front of the theater, and he paused underneath my name. He looked up. "So, how's it feel to have your dream come true?"

I looked at him rather than the marquee. "My dreams came true the day I met you."

Bentley

I stared at her in awe. Just the thought of being her dream come true filled my heart like nothing else ever had. To know that this beautiful and talented woman was all mine made me the happiest man on the planet. When she'd surprised me that day in the airport, she solidified my belief that we belonged together.

"Andi." That was all I could say. How this had all happened was like something out of a weird fairytale, and I didn't believe in fairytales. If I'd told Andi that, she'd have kicked my ass.

"We better go before they get wasted on the liquor in the limo." Andi giggled.

As soon as I opened the door to our home, my nose was overcome by the aroma of the Asian delights the caterers had prepared. I needed to excuse myself to write my review and e-mail it to my editor. I had all my notes carefully tucked into my backpack, but I needed to articulate them in a manner that didn't scream, "My girlfriend fucking rocks." My prose needed to be a tad more eloquent.

I placed a chaste kiss on Andi's head and went to my office. I fired up my laptop and reached into my trusty backpack for my notebook. I couldn't help but smile when a juice box fell out. Trying to rein in my emotions while I wrote would be more difficult than I thought, but once I'd begun, I couldn't stop.

When I was finished, I joined the rest of the party. Andi was beaming. Her parents were talking to Gina and Seth. I could tell by the look on his face that he'd rather have been alone with her, and I had to say I felt the same about Andi. Celebrating with family and friends was great, but I wanted to have a private party with my girl.

She stood in our living room and tapped a chopstick against a glass, making me smile. "Excuse me, if I can have your attention for a minute." Andi cleared her throat. "I wanted to thank you all for coming tonight to share this with me." She turned to face me. "And you, Bentley." Her voice could have warmed the champagne in her hand. "Saying thank you to you doesn't come close to what I want to say, but for now, I thank you from the bottom of my heart."

I raised my glass, and she followed suit. "Cheers, Andi."

"Cheers."

Everyone joined in, and crystal dinged as everyone saluted each other.

Once everyone had left and it was just us, I couldn't contain myself. I picked her up and took her to our bed. We lay on our sides, facing one another. I pushed her hair behind her ears. She smiled making my heart swell.

THE CRITIC

"Thank you for tonight. You really outdid yourself and are definitely the best boyfriend ever."

"Andi, I meant what I said. I love you—the woman who busted in on my quiet lunch to yell at me, the woman who always makes me want to use chopsticks, the woman who owns my soul and my love."

"You're the man who brings out my passion, who made me want to pull that slingshot as far back as it could go, and you made me realize I was stronger than I thought I was."

We sealed our declaration with a kiss.

The next morning, Andi stumbled into the kitchen in just a T-shirt and thong. I needed to rein myself in long enough for her to read my article, but that would be a challenge. My cock was already at full alert.

She poured herself a cup of coffee and sat at the table. "Good morning." Her voice was raspy and sexy as fuck, which didn't help my current state.

"Good morning. Did you sleep well?" Maybe idle conversation would quash the desire to throw her on the table and fuck her until she couldn't walk.

"Yeah, I did." She stretched, and her nipples poked into her shirt as she arched her back.

Shit. She was going to be the death of me. She finally saw the *Edge* folded neatly on the table, my review in plain sight. Her eyes shot to mine before she picked it up and began to read it out loud.

'Romance My Heart—A Story of Love
By Bentley Chambers, Managing Editor

For some reason, she giggled after reading the title. She regained her composure, cleared her throat, and continued.

> "'*Romance My Heart*, starring Stuart Maxon as Reese McCormack and Andrea Jordan as Fiona Masters was amazing and definitely a must-see. Considering my girlfriend has the lead role, I tend to be a bit biased. So this isn't the Edge's official review for this production, and rather than write a non-review, I've decided tell you a story of my own.'"

She glanced at me, and I smiled and told her to keep going. She took a deep breath and resumed reading.

> "'Five years ago, I saw a play. A beautiful young woman walked on stage, and my heart stopped. It was to be my first review for the Edge, and I couldn't wait to sing the praises of this gorgeous creature. I suppose I may have thought she would run to me to thank me and I'd have been able to meet her, but that didn't happen. Instead, my review wasn't glowing—it was negative. Who was this actress? Well, it was Andrea Jordan.'"

She paused and took a breath before continuing.

> "'After publishing that review, followed by several others, I couldn't help but want the best for this woman. I wanted her dreams to come true even though, at the time, I didn't know what they were. I didn't know her yet. So I continued to write reviews of her shows. They were mostly negative but still honest.
>
> "'One day, after I wrote an unsavory review of one of Ms. Jordan's performances, I had the pleasure of meeting her. She came to where I was eating lunch and ripped me apart. Then and there, I fell in love with her.'"

Andi looked at me, her eyes glassed over.

"Keep going." My heart raced as I waited for her to read the rest.

> "Once I got to know Andrea, her desire to be great and her passion for acting radiated from her pores. I knew that her dreams would become a reality one day, and I'm so happy I was there to witness it and share it with her.
>
> "Andrea once told me that people need to be conscious of how they choose their words and use them wisely, so that's what I'm going to do now."

A tear rolled down her cheek. Without swiping it away, she continued.

> "The first time I came face to face with Andrea, she refused to let me call her anything but Ms. Jordan. But someday, I will call her Mrs. Chambers because I want her to be my wife. I want us to support each other when we triumph and pick each other up when we don't. I plan on loving her with all I have and giving her everything she needs."

She sniffled as a tear wet the paper.

> "Andrea Jordan, you once told me there are over a million words in the English language. Well, I just have four for you—will you marry me?"

The paper shook in her hand as she laid it on the table. When she looked up, I was kneeling beside her. More tears left her eyes when she saw the two-carat, solitaire diamond ring with a platinum setting nestled in the navy velvet box I was holding.

"Bentley." Instead of going for the ring, she cupped

my face and wiped away the tear that had fallen from my eyes.

"Marry me, Andi." I swallowed hard, waiting for her response.

She closed her eyes, took a breath, and said the most important word I'd ever heard.

"Yes."

THE END

Read the first chapter of

Unexpected Chance

after the Author's Note & Acknowledgements

AUTHOR'S NOTE

One morning, I was watching a documentary on the movie *Ferris Bueller's Day Off,* which happens to be one of my favorites. The documentary mentioned that a critic didn't like the movie and, prior to its release, left a bad review. All I could think was, *Really? I loved this movie.* Then I thought, *What if that reviewer had held more clout than he did, and the movie was left on the cutting room floor?* We would've missed out on one of the most iconic movies of my generation. How many times do you hear, "Bueller, Bueller?" Yeah, my point exactly. I hadn't planned on writing *The Critic,* but because of that, *The Critic* and my critic, Bentley Chambers, was conceived.

What would happen if artists and people from all walks of life listened to negative opinions? We could miss out on famous works of art, great fashion, wonderful movies, television shows, Broadway productions, and great books—what a travesty that would be!

Everyone is critiqued in one way or another, whether it be their style, hair, or even the way they talk. Sometimes it's positive and sometimes it isn't. Either way it happens whether we like it or not. How we choose to deal with that criticism is what makes a difference.

Bentley told Andi, *"A critic doesn't slingshot you into*

stardom. You need to control the pull and release. The sling can only go back as far as you decide to draw it."

Which is my point exactly. Don't let anyone hold you back. Be like the makers of Ferris Bueller and go for it.

Joanne xoxo

ACKNOWLEDGEMENTS

A lot of people go into writing a book. Yes, I'm the author, but without the support of family, friends, and colleagues, this would not be possible.

My family are the ones who put up with me while I write and smile when I say I ordered pizza for dinner (again) and don't get mad when the laundry isn't folded. My husband has had my back and supported me not only on this writing journey but throughout my entire adult life. When I told him about this book, we were watching television. I was in the middle of writing a different one, and I grabbed my notebook and started making notes. I explained my idea, and he said, "You write what you feel you need to." Those words are enough for me, so thank you, Dave, for loving me and understanding when I temporarily lose my mind and can't locate my patience. My boys, Nick and Zack, this would not have been possible without your understanding. To say that I am blessed would be an understatement. I love you all so much, and you mean more to me than anything else in the world!

My beta readers, Lisa Paul, Erin Noelle, Vina Platania, Heather Ford, Mary Lou Moench, Katherine Katie Mac Crane, Lauren Collins, Lee Ann Parks, and Ann Marie Madden, thank you for taking the time out of your busy schedules to read for me. Your feedback, comments, suggestions, and more importantly, your honesty were incredibly helpful. Thank you from the bottom of my heart.

My friends who always have my back, thank you for supporting me. Without all of you, I know I wouldn't be where I am today. You all do so much, and I don't even think you realize it. Just by telling me you enjoy my writing and my characters makes me happy.

To my "Rockin' Street Team," thank you for "pimping," support, and more importantly, for your encouraging words. You're the best, and I'm so glad to have you on my team.

My critique partner, one of my closest, trusted, and funniest friends, Lisa Paul. I could write a short story about how wonderful I think you are! But you're going to have to settle for a shorter version. Spending my days writing and sharing pieces of this story with you has been invaluable to me. Your wit and incredible skills make me a better writer. Your friendship means the world to me, and we finally got to meet in person! To think I was fangirling over you a couple years ago, and now here we are . . . it's funny what brings people together. Thank you for writing *Thursday Nights*. Without that awesome book, we wouldn't be together. So thanks, Max and Janie! I look forward to many more years of friendship, many laughs, good times, and great books. I love you.

My teammate and close friend, Erik Fellows. It's been more than a year since we became friends, although I feel as if I've known you my entire life. You are more than a friend, you are family. I'm very happy your handsome face will be gracing another of my covers. The time you took to make sure I had just the right photo goes above and beyond—not that I'd expect less from you. You mean the world to me. Love you! XOXO Actor Boy

Madeline Sheehan, thank you for being you. I think you rock. You've been there to answer questions and to give me your honest opinion since my first book, back in 2013, and I'm very proud to call you my friend. Thank you for writing and for pushing me out of my "norm" when it comes to reading. You're truly are a wonderful person.

Ashley Suzanne, thank you for your help and confidence. I'm so glad we finally met in person. I think you rock and are a very special lady, talented author, and friend.

To all the bloggers, thank you for everything that you do. I truly appreciate all your support. I wish I could list all of you, but that would add several more pages! Thank you for all the time you spend supporting authors and reading our stories. You take time out of your personal lives, and I am very thankful.

Thank you to Otilia Villar Baker (About Time Photography) for taking an awesome cover picture!! Thank you for sharing your talent with me!!

Special thanks to my editor, Cassie Cox. This is the third book you edited for me, and I look forward to working with you many more times. I appreciate your honesty and your wonderful talent and mind. You're the best, and I'm lucky to have you!

Sommer Stein from Perfect Pear Creations, a thank you isn't enough. You create the most amazing covers, swag, and then some! I adore you and I look forward to working with you in the future. You killed it with this cover!!!

THE CRITIC

The Fictional Men's Room for Book Ho's group, thanks for your support! It's so great to have a group that shares the same love of books!

Most importantly, I'd like to thank the readers. We all love to read and talk about the books and characters we love, and I am so thankful to all of you for not only sharing your favorites but taking the time to send supportive messages. Your enthusiasm keeps me going, and there isn't a thank you big enough for that.

COMING SOON:

Brett & Julie's story in *A Heart's Forgiveness* (A Chance Series Companion Novel)

Bev & Dane's story in *Gripped*

Unexpected Chance
(Chance Series 1)

Chapter 1

When I was little and watched the Olympics on my family's television in our humble, middle-class living room, I'd get lost in my thoughts and would dream that I'd be the next great figure skater like Tara Lipinski or a great gymnast like Shannon Miller. Then I would go outside and attempt to ice skate on the pond behind our house and fall flat on my ass with my ankles going in opposite directions. I couldn't even do a cartwheel in our backyard and was far from graceful; I was lucky I could manage a somersault.

My parents always said, "You can be whatever you want to be, Aubrey. You just need to apply yourself." Yeah, that's the story of my life. Since I was a twenty-five-year-old college graduate with my Master's Degree in Journalism and Creative Writing, I should have been able to handle whatever came my way. At least that's what my mom said when my parents sold my modest childhood home and moved to their ritzy chateau in Paris. To say my mom had changed was an understatement. Apparently, my grandparents had invested wisely, and when they passed away, they left my mom everything. Now that my parents were well off, Mom decided she wanted to live the life of the rich and glamorous. I couldn't fault her really. My parents worked their asses off and deserved a great life. I just didn't expect them to move to Paris. *Oh well, I'll survive on my own.*

At my age, I knew I should be applying the education I earned by joining the workforce. I should also be partying with my girlfriends, meeting guys, and just having fun. Was I doing that? No. Instead, I sat in the small apartment that my parents rented for me in the city and I read. Life was going on right outside my window, but my nose was stuck in a book. My life came down to romance and mystery novels—some good, some just cheesy, some that just got me hot and bothered. Who was I kidding? It was all just fiction. That stuff couldn't possibly happen. That was how I thought of my life sometimes—full of fiction. I didn't have an ounce of romance in my life and had no clue how to remedy that.

I looked around my small bedroom at the pictures: my parents and me at Jones Beach, my best friend Julie and me just goofing around, but none of me with a man. I realized I hadn't had a true boyfriend . . . well . . . ever. At one point, I thought I did. His name was Garrett Reed. We were good friends, and I thought we had something special. He told me I was special, and I believed him, but once I slept with him that was the end of the relationship. Maybe that was all he really wanted, or maybe I just didn't get his rocks off. I don't know. Honestly, he didn't do much for my rocks either. I snickered at the thought; although, it still made my heart ache a little. I really liked him, or I wouldn't have slept with him. I wasn't that kind of girl, and he knew that. Maybe that's what hurt me the most. The feeling of being used is a horrible feeling, and that was how I felt. I had Garrett to thank for being guarded.

After graduation, I hoped to be an editor for the

Times, but my secret aspiration was to write a romance novel. I had a problem though; I didn't know a thing about romance. That wasn't a slight problem; it was a huge problem.

My friend, Julie, knew about it, though. She was confident, beautiful, and she turned heads everywhere we went. I was known as the pretty girl's friend, which was fine with me. I didn't exude the confidence that she did. I had been in school, so inundated with classes and homework and wanting to be the best in my class that I never took the time to apply makeup or spend a lot of time on my hair. Sure, I had great clothes because Mom sent them or the money to buy them to me and I loved to shop, but that was about it. I was going to have to confide in Julie to get her to help me with this. I trusted her with my life. We had been best friends since the sixth grade, and I knew she could help me. I just had to find the courage to tell her without sounding like a complete head case.

I looked in my bathroom mirror at the person staring back at me: long dark hair, empty light blue eyes, and skin that desperately needed some makeup or a spray tan. Exhaling, I picked up the phone to call Julie. She answered on the second ring.

"Hey, *chica*, what's shaking?"

"Hey, I need to talk to you about something. Are you busy or can you stop over?"

"I'm not busy. I can come over in a few. Is everything okay? Are you okay? You sound weird."

"Yeah, I'm fine." I knew I didn't sound convincing. "I just need your help with something." I felt like Sandy in the movie *Grease* calling Frenchy for a makeover. I guess in a way I was.

"Say no more. I'm on my way."

Julie really was the best. She showed up less than an hour later. We sat on the couch, had a soda, and I tried to muster up the courage that was needed to tell her why I needed her help. I ran my fingers on my microfiber couch, creating a figure eight pattern, around and around and back again.

Julie stared at the shapes I was nervously making. "So are you going to tell me what's going on, or are you trying to hypnotize me?"

Julie was tall with perfectly highlighted blond hair and big, gorgeous green eyes with sweeping lashes. She was taller than I was, probably about five foot seven, and had a gorgeous figure. Her personality was even more beautiful. She had the entire package. It was no wonder men loved her.

I took a deep breath and cleared my throat. "Well, I've been thinking about writing a book—a romance novel to be exact." I looked up at her through my thick eyelashes to gauge some sort of reaction. I didn't know why, but I felt embarrassed and a little shy. This was my best friend. I should have been able to say anything and know there wasn't going to be any snarky attitude.

She grinned ear to ear. "I think it's an awesome idea! You majored in this stuff, right? From what you've told me, you've read hundreds of those books, so, yeah, right on!" Then Julie's brows furrowed and she looked confused. "Why do you need me? I practically failed English, so writing a story is totally out of my realm of expertise."

Okay, here comes the hard part. "I know my studies prepared me, and I aced my writing classes, and, yes, I've read a ton of books, but when it comes to actual heart-melting, making-me-want-someone-so-bad-I-can-feel-it-in-my-legs romance, I'm clueless."

I looked down at my hands, which were now twisting in my lap. "I haven't had a boyfriend in years, and the last one was crappy at best. I want to feel romance, the swept-off-my-feet-I-can't-believe-this-is-happening-to-me type of romance."

Realization dawned in Julie's eyes, and they grew bigger. She bounced up and down on the couch cushion and clapped her hands as if they were on fire and she needed to extinguish them. "Oh my God, we are so going to do this! I'm so excited! We need to find you a muse and get you a sexy outfit! Then we need to make sure that you're trimmed everywhere if you know what I mean!" She winked after that.

I wanted to smile at her enthusiasm, but instead I felt a little nauseated. Maybe this wasn't a good idea. "Okay, so the outfit seems easily attainable, and, uh, I don't need a trim anywhere, except maybe the ends of my hair, but finding a muse will not be as easy." I made sure to use finger quotes when I said "muse."

"That's where you're wrong, Aubrey. We can totally do this. As a matter of fact, I'm working at a Speed Dating event tomorrow night at a hot club called The White Orchid. Walker-Stone is in charge of its marketing and advertising. It's a sold-out event, but I can get you a ticket. I'll be there with my boss, Brian, to make sure everything goes as planned, so you'll have a wing man, well, wing woman."

Julie laughed; apparently, she found humor in my despair. I suddenly felt as if we were no longer Sandy and Frenchy, but now Maverick and Goose from the movie *Top Gun*.

"What the hell is speed dating and why doesn't that *sound* romantic?" *Top Gun* flashed in my head again. "I feel the need, the need for speed." I almost laughed out loud. What was next? Going to a bar and singing "You've Lost That Loving Feeling"?

Julie rolled her eyes. "It isn't romantic. Well, I guess it could be if there were such a thing as love at first sight, but the goal is to meet a guy, right? Not necessarily fall in love. You just want someone to make your panties a little damp."

Julie enjoyed this banter a little too much. She was so comfortable with guys and sex. She wasn't a slut by any means; she just knew how to have safe fun and not get heartbroken.

"Look, I don't need my panties damp. Knowing me, I'll have an anxiety attack and probably pee a little; that'll make them damp."

We both laughed. Although, I inwardly cringed; it really wasn't that farfetched. I was known for my anxiety attacks. They started in middle school when I was picked on for not having the right brand of clothing or something like that. I ended up at the nurse's office, and that was where I met Julie. She didn't feel well that day. Well, that's what she told the nurse. She really didn't want to go to Algebra. She confided in me that day, and we'd been inseparable ever since. Julie was one of the cool girls, so my being picked on was instantly over. Back then, I was so thankful for Julie, as I am now.

"How does it work anyway?" I felt my anxiety building already.

Julie adjusted herself as if she were going to give me a marketing presentation. Her posture was perfect; she flipped her hair over her shoulders and flashed her perfectly white teeth. "There will be tables lined up, and each of the ladies picks one and sits down. Every six minutes or whenever the bell rings, a new guy will sit at the table. Both the men and women will have rating cards where they can make notes on whomever they meet. At the end of the night, Brian and I will collect the cards to see if there are any matches and take it from there. Voila! You could have your muse!"

I was shaking my head in disbelief, and my head was spinning. I felt as if I just drank a pitcher of margaritas. "So I'm going to be rated by men I've only spoken to for six minutes? And you expect me to find a match? What the hell do I say in six minutes that gets me a high rating? 'Hi, you're hot. Want to have sex?' Will that do it?"

"Oh, Aubrey, you're so dramatic! Listen, you'll never know if you don't try. What do you have to lose? If all else fails, we'll call it conversational practice. It's a win-win!"

"Yeah, win-win or lose!" I covered my face with my hands. I couldn't believe I was considering doing this.

Julie pulled my hands down and looked at me. "What do you have to lose? If you don't meet Mr. Romance Hero, you don't lose anything. But you could meet someone. You won't know if you don't give it a shot. Just have faith."

Julie was right; I had to admit at least that much. If I really thought about it, the idea wasn't that bad, and I really didn't have many other options. I was just trying to think of what to say that would be so amazing in six minutes. Worse yet, what would a guy say? And what were these guys like? They were probably creepy losers, and this was the only way for them to talk to women. Or worse yet, they were players looking for their next piece of ass, like Garrett. Either way, I couldn't believe I was going to do this. Did that make me a loser too? *Oh hell, who cares? I need to do this.* "Okay, I'm in. What do we need to do first?"

"First, we call the spa and make appointments for tomorrow, and then we shop and figure out what questions you're going to ask in your six-minute time frame." Julie was so excited; it was as if she were the one who would be speed dating; she definitely had faith.

"How come you never told me about this event or club?"

"I don't know. Honestly, it never dawned on me. I never thought you would do this or even want to."

"You're right. I wouldn't have done it if I had any other choice. I really need this for my research, or I wouldn't be going."

"Yeah, about that . . . What happens if you do meet a great guy? You know that's a possibility."

I shook my head and rolled my eyes. "I honestly don't think anyone who would attend an event like this would be my type—no offense. And what do you mean by 'what would I do?'"

"I mean if you meet some delectable, stunningly handsome, want-to-make-you-strip-naked creature of a man and you end up dating him, will you tell him about the book, about him being your muse, or will you keep it to yourself?"

I shrugged, "I don't know. I never thought about it. Anyway, I highly doubt I'll meet someone who'll make me melt and be gaga over. Do you know what kind of guys signed up?"

"We ran limited background checks on the guys. They have to be gainfully employed, between the ages of twenty-five and forty, single, and not on any sex-offender registries."

My eyes went wide. "I guess those last two would be quite important!"

We both laughed. We called the spa to make appointments for nails, hair, and makeup for the next afternoon, and then we were off to find some nice little boutiques off the beaten path.

I had money, but I didn't want a cookie-cutter outfit. I didn't want to look as if I tried too hard, but I definitely didn't want to look like a mall rat. I purchased a black pencil skirt that came just above my knees and a tasteful blue, sleeveless top that had a scoop neck and just grazed the top of my cleavage. I didn't have much in the breast department, but the padded black lace bra Julie picked out for me helped fill me out nicely. She also made me buy a matching black lace thong and confirmed that I was okay in the waxing department. She wanted me to wear a garter belt and silk stockings. I just laughed and told her that I was all set. We finished our day with some good food and wine.

That got me thinking. *I'm probably going to need wine to get me through tomorrow night. I should stop and pick up a bottle—no, a case!*

STAY IN TOUCH

Website:

www.joanneschwehmbooks.com

Facebook:

www.facebook.com/joanneschwehm

Twitter:

www.twitter.com/JSchwehmBooks

Google +:

www.plus.google.com/jschwehm

Amazon:

www.amazon.com/Joanne-
Schwehm/e/B00GBC1X2K/

Goodreads:

www.goodreads.com/author/show/7209983.Joanne_Sc
hwehm

Goodreads Group Page:

www.goodreads.com/group/show/156533-joanne-
schwehm-s-romantic-reading-friends